On Desecrated Faith and New Found Religion

These words that follow are an account of the author of this book,
Absolom Teendyth IV,
High Priest of the Great Perversion, Cha' Ush.
Praise Be His Name.

Teendyth: On Desecrated Faith and New-Found Religion

Steven-Mark Maine

Published by Steven-Mark Maine, 2023.

This is a work of fiction. Similarities to real people, places, or events are entirely coincidental.

TEENDYTH: ON DESECRATED FAITH AND NEW-FOUND RELIGION

First edition. October 27, 2023.

Copyright © 2023 Steven-Mark Maine.

ISBN: 979-8223743613

Written by Steven-Mark Maine.

Thank you to Ladonna Friesen, without your guidance as my professor I would never have loved writing as much as I do now.

Mom, there's a swear on page 33. Skip that one.

Prologus

In the year 1786 a thirty-year-old Dutch man changed his name to David Absolom Teendyth and moved to what was then known as New Amsterdam in order to help settle the East Coast of the New World. In fact, everyone in his village had left, leaving David not much of a choice but to leave his position as pastor. It saddened him greatly, as his father was a pastor, as was his grandfather. They had all three taken care of and preached at that same Dutch church, and he would be the first to abandon it. With that, he uprooted his wife and traveled to America. Not long after he arrived, he was given the role of the local reverend as he was the man with the most education in the field of Theology, and the town felt as if they required a godly man to keep the demons that stalked the mountains at bay. David jumped at the chance to continue his family tradition and spent his years in that settlement. He could recount in his old age remembering when New Amsterdam became New York not only two years later. A few years after that his wife gave birth to a son, who they named David Absolom Teendyth II. David the II would go on to become the next pastor of the church in what was then known as Jericho. David I died after a long and full life, living to be over a hundred years old. He died the same year that the portion of Jericho we lived in, now known as Bainbridge, split off into another town called Afton. His family lived in Afton for generations to come.

David I witnessed the birth of his grandchildren, and even his great-grandchildren. David II had two children, twin boys. The one who was older by a few minutes was David Absolom III, who would later take over as reverend when his father retired. The younger was Eli, who would travel to seminary and further his enlightenment. Eventually, in his thirtieth year, David III would give birth to David Absolom IV.

The words you are reading at this moment are of David Absolom IV.

At the day of my birth, four David Absolom Teendyth's existed on this earth, and each one of them had been, or were, destined to be a pastor. More specifically, a pastor of the same small church in Afton, New York. It was tradition at this point, and even though only four of us had served in America, the chain of ancestors who had served in some sort of leadership position, more times than not as a pastor, went back over ten generations. At last, over hundreds of years, my father had reached his destiny.

And when time came for him to fulfill that destiny, he fulfilled it with ease. He even looked as if he were specially crafted for this role, as his countenance held a kind and pious nature, his body gently molded into a figure of grace. In his prime, he would have been a fairly lithe man, but the long years and my mother's cooking had given him a thick but firm layer of paunch over his stomach. This chub did not stand out with the rest of his body, as his legs, which were as thick as cedars, were long and strong from years of walking to the houses of his parishioners. His arms were just about as thick, but a lack of regular arm exercise caused the muscle to be affected by gravity and attach itself to the bottom of his biceps. His jaw was like a brick that had been taken over by moss, strong, but not as chiseled as it was when first made. His light blonde hair was kept tight to his head. His facial hair was kept just as tight, providing a golden sheen to his pale face. His eyes were stern, yet were betrayed by a glint of kindness that reared its head whenever he felt it needed.

He looked the part of a pastor, spoke as a pastor, loved as a pastor, and above all he acted as a pastor.

His wife was in stark contrast to him in terms of height, reaching only five feet tall when she stood on her tippy toes. She was a brute of woman, forcing herself through any sort of pain that she suffered. Had she not been able to do that, she would have been more bedridden than she already had been. She dealt with chronic pain and weak lungs. She always struggled to keep weight, and would try her best to make the most fattening and rich foods she could on our meager budget in an attempt to keep herself from becoming too thin. Her dark hair was usually tied up to keep it out of her face. She made it her duty to keep the house clean, but was willing to admit that all women may not want such things. Many of the wives of the deacons of the church looked down on her for such thoughts. She always paid them no mind.

As their son, I looked as if I were my fathers reflection. By the age of seven I was already reaching the height of my mother, and would very quickly surpass that by the age of nine. Despite having the height of my father I shared a fair amount of qualities with my mother - most notably my health. I was an asthmatic who lacked any sort of musculature, leaving me to be a fairly gaunt child. As I got older and my height increased, this only furthered the work that my body required to produce any muscle tone or body fat in my body. I was borderline skeletal, but I pushed past my struggles much as my mother did. For a while I was well enough to even carry on the tradition of spending the weekdays with my father studying, in order to carry on the Teendyth family pastoral duties, which was no easy task.

Those who have not been involved in the profession of pastoral duties would usually think that being a pastor just means sitting around all day thinking about how you want to tell your congregation that they are doing something wrong. They do not realize *that* is a privilege reserved for only the worst pastors. In fact those people are not pastors, they are *preachers*. The kind of man that tells you he knows how hard you have had it your whole life, but never had to give up his weekly steak, and he for sure was not one to give up that same steak to someone who was hungry.

My father was not one of these preachers. He was a pastor, and a fine one at that. If anyone as far down the picking order as the town drunk had the sniffles he would be at their doorstep with a hot drink to soothe their throat. He used everything in his power to ensure people received what they needed to survive and had joy running through them. This eagerness to make sure all in his care had not only their needs, but also their wants met would eventually cause problems to arise within our own family.

It was not only every elder Teendyth's duty to lead the church, but also to make sure that every younger Teendyth was prepared when he was handed control of the church. It was not uncommon to see each Teendyth traveling the streets of Afton hand in hand with his son. From the time that I was four I would sit with my father reading scripture until the late hours in the sanctuary. I would caravan through the streets while he modeled to me how to love and look after those who needed help. I saw the kindness in his eyes as he saw those who were struggling. I also saw the men going into the local bar immediately after my father had given them money for food. We would pass by those same men later in the day, asleep in the gutter. I did not know what they were doing, but I did know my father gave them money for food and that was not what they were using it for.

One such example was from that of a man by the name of Charles Willith. He was an obese man that would, if given the chance, literally steal candy out of the mouth of a child. His entire family shared this trait, an obesity that was fueled by other people's food. They seemed to have a fetish for stealing food from others; a gluttony that was interlaced with envy. One year they asked my father to help them with a "Christmas family tradition" in which his child and his wife would make as many homemade sweets for the community as they could. That year was particularly povertous for my family as someone had been skimming funds from the tithe, meaning my father was not bringing in as much income as normal. My father gave them every single ingredient they asked for, and then some. Issues arose as my mother and I had the exact same tradition. Due to both of our inabilities to gain weight, my mother and I made extra sure to cook as many sweets as we possibly could in order to gain weight for the cold winter months. We began the tradition when I was only five years old, my toddler mind creating the idea after learning about the hibernation cycles of bears. My mother agreed, and for the first time I had ever experienced my mother managed to gain some weight. The winter was much more bearable, as both my mother and I could stand walking past an opened door without getting chilled. From that point on, we held this tradition every year.

In fact, it was the fifth year we had observed this tradition when the Willith's asked my father for those groceries, and the first year since its creation that we were not able to see its fulfillment. The aforementioned tithe stealing made it impossible for my mother and I to replace the groceries my father gifted to the Willith family. That winter seemed even colder than the previous, and my mother was bedridden for the entire season.

The irritation of the subject was exacerbated by the fact that Benjamin, the Willith child, was known by all to be my childhood nemesis, of sorts. To little Benji, as his parents called him, I was nothing more than an item to take his aggression out on. He was loud-mouthed and spoiled, with a penchant for striking anyone who did not let him get his way. The only thing that I could figure was that my existence somehow kept him from receiving what he wanted, as I was the usual target of these blows.

The blows were not always physical either, as he had the rare ability to verbally abuse someone until they were an inch from mental death. This came at a price though, as he could not keep something secret if he knew revealing it would cause someone harm. It was that inability to keep a secret that led me to learning that it was his father who was the one that was skimming from the church offering. No one had known that this was even occurring, and I had never made mention of the situation to the little bastard before.

There was no reason to doubt his words.

He also snidely confided that his parents did have more than enough funds to pay for ingredients for their "tradition", they just felt an unholy need to watch my family suffer.

I ran to tell my father as soon as I had been told.

"Son, it is not my job to care that I was deceived. It is my job to make sacrifices to those who say they need help. They will answer to God for their trickery."

I never questioned my father's lackadaisical attitude to his family's persecution. Having to turn the other cheek was something that a person who was a member of a pastor's family had to do. It never occurred to me to hold deacons, which was the caste Willith was a member of, to the same form of persecuted decorum.

"I understand, Father. I just wish there was something I could do. It seems that I am being bullied just for existing. I wish there was some sort of way any of us could do something to stop them from being mean to us."

"Turning the other cheek is the only thing we can do, son. The Bible says that those who follow Christ will be persecuted for their actions. I promise, it will be easier with age, but until then you will need to trust my guidance."

I did trust his guidance. I always trusted his guidance, and it would be another decade before I knew what it meant to protect myself.

That was not the only case of abuse I suffered at the hands of not only Benjamin, but the other children that were around my age. I was easy prey for those evil machinations that only children can create. I was frail and easily broken, and my peers, all children of deacons, loved to watch things break. Their parents never saw fit to punish them, as they never believed there was an issue in the first place. Most did not believe my pleas for help, as their children never acted so viciously around other children or their siblings.

But I was not other children.

I was their lesser.

I could not chase after a ball without becoming winded, nor could I wrestle in the mud pits that formed in the fields without one of my bones breaking.

It was unheard of that their precious children would do anything that was considered imperfect.

They simply did not care. I was frail, and to them frailty could be cured by harassment. After all, Jesus simply looked at the lame man and proclaimed "get up and walk" and the man did. Why should their childrens' jeering be any different? All the name calling and beatings were simply encouragement akin to Christ, nevermind the hatred that shone through the eyes of my tormentors. Their perfect children just wanted me to overcome my sickness and were doing whatever they could to help my ailing body. At least those who simply saw their children as perfect did not

encourage their behavior, but this caste of bully was treated as if they were
my saviors.

Benjamin was neither of these. His parents knew about his poor behavior, and did not attempt to portray it as anything but abuse.

Instead, they joined him.

The entirety of the Willith family were more pig than human, but did not realize most saw them as such. They always walked with their heads high, dressed in the best clothes they could afford. They saw themselves as the de facto governors of Afton, flaunting their wealth as if it actually belonged to them. If it was not made obvious by my previous anecdote, they procured their wealth through coercion and thievery. Their thievery was only unparalleled by their penchant for believing they could punish the children of other families for anything they believed to be inappropriate behavior.

Willith verbally stated at one time that my birth was inappropriate behavior, so to him, my mere existence was a punishable offense. Whenever he experienced me standing up for myself against his brat, he would promptly shove his booted foot directly into my limbs. Most were afraid to call him out on this, and those who did noticed an increasingly large amount of items missing from their property.

My father saw all of this and firmly held onto the sentiment that I should turn the other cheek, and I took pride in the fact that I was more Christlike than those who abused me. But that sense of pride was not enough to keep my ribs from cracking under the heel of a grown man's foot.

With my bones being cracked more and more as I aged, I began to shut myself in. My mind began to give way to the incessant bullying from Benjamin and his ilk, and my body took a turn for the worse with it. Thankfully my father never forced me to join him on his walks, or join him in his late night readings at the church, as he respected the fact that I was ill. Despite that, he never truly faced the deeper issues that were the root of my new found reclusive behavior. I never expected him to. I spent most of my teenage years in bed coughing or helping my mother around the house.

A positive that came with my sickness and need to stay home is that I developed a skill that not many bachelors at the time had learned: The art of taking care of one's living space. While I would not leave the house, it was important that I keep the interior clean for both my mother's and my own sake. Any sort of dust in the house would cause our weakened lungs to go into fits so severe it would almost cause suffocation, and while my mother's condition worsened with age, mine began to improve as I worked around the house. The regular lifting and housework caused my body to finally take on some sort of mass. At first I could only just manage to dust the house to ensure we would not choke. Then I became strong enough to cook small meals for myself, and then my mother when her ailments acted up. Over time I had finally built enough muscle to chop wood to keep the house warm.

By the age of sixteen my body was finally in a state that fit my age, and while still weaker than most, I could very easily take regular trips outside of the house again. My lungs were still stricken with asthma, and I continued to keep to myself and spent my time caring for my mother. She could scuffle about a little, but still needed help around the house. I neglected my pastoral training and became my mother's assistant until the time would come for me to take over my father's position.

THE TIME THAT LED TO my consensual usurping of my fathers position was wrought with long hours of not speaking to nor seeing my father. He had become increasingly submerged in his work in all ways, may it be spent in his office preparing for Sunday service or in meeting with the church members. While my mother and I saw him commonly in the mornings, his presence became more and more uncommon in the evening hours. He had taken to the habit of eating with the families of members and deacons in an attempt to further love them. It was unthinkable to some that he would willingly opt out of eating the food that my mother made, as Mrs. Teendyth's food was considered nothing short of sacred by all who lived in the town. Even when he came home in time for supper, he would often be satisfied by the food he had already eaten and refuse to dine with us. My mother often said "I know your father loves the food I make, but I can't expect a man to only eat his wife's cooking and no one else's."

I was never quite able to discern why she sounded so melancholy when she would relay that sentiment. Perhaps she simply delighted that much in her husband indulging in her cooking. Whatever the reason for her sullenness, she had always made it clear on those nights that she wished father to be with us.

There were, of course, still times my father would be present for dinner, and even more so times when he would be working in solitude at the church. On those nights mother would cook for all of us, then have me deliver my father's dinner to him so he could eat without ceasing his work. It was a short jaunt to the church, so the request was never too burdensome. My mother depended on me in her sorrow, and my father depended on me in his labor.

These nightly treks, while less common than those times that my father failed to appear, became more common than the nights he ate at our table. I traveled those same streets so many times I could traverse them with my eyes closed, even being able to avoid the drunks that laid about the streets. The back and forth become monotonous, not dissimilar to the trek one took to the restroom from their bed. That is, with the added inclusion of the aforementioned drunks. Thankfully they were not an issue when I needed to use the restroom, though inviting them in to spend the night would not be an unheard course of action from my father.

All but one of these nights could be considered forgettable, a drop of ink on a story preoccupied with other matters. The one night that broke the norm began in a similar manner. I dodged the inebriated and precariously balanced the hot jar of soup in my hands. Most of the lay-abouts had already gone off into unconsciousness, but one specifically stood out. Benjamin Willith had grown from the spoiled brat of a child I had known into a spoiled brat of man, with the addition of a crippling drinking problem. By now I was used to him being faced down in the street water, but tonight he held himself as upright as possible.

"Heeey junior, you bringin' your daddy dinner because he refuses to come home
to mama?"

Let it be known that that is not exactly as he said those words, as if I wrote them down exactly as he said them they would be unintelligible. I had experience speaking with drunks, so I knew their language.

"I wouldn't wanna be home with a pansy son either."

"Benjamin, we are adults. Playground insults are beneath us." I said as I went to press past him, but he blocked my way. My defiance against his harassment seemed to sober him up a bit, and his words were finally legible to those who were not well versed in alcohol. He slurred out words again.

"Dangerous thing to say to the future pastor. You know, I could turn this entire town against you. Get 'em to burn down your house. Hell, I could get 'em to burn their own
houses down."

The look of incredulousness on my face conveyed more than any words could, as Benjamin continued without my dialogue. "Look, I have no reason to explain it to you. You're going to the church anyway, so you might wanna hurry before your dad signs away your birthright."

I normally would have trusted any of the eerie noises we all heard coming from the woods every night more than I would trust a drunk Benjamin, but the conviction in his voice was all that anyone needed to determine this man truly thought he would be the next in line to lead the local church. Had I not known his father, I would have thought these were just the words of a blathering drunk. If what he was alluding to was true, I needed to make haste to the church. I pushed past Benjamin, spilling soup on both him and myself, and sprinted towards the church.

I heard the voices barking at my father before I could even enter the building.

"Well, David, if you truly want to retire, I find it only fitting that my son take the place of the local reverend." I could already tell the loudest voice in the room belonged to Charles Willith, Benjamin's father. It was not hard to pinpoint when it was him who was talking, as it was always loud and accompanied by the rattling of his thick jowls. Each sentence was punctuated with a wheeze, as his lungs were made for a man a sixth of his size. Stealing sugary goods tended to cause a man to balloon in size, especially when done as often as he did.

"Charles, your son is nowhere near able to take on the church." The timber of my father's voice was shaky, holding back an anger that was rare for him to express.

"You and I are both aware my son is the most prepa-"

"Is he the most prepared, David? Your son has been disinterested in the church for quite some time now, and dare I say, disinterested in *you*. It has been years since you have done any sort of pastoral work together."

"Charles, my son has been sick. He just recently has been able to leave the hou-"

"And besides, you may think my Benji isn't prepared, but the fact of the matter is we've been studying and working together the last few years. I thought it would be intelligent to prepare my son in the event your son isn't ready to take on the position. As it seems his father hasn't prepared him adequately..."

It had taken what felt like a millenia to reach the doors to the sanctuary, despite it only being a short trek across the crimson carpet. Perhaps I had not realized that I had frozen in shock at the words I heard, but by time I reached the inner chambers of the church I could no longer stand the insults being hurled at both me and my father. I burst through the door, ready to shout "Would you louts cease harassing my father", but barely a syllable was uttered before I was spoken over.

As was typical with Willith, he felt the need to interrupt. I could not fault him for his rudeness, as the flab from his neck had devoured his ears and muffled the voices of all who spoke.

"Ah, speaking of the young Teendyth. From the look on your face I take it you've been listening to our conversation. Tell your father you have no interest in taking over the church."

"On the contrary, Deacon Willith. I actually have come to speak with my father about just that." I lied, trying to hide the jar of stew I had brought for my father.

"Absolom, don't you know that lying is a sin? You don't need to defend your father. The fact of the matter is this - if your father wants to retire, there will have to be a suitable candidate to take the pastor's place."

A smug grin rippled through Willith's jowls.

"Besides, both I and the other deacons agree your father has failed in preparing you for this duty."

"As I was saying earlier before you so rudely interrupted, Charles. My son has been sick. We all are aware that he inherited a poor constitution from his mother." My father interrupted.

"It's a shame that your son has to suffer due to you engaging in poor breeding."

The group of the deacons chuffed at Willith's comment, but my father continued and ignored them.

"Even in my son's inability to study with me, I think most can agree that he is more prepared than Benjamin to run this church. Being a pastor does not involve drinking in excess, which seems to be the only skill your son has developed so far."

I had never seen my father so aggressive in his sarcastic defiance against those he felt attacked by. For once, he had decided not to turn the other cheek and instead allowed himself to be defensive. Whether he was protecting me or the pulpit, I was unsure, as both were being actively insulted.

"Besides that, you have attacked my ability to raise my son. Do you really expect me to force a sickly child to undertake vigorous training?"

"Don't fool yourself, David. We have all seen him traveling throughout the town, strolling as if he has no care in the world. Even if he was ill at one point as a child, he has been in fine health ever since. You were just not manly enough as a father to force him to continue his studies. Your family no longer being in control of the church is recompense enough for being such a failure of a parent to your own spawn."

At this point I was raring to brutalize Willith, whether it be with my hands or my words. I had sat back and held my tongue long enough. There was no feasible reason for me to allow my father to be destroyed by such an oaf of a man.

"You, the man with a drunkard of a son, is telling MY father about how much he has failed in raising me? Why not do every person in Afton a favor and swallow a hot coal!" I yelled.

"ABSOLOM!" My father barked. "How dare you stoop to such a level as this man! Perhaps I was not forceful enough in your upbringing, as you seem more than well enough to open your mouth to spew hatred."

He was right, of course, and his scolding took any moxie I had and ripped it out of my spirit. He had finished berating me, and found it to be his turn to berate himself.

"Apparently I have not been strict enough in my teachings, for if I had been, you may have not been so quick to open your mouth."

Willith tried to scoff at my father's admittance of guilt, and began to speak of Benjamin being made pastor again, as if he was a bird repeating the only words he knew.

"So all are in agreement. Benji will become the pastor of Afton Assembly once Teendyth the Senior retires."

My father rubbed his eyes and spoke in a tight voice. "Charles, I never agreed that I would allow your son to take my place as pastor. I simply admitted that you were correct in saying I neglected my son's education. Yes, he was sickly and yes, he stayed home instead of joining me even when he was in good health. That does not mean that he was loafing about, as he was helping his ailing mother take care of the house."

A few of the deacons chuckled to themselves, amused that their future pastor was doing anything outside of the parameters of their perceived notions about a man helping with "woman's work".

My father continued. "Even then, it is no excuse. I should have taken better care to raise him in a manner that would befit his future status, so this conversation would never have had to happen." My father's face relaxed as he continued to speak in a more subdued manner.

"But it's too late for that now and the answer is simple. I won't retire."

A synchronized gasp left the mouths of all in the room, including mine. My twentieth birthday was coming at the end of the month, and it was unheard of for any Teendyth man to

break tradition.

"You cannot pastor this church forever!" Willith seemed as if he was now grasping at straws, trying to find a way for my father to step down and give his precious Benji control. Whether it was for some petty squabble or some deeper conspiracy, I had no idea. All I knew was that my father would not be allowed to have me continue in his footsteps as pastor when he retired. I began to sink into my self pity, thinking of how I had forced my father to deny his want for rest and fulfillment of tradition. I had fully realized my lack of preparation, and had only hoped that no one else noticed it either. My heart sank as the realization that not only the church elders but my father seemed to be in agreement. My father spoke again.

"I know Charles, that is exactly why I will be sending my son to seminary. There is no possible circumstance that I would allow Benjamin to lord over this church as we all know that he has become the worst of all the drunks in town. He spends his days traveling between the bar and the whore house; whether he travels by feet or belly is up to fate itself. I also recognize that in no way will you allow my son to take my place, despite him being adequately prepared. So, I will do as you wish. I will stay as pastor. My son will go to study. If he returns and you still refuse his leadership, it will be known by all the people of Afton that you are corrupt."

The countenance of all present had already dropped, and with that they were completely shattered. It was clear that all of them, for some reason or another, had become reliant on Benjamin Willith becoming the next pastor. One smug face remained though. Hidden under a layer of fat was the curling upper lip of the apparent ring leader. "Tell me then, David. How will you afford to send Junior here to college? All your years of using your income to provide for the town... you surely don't have enough to fund it yourself? I would offer to help myself but I simply don't have anything to spare..."

"I have it arranged already, his schooling has been taken care of."

"Surely you jest. University is expensive, and there's no way they would give your son free tuition for no reason."

I looked over at my father and saw his calm demeanor get replaced by the same smug look that was splayed across Willith's. It was a fitting look for him.

"Do you remember my brother, Eli?"

Willith's face turned red in anger. My uncle Eli, over the years of ceaseless study in the fields of academia, had become a professor of theology at the same seminary he had attended. He had become somewhat of a local celebrity. It had been unheard of for someone from our little town to uproot and make a name for themselves, but Eli Teendyth had become very well known for his upward mobility.

"We all do, David. What about him?" Willith was speaking through gritted teeth. If he could be said to have disliked my father, it was just as easily said that he despised my uncle. What Willith craved was power, and the only way he could exert his authority over others was in his position as a deacon. The thought of anyone with more power than him was repulsive and made his flabby face curl into the worst of grimaces.

My father continued his speech. "You see Charles, I had a feeling that if I tried to step down when my son came of age you might raise an objection."

For once my father did as I always wished he would. He bit back at the one trying to trample him. "And while I feel that my son is more than ready, I will sate your worries. I have spoken to my brother about the situation at hand, and he is understanding of the circumstances. He has put in a good word for my son to attend his college. He will be attending next month, and while he is away I will delay my retirement. I would rather break a smaller tradition in order to make sure my son can take my place. It is not right for a non-Teendyth man to pastor this church." That last comment was added for the extra twist of the dagger that my father sunk

into Willith.

No one had expected this response. Not the deacons, not Willith, and definitely not myself. Willith looked as if he was going to strike my father, but somehow held himself back. While he showed no positive attributes classically held by an elder of the church, he at least was able to keep himself from resorting to violence. While this was a pretty low standard for a deacon, it was still surprising to see where he would draw the line. It may have also been that he was too much of a coward to strike a grown man, despite being so willing to strike me as a child.

"David, I strongly advise you to give control over the church to my son, for I will fight any other outcome." Willith all but growled out the words through his teeth.

My father parried the thinly veiled threat. "Charles, it seems you care less about my son being ill-prepared and more that your son is given this position of power."

He paused to catch his breath. "Seeing as we are at a bit of an impasse, why don't we put the fate of the church up to a vote."

The gathered men shifted and murmured as they waited for Willith's response. Willith looked around at the other deacons as he answered. "Alright. All in favor of my son Benjamin being the next pastor of Afton Assembly, raise your arm."

Every single deacon present gave each other knowing glances while they raised their hands in unison.

My father's voice was flat as he spoke. "I will not be conspired against, Charles. We will ask the *people* of Afton what they believe should take place. What does it matter to have a church that people will not attend? There would be no worship, no teaching, and as some of you are concerned, no *tithe*."

At this, a spike of murderous intent lept into Willith's eyes.

"We will hold a vote with the people of Afton, and they will decide who will be in charge of the church."

Willith tried his best to save face as he ranted against the words of my father. "There really is no reason for that David. We did not call this meeting to ask your opinion on this matter. We have more than enough power over this church to make the decision whether you agree with it or not, and the people will still very willingly come to the church no matter who the pastor is. The residents of this place care nothing for religion or worship; all they want is to feel safe from superstition and hell. To them, coming to church is not about the relationships you prattle on about. To them, church is nothing but paying for a service."

By now my father had settled back into his docile mannerisms again.

"Even so, Charles, people do not care for a decision being made for them. You may be right that these people do not care for any of this religion, but even if they don't, they will not appreciate being tricked."

Willith's confident air dropped at this, knowing that if they did instate Benjamin against the wills of the townspeople, the church pews would never be full again.

Even if Benjamin was John the Baptist incarnate, the people would reject him if he was forced upon them. While the previous pastors had all been determined by their birthright, no vote was ever needed as everyone agreed that the position belonged to a Teendyth. Most did not even refer to the congregation as "Afton Assembly", instead calling it "Teendyth's Church". It was the way things were, and there would be uproar if that ever changed.

Willith sputtered one last attempt to gain control. "But even if they do vote for your son, he is still required to attend college. He is in no way suited for this job in his current state."

"I wouldn't have it any other way, " My father agreed.

They shook their hands in view of all attending to sign the pact that would speed me onto the next chapter of my life.

Congregatus

The morning of the next day was rife with business as my father and I went about the town to ensure that the entire populace would be able to vote. My father and I took extra care to make sure that all the townsfolk, including the down-and-out of the town, had word of what would occur that night, as we speculated that the deacons would pay the same amount of care to ensure they would *not* be invited. We started the day by visiting the local bar. The moment we walked into the tavern we were met with confused looks from all the patrons, then with dismissive glances as they returned to their raucous conversations. My dad walked up to the bar, took a seat, and gestured at me to join him. Mr. Sterling, the bar keep, walked over to

greet us.

"Hello Reverend! What do you need today? I know you aren't the one for drinking."

Jonathan Sterling was a large man, usually being the tallest man in the room. My father, who was considered fairly tall, only came to his shoulder. Mr. Sterling was burly on top of that, being akin to a mobile mountain. He had to stoop low to talk to any who sat at the bar.

My father chuckled at Mr. Sterling's comment. "Yes, I am going to refrain from my drinking today, as per usual. I actually came to ask you a favor."

"What would that be, Reverend?"

"Well, the deacons and I are undergoing a bit of a disagreement."

Mr. Sterling raised an eyebrow, curious as to where my father was going with this information. "We have decided that in order to agree upon a decision, we are going to the people. It is important that you all have a say in this decision as it affects the community as a whole."

"And what is it that you need from me?" Mr. Sterling heavily respected my father and paid close attention to his words. There was no reason that he should believe my father would cause him any trouble, so it was clear that the answer to whatever favor he asked would be yes.

"I need you to announce to everyone in here that there is going to be a vote tonight. I would like them all in attendance."

Mr. Sterling nodded, stood up straight and made a cone with his hands to amplify

his voice.

"QUIET!"

His voice was large and booming. I swear I felt the ground tremor. Everyone stopped and turned their heads towards Mr. Sterling, fully expecting that someone was about to be permanently removed from the establishment. Once he had everyone's attention, he shouted across the tavern my father's message.

"TONIGHT AT TEENDYTH'S CHURCH IS A-" he stooped down low and spoke to my father. "How important is this meeting?"

"Highly."

"A HIGHLY IMPORTANT MEETING!"

I was startled by how abrupt the yelling began anew.

"HE ASKS THAT EVERYONE PRESENT ATTENDS!

Someone from the crowd shouted in response. "What's the meeting for?"

"REVEREND DIDN'T TELL ME, BUT THERE'S GONNA BE A VOTE!"

It felt as if we were attending a rally with how passionate Mr. Sterling was.

"ALL I KNOW IS THAT HE AND THE DEACONS ARE HAVING A DISAGREEMENT AND THEY WANT US THERE TO HELP SETTLE IT."

Someone shouted from the crowd of drinkers, "Yeah! Fuck the deacons!" That exclamation was promptly followed by one in attendance throwing a glass at the head of the profaner. "Watch your language around the Reverend!" The crowd began to berate the profaner with more profanity and threats of death for cursing around the pastor. My father chuckled and Mr. Sterling quickly restarted his yelling.

"ALL OF YOU SHUT YOUR MOUTHS AND SHOW SOME RESPECT! YOU'RE IN THE PRESENCE OF A HOLY MAN! AND WHOEVER THREW THAT GLASS IS PAYING

FOR IT!"

My father continued to chuckle as he got up to leave, having his invitation to the meeting sent by means of screaming man. "Thank you for your cooperation, Mr. Sterling. I hope to see you tonight as well?"

"Wouldn't miss it for anything, Reverend." Mr. Sterling went to shake my father's hand then stopped. "Oh yeah, one last thing before you leave." Mr. Sterling stood at attention once again and shouted.

"THE BAR WILL BE CLOSING EARLY AS I WILL BE ATTENDING

THE MEETING!"

A mass of boos rose out of the crowd until Mr. Sterling growled loudly at them.

"ANYONE I SEE IN ATTENDANCE TONIGHT WILL RECEIVE THEIR BOOZE ON THE HOUSE TOMORROW."

The crowd rose up into a cheer, shouting so loud that I felt my ears begin to ring. My father laughed at Mr. Sterling. "Sterling, I am trying to get these people to stop drinking and here you are making the problem worse!"

Mr. Sterling patted my father's shoulder and chuckled quietly. "Reverend, you can either have your attendees, or you can stop the drinking problem of the town."

"I guess I cannot complain. Take care Mr. Sterling, as I must take my leave now. Be safe in this crowd."

"Take care yourself Reverend."

AFTER OUR ADVENTURES at the tavern we spent the rest of the day pulling alcoholics out of the gutters and flattering the ladies of the night. All who we asked said that they would be in attendance. We could only hope that they would hold their word.

By the time the meeting had arrived both my father and I had become sore from a full day of meandering the town and asking all who could to attend the meeting tonight. When we entered the church we were both coated in sweat from a full day of speaking to the people.

When we saw the contents of the chapel we were both overjoyed that our labors had paid off. Almost everyone we had asked to come had made an appearance. From every drunkard to every prostitute. Even the worst of them all, the catholics, decided to make an appearance. The deacons were standing near the pulpit, conversing with themselves and entirely ignoring the makeshift congregation that stood before them. It was the largest number of people to ever sit in the pews of this chapel, there were even some standing in the back. Had we been collecting offerings that night I can assure you Willith would have been much more friendly with the people who sat in the pews.

As my father and I walked up the center aisle of the church everyone turned their heads to look at us. None of us had told them what the purpose of tonight's meeting was as we wanted to avoid any chances of the deacons interfering with the outcome. Whispers started to float about as they saw me shadowing my father to such an important meeting. The last time my father brought me along during his work was when I was very little, and it was a strange sight for them all to see me standing next to him in the church.

Once we reached the pulpit my father took his place behind it and gestured for me to stand by his side. He also called over Benjamin, who was standing nervously in the corner. It seemed that he, by order of his father, had sobered up for the night. He would not make any sort of eye contact with anyone in the room. It seemed as if sober Benjamin had none of the machismo that the drunk variant had.

My father cleared his throat, gaining the attention of everyone in the room. "You must be wondering why I have called you all here tonight, and I assure you that you will find the answers to your questions soon enough. Let me preface tonight's meeting with a bit of background to the situation. As you all know, my son is reaching the age of twenty and as is tradition it will soon be time for me to retire and give the church over to him."

My father paused, sighing long and deep, nobody daring to interrupt his exposition.

"But, the deacons feel that I have not prepared my son to be fit for this position and instead feel that we should have Benjamin Willith take up the title of reverend."

The moment my father even uttered the words "Benjamin Willith" and "Reverend" in the same sentence an uproar started. Anyone who would insinuate that those two things should be said at the same time were instantly considered an enemy. The congregation was on its feet and if my father hadn't intervened the people would have left and started building fires designated for the deacons.

Speaking in a slightly louder, but still in the same calm voice, my father urged the crowd to settle. "If you all would please simmer down and let me speak, I have more to say"

Silence slowly returned, allowing my father to continue. "We came to the decision that you, the people and lifeblood of the town, should have the final say in the matter, which is why we gathered you here today. We will be putting this up to a vote."

The deacons were glaring fire and brimstone at my father. None truly believed that they had *all* decided it was up to a vote. But it was crystal clear to those present that the elders, other than my father of course, would do whatever they had to do, if it meant they would have their way in the end.

"The options are as follows. I will resign from my position as pastor immediately. Benjamin Willith will then be instated as the new pastor of Afton Assembly, taking over in place of my son."

This time, there was no violent uproar, just a wave of the congregation awkwardly shifting in their seats. They managed to hold onto their respect for my father, refusing to lose control of themselves again.

"The other option is that my son is sent to seminary, then after his tenure, return to Afton to pastor over the church."

Mr. Sterling stood up from his seat and boomed out from the pews.

"WHY SEND HIM TO SEMINARY? I SAY MAKE HIM PASTOR RIGHT NOW!"

The blood rushed to Deacon Willith's face and he ran towards the pulpit with a speed that was shocking for a man of such rotund stature. After roughly shoving my father away, he smoothed his mussed hair and spoke his own greasy words to sway the crowd.

"The other deacons and I strongly feel that young Teendyth has simply not been trained enough to know how to handle a church. We worry that the stress may be too much on him, as we all know he inherited a weak disposition from his mother."

"He looks fine to me!" One of the local women known for her profession chimed in. The gentle noises from the doves that had been nesting in the church rafters managed to be heard over the congregation's cacophony.

"Sure, I mean he *looks* fine, but does that qualify him to *be* fine? The boy only has enough energy to do housework and that dictates he needs to stay home with his *mother.*" Venom dripped from Willith's words when he mentioned my mother. He held a special disdain for her, and the same disdain was held by all the deacons, and especially the deacon's wives.

"She has always insisted that she has young Teendyth stay at home to help complete her homely "duties". How does one use clothes washing and cooking to lead a church? Much less to speak from the pulpit? No no no, the boy simply does not have the QUALIFICATIONS to lead

the church!"

Willith was getting worked up and sweat was beading on his tomato face that he uselessly dabbed at with his shirt sleeve.

"She never was one for strength of mind or body, and never thought of Absolom's future or upbringing, but only of her own selfish need for someone to cater to her every want."

I felt a silent growl leave my throat as I heard Willith speak of my mother in such a tone, but I could deal with him at a later date. Right now I needed to prove to the town that

I was fit to be the pastor, and to do that, I needed to hold my tongue.

Mr. Sterling interrupted Willith's soliloquy and spoke up again. "WELL WHY DON'T YOU JUST ASK THE BOY? ALL I AM HEARING IS ASSUMPTIONS ABOUT HIS HEALTH."

The crowd echoed Mr. Sterling's sentiment and started to shout my name. Ripples of anger washed across Willith's face as he begrudgingly motioned for me to stand beside him.

My voice was tiny compared to the previous spoken words, but my spite for the deacons banished any nervousness. "I feel well. I do still have a touch of asthma, but as long as we keep the church free of any dust, I can breathe well."

I was understating as I had much more than "a touch of" asthma. In fact my asthma was pretty severe, but it took a large amount of factors to trigger it. The people did not need to know that. They only needed to know that they could trust my health. The crowd murmured in happy burbles and seemed ready to accept me as the new church leader right then and there. Willith began to scramble, attempting to gain control over the public opinion of me.

"Well, even then, I think we can all agree that he is severely lacking in any sort of experience that may lend him skill in a position of this nature." He motioned his son to his side. He gripped Benji's arm tightly as he spoke again. "I, on the other hand have vigorously trained Benjamin all these years while the young Teendyth has been slacking at hom–"

He was barely able to finish his words before the uproar began. All present were down right insulted that anyone would insist that my lack of training had been due to me slacking off instead of being ill. Their raucous sentiment would have been much more welcome to me if they had had a history of supporting me in the past during the days of my bullies beating me, but I found a small sliver of solace in their pure willingness to stand up for me now.

Shouts came from the crowd hurling a menagerie of insults towards Willith. Some were simple curses, while others got more creative. I heard more than one man hurl insults about being intimate with Mrs. Willith. I think my father allowed himself some sort of satisfaction at that, as I saw him smirking to himself as he made his way back to the pulpit. He pushed past Willith, usurping him in the same way Willith had usurped my father earlier. He placed a hand on my shoulder to guide me beside him as he faced the crowd. My father then slammed his fist into the pulpit repeatedly, demanding everyone's attention. With a voice of fatherly sternness he spoke to the crowd as if speaking to a disobedient child.

"I would ask that you all refrain from another one of these outbursts. I also ask that you show Willith the same decency you show to me for the rest of this meeting." The masses of people immediately quieted and awkwardly shuffled back into their seats - chastised.

"It is time that we call a vote. I ask that you all be silent during this time. We will ask in a moment for you to raise your hand on who you will choose to lead this congregation. The deacons will be standing on the sidelines counting the hands." Each of the deacons, excluding Willith, shuffled out and took post beside the pews.

"Let us start with Benjamin. All in favor of Benjamin leading the church, raise your hand." There was some silent murmuring as the attendants deliberated amongst themselves. In the pews, a scant number of hands rose. Most were understandable that they would vote as such, as they were Benjamin's closest friends and some of my biggest tormentors. A few hands raised that belonged to other men of the church. They held scowls on their faces; grimaces so tight it seemed as if their skin had been forcefully stretched against their face. They kept their hands up for a moment, allowing the votes to be tallied.

"Twelve votes for Benjamin." The deacons exclaimed from the floor. Willith shifted nervously on his feet.

"Alright, you all can put down your hands." Everyone who had already voted lowered their hands.

"Now, we will move on to the next. All in favor of postponing my retirement and sending my son to seminary, and upon his return taking up my mantle of reverend, raise your hand."

Hands extended to the sky throughout the entire sanctuary. Even the wives of all the deacons, including Mrs. Willith herself, raised their hands. Deacon Willith glared at his wife. If he had had his way, only the "respectable" men of the town would have been present for this meeting, and the vote would have been in his favor instead. He hated my father for many reasons, but the biggest conflict they fought on was the presence of women in the church. My father believed that as long as there was no disruption, they were welcome to join the congregation, and even have a voice in the matters of leadership. Willith despised every action my father took when it came to women, but since he was the pastor, my father had the last word on the matter.

The deacons finally finished completing the tally of votes, which I thought unnecessary. "Sixty-three votes in favor of young Teendyth!"

An uproar spread through the church for the third time, but this time it was in celebration. Everyone was certain from the moment the meeting started, and the purpose revealed, that I would receive the position. Almost everyone present knew that Deacon Willith would try to scheme his son into the position, but for the time being the masses decided to ignore that worry. To finally have the worry of a despot being placed in power assuaged was as exhilarating as rain during the drought seasons.

My father allowed applause this time and for a moment, stepped out into the sea of attendees. All of them patted him on the back, insisting that he must be proud of his son. I was proud of myself as well. To know that the people of the town so explicitly wanted me to be their pastor inflated my ego, but a nagging feeling permeated throughout my mind. Had they chosen me because they approved of me, or was it because I was a Teendyth? Or, even worse, was it simply that my opponent was just that despicable? I pushed it down, and accepted it as a means of keeping myself humble.

After a moment of celebrating my father regained order, he thanked everyone for their time and attendance, and dismissed them all to their homes. No one lingered as they

wanted to cling to the elation of victory without the soil of Willith's pandering and weaseling for
a re-vote.

My father and I also rushed out of the church as soon as we could, making our way towards home. My father was beaming. I had not seen this much emotion from him in years and it held a smile on my face as we walked.

He was proud and for tonight I believed he was proud of me for just being his son. He smiled an almost boyish grin and he told me he was proud of me for speaking my piece clearly. We talked together as if we were friends for the first time and when we burst through the door of our house we were both out of breath. Before I laid eyes on my mother I began shouting for her, rifling throughout the house in an attempt to relay to her the news before my father could. I first checked the kitchen, then I ran through the dining hall. The journey wasn't long, as I found her reclining in the sitting room with her feet up. When she saw me, she looked up from her knitting and smiled.

"How did the assembly go, dear?"

"It was almost unanimous, Mother!" I said, shaking with excitement. "Sixty-three votes in
my favor!"

She smiled a gentle smile. "I knew it was destined to be so. We all know that if God meant a Teendyth to be pastoring this church, he would make sure one would be in place." She then started rambling, words spilling out of her mouth and overlapping each other.

"When will you be starting?"

"Oh I simply can't wait until your father retires!"

"We'll finally be able to spend some time together!"

'I will need to make you some new clothes!"

She stopped abruptly and a smile crossed her face. "David Absolom, do you know how long it has been since your father and I have shared a bed?"

I soured my face. "I would rather not think of that, mother. The sad news is that it will be a few more years until I can fully realize my vocation."

My words slowed her questions and her smile fell, but not to sadness, but instead to confusion. "But you said they agreed that you would be the next pastor?"

At that point my father had entered the room. It seemed he had taken a detour in the kitchen to get himself a glass of water. Mother looked towards him. "What is it that our son is talking about, dear? A few more years? I thought it was your time to retire?"

My father took a sip of his water. "Ah yes, that is the portion I forgot to tell you. Absolom is going to be attending seminary."

She glanced up at me quizzically. "Is what he is saying true?"

I grinned and nodded vigorously as my mother's smile forcefully returned to her face.

"What? Why didn't you tell me about this David?"

"I figured Father told you."

"I know you would dear, I'm talking about your father." She said, brushing me aside.

"I was going to wait to see if he would be required to attend." My father explained his machinations and thoughts. "I knew that Willith would try to attempt some sort of scheme to put his brat in power, but I knew not to what lengths he would go. If they would have just allowed a simple vote for who would get the position I would have forgone the entire vote and instead initiated my retirement post-haste. I had to promise that Absolom would be getting a higher education or they would have vetoed any sort of decision that was made and would have ordained Benjamin to the position instead immediately."

My mother's face scrunched tight. "And how exactly are we going to be able to afford that, David Senior?" You could always tell when my mother was angry when she added the "Senior" to my father's name.

"I've got that entirely taken care of, dear. He will be attending Eli's college. Isn't that grand!?"

My mother went silent and her face blanked like it always tended to do that when my uncle was mentioned.

"Margaret, there's no reason to sulk like that," my father scolded her. "I know you don't care for Eli, but he is an excellent man of God and a fantastic scholar. Absolom will be in

good hands."

My mother somberly agreed with her husband and nodded. "You are right of course my dear. But as his mother I have every right to worry about my son. That being said, you still haven't told me how we are going to pay for this."

My father proceeded to explain his earlier correspondence with his brother, requesting that he put a good word in for him. The seminary dean, being very fond of my uncle, agreed to allow me a full ride scholarship and consider it a charity case. The addition that my competition was a blithering alcoholic was what fully convinced the dean, a staunch fundamentalist, to allow me to attend.

My mother pursed her lips for a moment, pondering over the story she had just been told.. After a moment of thought, she spoke. "I'll allow it. But if I hear anything about my son being hurt by anyone I'll have the head of whoever caused it."

My father laughed. "Of course, dear. And you know I would help."

Mother stood up to go to bed and as she walked by my father, she stood up on the tips of her toes and looked my father in the eyes the best she could, giving him a very stern expression. "I mean *anyone,* David Absolom."

I had no clue who that threat was towards, but my father took it to heart.

"I promise you, no harm will come to our son." My mother's stern expression melted into a small smile as she nodded in acceptance. "Well then, David Junior. Should we start planning your trip?"

Iter

My uncle arrived a few days before we were set to depart. It was important that he get some sort of rest before we made the trek, as he had just returned from a trip overseas, and the seminary was located about a half-day's trip by train to the east of Afton. After he arrived my father, uncle, and I sat in the living room while my mother kept to herself in the kitchen. My uncle was grilling me on whether I was prepared for the trip or not.

"You've packed everything you'll need, correct? You won't be able to come back for anything you might have missed."

"Uncle, I will not forget any of my things." I assured him. "Admittedly, I have been packed for weeks now."

Uncle Eli chuckled. "Let me guess, your mother insisted as soon as she knew"?

"Of course she did, but I'm thankful that I can be certain that I have everything." I will admit, living out of suitcases since then had been a tad irritating, but I knew it was how my mother showed she cared for me.

"Speaking of your mother..." Uncle Eli diverted. "How are you doing, Margaret? We haven't spoken in a while." Uncle Eli raised his voice and craned his neck towards the kitchen so my mother could hear him. There was no response.

Eli chuckled to himself. "I guess she still can't seem to speak to me."

I gave my uncle an inquisitive look. I had always sensed some sort of disdain from my mother whenever my uncle was mentioned, and she had always refused to be in the same space as him. It was most likely due to her chronic tiredness and it being my last days at home that she refrained from leaving the house entirely.

"Oh, you've never told him, David?" Uncle Eli asked, clearly insinuating there was some reason behind my mother's hatred.

My father, who was reading a book in the corner, looked up with an uncomfortable frown on his face. "I've refrained from doing so, and I would rather you not tell him either."

"Oh it's no harm done, the story is completely innocent." My uncle insisted.

I looked at my father with a begging look unbecoming of a twenty year old, for whenever my uncle was present my mental age devolved by ten years.

"Alright fine, but I will not be around to hear it."

At that my father got up and left to accompany my mother in the kitchen. I scooted myself towards the edge of my seat, leaning forward and looking intently at my uncle as I waited for him to recount the tale.

"Well, out with it, Uncle!"

"Don't get too excited Abb, it's not that interesting."

"That does not mean I am not excited to hear it."

"Very well then," Eli snickered to himself. "When your father and mother started courting I had feelings for your mother. I tried many times to woo her myself, but she was head over heels for your father and there was no way that the two could be separated."

"And that is why she does not speak to you? That seems out of character for her."

"Normally, I would agree. In a final act of desperation I attempted the largest gesture I could think of, but ultimately it ended up encouraging your mother to never speak to me again."

"What was it you did?"

At that moment my father all called us to the dining room so we could sup before we retired for the night.

"That, nephew, is a story for another day."

MY MOTHER WAS QUIET through dinner, forcing herself to sit with us all as it would be our last dinner together for a while. The rest of us, emotionally oppressed by her hateful and mournful looks, remained quiet as well. We all inhaled the stew my mother had made for dinner and headed to our separate rooms to rest before the early morning. Even with the early hour we were going to sleep at, we would only be able to get by with around two hours of sleep.

And those two hours passed by quickly.

We awoke, all three men currently residing in the house all overwhelmingly groggy, while my mother was more energetic than ever. It seemed her anxiety that I would be ill prepared overwhelmed her need to shun Uncle. She zipped around the house ensuring that both Uncle Eli and I had everything we needed packed. It was understandable that she was so concerned about me, but that she was worried about Uncle was strange. When asked why she was so helpful towards him, she responded matter-of-factly, "I just want to ensure that nothing of his stays in my home for longer than necessary. Besides, if he forgets something he will have to come back to retrieve it."

We loaded up all of the trunks and bags and things and all got onto the carriage. My parents would be traveling with us until we reached the train station, at which my uncle and I would depart and my parents would return home. It was only a few hours trip, each moment of which was filled with my mother mulling over everything that I may have forgotten and ensuring I had everything I needed. I assured her multiple times that, yes, I had triple checked over the past weeks that I had packed everything. We had had this conversation multiple times. She even insisted as such when we pulled into the train depot, and only ceased once our feet touched down on the gravel.

"Well, if you left something behind it's too late now and out of my hands," she declared.

"I did not forget anything..." I said to myself in exasperation.

My uncle pulled the watch out of his waist coat to check the time. "We've arrived just in time. Had we been a moment later, we may not have had the chance to get all of your stuff on the train, let alone the things you forgot."

"Not you as well, Uncle."

Uncle Eli let out a hearty laugh at my feelings of betrayal. "I'm just ribbing you, Abbs. I know you remembered all of your things."

My mother had developed her own look of irritation at this point, feeling somehow targeted by both my exasperation and my uncle's ribbing

"Eli, you would do well not to refer to me in any manner." My mother stated.

My uncle moved towards my mother, attempting to put his arm around her shoulders as if they were the closest of friends.

"Oh sister, do not treat me so harshly. You're here to see us off, I wouldn't want a

sour memory."

"I am not your sister, and I am barely your sister-in-law. I am here to see my son off, not you." She shrugged his arm off her and stepped away with a huff. There was clear aggravation on her face, but that soon melted into an expression a mother bird may make when its young learns to fly. She had been such a tempest of emotions until this point, that when the time came to bid her son goodbye, the dam relinquished its hold.

"Oh goodness that's right..." she said to herself quietly. With that, she broke. That dam broke loose into sobs as she lunged forward, wrapping her arms around me. I hugged her back, resting my chin on her head as she dampened my collar with a wave of tears.

My father patted me on the shoulder as I hugged her and said "It's your job to console her this time. Your uncle and I will take care of the luggage." I nodded in response.

"It is okay, Mother, this is not some sort of forever goodbye. I will be seeing you again in the winter months. It will pass quickly, I can guarantee it." More sobs eked out of her throat as I petted her head. Finally, she calmed down.

"You have taken such good care of me, Son. I want you to know that I am so proud of you." She said in a cracked voice. "I would not have made it these past years without you. Thank you for helping me despite your sickness."

"Of course mother, I only knew how to treat you so well due to Father's teachings."

A sad look washed on her face for a fleeting moment. Not the same sadness that was caused by my departure. No, this was something deeper and much older.

"Don't tell your father, but I personally think you exceeded his teachings."

"Well that is very unfair to Father!" I exclaimed. "Though I will not deny that I am flattered, Mother. Making you and Father proud is something I have always wanted to succeed at."

"And you have."

"I could agree," My father said as walked up behind me, my uncle trailing him. "You are an amazing son, Absolom. We are proud of you. To have a second member of the Teendyth family attend college is reason enough, yet it is still only a fraction of the reason of why we are proud of you." He wrapped his arm around my mother while she nodded in agreement.

"All your things are loaded." My uncle cut in. "We should go on and board the train. Your parents will follow us so we can say our last goodbyes." With that we started in the direction of the passenger cars.

"We also do not want to arrive back home too late ourselves." My father added. "It will be the first time in almost twenty years your mother and I will have the house to ourselves. We have many....tasks, to attend to". He had a twinkle in his eye as he said this and my mother quickly scolded my father. "David Absolom! You shouldn't say anything like that in front of
the boy."

"Oh, he's old enough to know these things."

I will say, it was strange seeing my father act this way with my mother. He was generally distant from her in all manner for almost a decade now, and possibly even longer than that. To hear them make such playful comments was an alien concept. Much to my mother's horror, my father continued this line of conversation.

"Perhaps we should have his opinion then! Absolom, I know this is not how things generally work, but tell me son, what is your preference? A brother or a sister?"

"Disgusting." I declared flatly as we finished our short trek to the train.

"Alright, enough flirting. You two are going to make me commit the sin of jealousy." Uncle Eli finally saved us all from my father's apparent arousal.

He gave me a verbal push towards my parents. "Give your goodbyes so we can board." Again, my mother wrapped her arms around me sobbing that it would be months since I could accompany her. I tried to gently brush her off of myself as the conductor called the all-aboard.

"I am sorry mother, I cannot continue the goodbye as long as usual. I need to board." She nodded, tears in her eyes, as she unwrapped her arms and backed away.

"Come on Abb, no dallying!" Uncle Eli yelled, hanging off the steps into the interior of the train, gesturing at me to hurry up. I told my mom I loved her one last time, then dashed into the train as it began to creak to a start. The train had saved me from any more lingering, awkward goodbyes that I felt such disdain for. I hated seeing my mother in such a state, and while I generally was the one to comfort her, I took no joy in comforting her this time.

UNCLE ELI WAITED FOR me at the doors, which I was grateful for. There would have been no way that I would have found my way around the train to locate him had he went ahead to our seats. He led us through corridors of seats with many different faces sitting upon them. These seats were mostly the common folk; mothers and fathers shushing their antsy children and the elderly traveling to visit loved ones who had moved across the country. I found an empty row and began to slide into the booth. As I did I heard Uncle Eli curse under his breath, very

clearly upset.

"Get back up, Absolom. These aren't our seats." Confused, I got back up and continued down the aisle.

"Whatever do you mean? Can't we just take any seat we would like?"

"Well of course we could, but I booked a specific spot."

"Where would that be? Is it over there?" I pointed towards an empty booth in the back corner.

"That's the problem."

"What is?"

"We're in the wrong spot, Absolom. Your mother distracted me and I entered the wrong car ." My mother's show of emotions were quite distracting, I did not blame him for the faux pas.

"Well, I guess we will just have to find a seat in here. It should be no worry." I went to sit down again, but was interrupted before my rear end could hit the leather a second time.

"No, Absolom, it's an easy fix. Just follow me." Uncle began speeding towards the end of the train. Once he reached his destination, my uncle opened the door at the end of the car. There was open air, then a door with a large "11" painted on it.

"Good, It's just the next cab over."

I stopped him right as he went to step through the door. "Assuredly you aren't allowed to do that, Uncle."

"Abb, have you ever ridden on a train before?" Uncle Eli said with a tint of exasperation in his voice.

"Well, no..."

"And have I ridden in a train before, Absolom?"

"Yes..." I said dejectedly.

"Case and point. Now hush up and follow me, I know what I'm doing."

He cracked open the door between train cars and stepped out of the door, and I followed suit. Outside was a small patio that had a guard rail made of wrought iron to keep one from teetering off the side. The guardrail was absent from the end of the patio, allowing the open air over the coupling to be completely accessible. Uncle Eli gripped his briefcase, and holding it tight, leapt over the speeding chasm that could easily cause his death. He was fox-like as his feet touched down on the opposite platform, the loud rushing of wind making any thud he might have made, inaudible. He was in stark contrast to me, who was currently grasping the iron guard rail as if it were the only thing keeping me from tumbling into the rushing railway tracks below. From all my experience, it very well may have been the only thing keeping me from being taken off this mortal coil

"It's only gonna get worse if you draw it out, Abb. Now leap over."

"I think I would rather not, Uncle." I cried.

"Oh come on, you don't even have any luggage to hop over with! All of your

things are in the luggage car!"

"I really don't think I..."

"Absolom, you're a man now. You're going to live on your own for the first time in your life. Consider this leap a right of passage!"

I wouldn't say those words emboldened me, but they did make me feel some sort of shame at the thought of turning back now. Yes, I admired safety, but my uncle desperately wanted to get to his "special seats" and what kind of man would I be if I were to be the reason he could not make it? Though different from the drunkards and prostitutes, my uncle had something he needed and wanted. It was on me to make sure that he received that. I stood up straight and inched towards the edge.

"Yes! That is it Abb! It's not even that large of a jump."

I looked down and saw the speeding rails beneath me, filling me with even more panic. I couldn't bring myself to jump. Instead, I reached forward and grabbed the wrought iron bars on the opposing patio. Taking a giant step, I brought one foot forward to the opposite floor, then dragged the other leg, along with the full weight of my body, safely to the other car. I silently thanked the heavens I had inherited my father's height.

Uncle Eli let out a chortle, "You see Abb? You didn't even need to jump!"

The exertion from the leap mixed with the anxiety caused my health to temporarily tank. In between wheezes I managed to eek out two words and nothing else.

"Shut up."

"Of course, of course." Uncle Eli said, giggling to himself. "Now let's get inside."

He popped open the door, revealing the contents of the next car. The inside of this one was entirely different. The open pew-like seats were replaced by large cubicles that stretched the length of the cars. Instead of moving down a middle lane, Uncle and I veered towards the wall and traveled past several doors that let passengers enter the "business class" seating. Most of these cubicles were filled with men in suits discussing, sometimes arguing, about whatever deals they dabbled in. I did not seem to get a good listen at the topic of their discussion, as they all stopped and looked my way as I passed. It seemed as if they had seen a corpse. I felt like one, so their eyes may not have been deceiving them.

Uncle Eli stopped at the last of these cubicles. He seemed spry compared to my heaving brought on by our adventures in train-car hopping. I leaned on the wall outside the box, but my uncle gestured for me to go ahead. He gently shoved me through the door, unintentionally causing me to stumble on the way through. I caught myself and sat down hard on the seat. My uncle looked worried at my stumble and began to apologize for pushing me too hard. I waved Eli off, trying my hardest to convey that I had no ill feelings, all while feeling as if my lungs were going to fall out of my throat. The August heat caused my brow to bead with sweat as I gasped for air. Thankfully, he was able to decipher my waving and wheezing. We both waited a minute, letting the moment pass so I could form full sentences again.

"I am not ever doing that again, Uncle."

"I will try my hardest to make sure I get the correct car next time." Uncle Eli did not seem remorseful in the least. In fact, he seemed rather proud of the discomfort he had caused me.

"But, now that we are here, I can finally show you why I wanted my specific seat."

"Show me?" I questioned. "You have told me nothing about showing me anything."

"Well of course not!" He proclaimed with a wild grin across his face.

"Well... Why didn't you?"

"Absolom, did my brother fail to teach you what a surprise is?"

"Of course he taught me what a surprise was!" I felt almost as if I were being scolded.

"You could have at least hinted towards it!"

"And distract you from the packing you needed to do? Lord boy, you already forgot things enough!" Eli let out a deep belly laugh that shook his entire body. I did not share in

his elation.

"I thought you said you would not make those jokes again." Ever since I had stepped on this train I felt as if he were mocking me in some way. I often struggled to decipher his intent, but I had seen him treat my mother in the same way, so I figured it was part of his playful nature.

Eli wiped a tear from his eye, his laughter slowing down. "You are correct, that was uncalled for. Let us get on with it then."

"Thank you."

"You are welcome." Up until this point Eli had been leaning against the door frame, so distracted by his own wit that he forgot to sit down. It was now that he slid into the booth opposite the cabin from me, then slammed his oversized briefcase on the table between us.

"Now to what is really important."

"And that would be...?"

"Your birthday present, Abb! I know it's a tad late, but you know I would never forget my favorite nephew's birthday." He smiled broadly in excitement, then gestured towards the case in front of him. I felt so intensely confused by his behavior.

"You are giving me your briefcase?"

"No no no." He slid the case around so the latches faced me. "Open it."

"Uncle, you are a very confusing man." I reached down and undid the leather case's straps, flipping the lid open. I was dumbfounded by the contents.

It was a sheath of sorts, an object painted in a gaping black that consumed the light that shone on it. It was a heavily treated leather, being hard and malleable. Out of the very top was a grip made of an ashy wood, cylindrical in shape yet cinched in at the middle. It looked as if it had a girdle hidden under the wood, tightening the waist of the grip. A semi-translucent black seam bisected the wood of the handle, then fattened into a round disc that covered the end of the wood. This was clearly the blade's pommel. The shape of the sheath was strange as well, almost as if someone had taken a curved fruit and flattened it. The tip of the sheath curved backward as if it were trying to make contact with the exposed grip. Slid into the top of the sheath were two small retaining knives who's handles matched that of the main blade's.

I was astounded by its beauty.

"What am I looking at, Uncle? I have never seen anything like it, yet I can tell this is the most beautiful version of... whatever it is."

"It is a knife, Abb."

"Well I assumed that, but what *is* it? Where did you acquire this?"

"Are you sure you want to know? It is highly likely you will cause your uncle to go on a fairly large rant about his passions." It was clear he was being cheeky, he knew I wanted to know. He just wanted me to beg him for the details.

I rolled my eyes. "Yes Uncle, I am absolutely sure."

He puffed out his chest, clearly proud of the work he does. "That knife that you are holding is a kukri. They are a weapon that comes from the southern regions of Asia".

I could not take my eyes off the blade sitting before me as I asked more questions. "Are they all this beautiful?"

"Oh no, not at all. I mean, some say that the kukri is used for worship purposes in many Hindu beliefs. I have seen many of those, whether carried by the common man or the local gurkh, which is their version of the military. Those are usually made with steel or iron, nothing quite this ornate."

I gingerly picked up the weapon by its hilt. "Would you happen to know what is so special about this specific blade then?"

"It's intended for sacrifice."

I fumbled the blade, dropping it back on the table. " I assume I should stop holding

it then."

Eli grimaced as the blade hit the table but assured me that there was no reason why I should not be handling it.

"It should be fine, the group that used it is no longer functioning."

I cocked my head, curious to know more. Eli began to explain."Well, before the rise of Hinduism 30 years ago-"

I raised my hand, trying to get his attention. "What exactly is Hinduism, Uncle?"

"Oh, much apologies. I forget you have never left Afton. It comes as no surprise you wouldn't know much about the goings-on across the ocean. Hinduism is a religion that came to light just a few years before you were born."

"A new religion?" I asked, confused by the fact that more were still being made. "I thought that religions were a pretty well set thing..."

"One would think, but Joseph Smith started a new one back in 1830 right over in Manchester..." I could tell he was about to go on a tangent, but he caught himself. "You'll learn about that in due time. Anyways, the beliefs of the Hindu religion are actually fairly old, it's just the title itself that is new. Hinduism is a conglomeration of different family and village religions all came together under the same name."

I was intrigued. I had spent the majority of my life inside the four walls of my house. The few times I left I was still within the four walls that were Afton. In fact, I had never left the town. To finally hear stories and history of places other than my tiny hometown brought me joy, if not a singe of jealousy.

My uncle stopped and caught his breath. "Am I boring you?"

"Of course not, Uncle! Please continue!"

I was emphatic about hearing more. It was less of a want and more of a necessity. "Why did they conglomerate in such a manner? Would it not be confusing to keep track of all the different familial beliefs?"

A wide grin spread across Uncle Eli's face, clearly pleased that I was so very intrigued. "Well, in answer to the former, they did it due to pressure from the British Empire. Before they declared themselves a religion they were being forced to declare whether they were Christians or Muslims. To the British they really only saw those two religions.. The people got fed up and coined the term "Hindu" in order to get them to stop hounding them about it."

"I see. And what about my other question?"

"Ah well, you see there isn't really a set guideline for the religion. It mostly still varies from house to house and god to god, but now they have a common banner. Which brings us back to the history of the knife, now that you have context."

I inched forward on my seat, very much so engaged.

My Uncle continued. "As you know, when I graduated seminary I was sent overseas to minister to the impoverished people groups in southern and eastern Asia. On my most recent trip, the one I just returned from to be exact, I was sent out to India to study Hinduism. Despite being formed of some fairly old beliefs it wasn't really something of notice until recently. While I was there I ended up having the pleasure of being hosted by a man named Anvit. He was a small man with incredibly scruffy features. Years of poverty had made him nothing but skin and bones, and even now, in his most affluent stage, he struggled to keep on any weight due to previous malnutrition. He very clearly never shaved nor cut his hair, and it puffed out in a curly salt and pepper colored mass. He housed me and fed me so I could focus on traveling and asking the locals about their beliefs."

"And he gifted you the knife?"

"Well, not quite." A troubled look rippled across his face. "One night while speaking to him he told me that he had recently lost contact with his brother who was a blacksmith that lived a town over. Not only had he not heard from his brother in weeks, the times he did meet up before, his brother seemed to become more and more enamored with one of his new house gods. He had not been overly zealous beforehand, so this perturbed Anvit greatly. He would have gone and checked on him himself had it not been for a bum leg he developed in an accident years before. It was unsafe for him to travel to different villages alone and the others in the village would brush away his pleas. They swore that the silence was purely in character for the man. In fact, it seemed that the man had a penchant for disappearing like this on a regular basis. But that silence had never been directed towards Anvit before, as they were incredibly close."

"I am guessing you helped him?" I inquired.

"Of course! Anvit was one of the kindest men I had ever met in my travels, it would have been rude of me not to offer. Besides, my itinerary was incredibly open. I could log this down as "missions work" and my higher ups would never question it. We left the next day, as it was only a day trip to said town. It was a pretty craggy trek but I was much younger at the time. The worst of it all was the heat, and we had to be sure we traveled with plenty of water. Overall, it was a pretty enjoyable hike..."

His voice trailed off and his gaze became long. I may have not interacted with him much growing up, but it was very clear that this new countenance was rare for him.

"...Are you okay, Uncle?"

He responded in a grim tone. "Before I continue, I need you to tell me how well you handle the concept of death."

"What do you mean?"

"Viscera. The macabre. The grotesque. The final sleep. Do you become queasy at hearing about these things?"

"I would not say so..."

"Okay. You've been forewarned," He cleared his throat. "The village was quiet when we first entered. There wasn't even any activity towards the village center. No noises came from the houses. Children's toys lined the streets. There was absolutely no one. It unnerved us as we traveled to his brother's house. We could rest there and ask any questions we had about the stillness, but..."

"I'm guessing you did not find him?"

He ignored my comment and continued. "There was nothing on the way to his house. Any sign of children was just abandoned toys. We were surprised when we knocked on the door and his brother answered. It was a strange sight to see such a large man be in such a state of panic. You see, Anvit's brother was very large, and not one bit overweight. His profession had caused his muscle to tone to the point that they rippled down his arms. His dark skin glistened with sweat in such profound levels that it could only be explained by anxiety; even the Indian heat couldn't explain such profuse amounts of perspiration the man was covered in. His head was clean shaven, and his beard was kept close to his jaw. That way he had no risk of harming himself during work due to stray hairs. He rushed us inside, adamant that we not stay outdoors for too long."

The story unnerved me. I was nowhere near deducing the ending of this story yet I knew deep down nothing good would come of it.

"Bishanpal- that was Anvit's brother- refused to tell us anything about what happened. Whenever we asked about it he would just insist we went to sleep. 'I'll tell you in the morning, you need rest" he repeated over and over. We finally gave in to his requests and laid down on the floor to sleep. It was short lived though, as I almost immediately heard scuffling followed by someone sprinting out the door. Bishanpal had knocked his brother unconscious and was sprinting out the house. I shook off my sleep and followed in pursuit as quickly as I could. Bishanpal was both fast and strong from years working in the forge. In contrast Anvit was rather small from years of poverty due to his injury. It didn't take long for Bishanpal to create distance between the two of us."

"Were you able to catch him?"

"I caught up to him, yes, but I did not catch him. I-"

He stammered over his words as if his vocal cords seized. "I didn't make it-" He let out a deep sigh, regulating his breathing. "Nevermind that. No, I didn't catch him. I chased him through the village for a good five minutes until he stopped. When he did stop, it was too late. I froze when I saw our surroundings. There were piles of bodies, Abb. Men, women, and children. The elderly. Livestock. All were piled up, and streams of dried blood flowing from underneath the piles. He had exsanguinated all of them. Even the crops from the village were piled up, all charred to a crisp in some sort of burnt offering. As soon as I saw Bishanpal, it was already too late. He threw Anvit on the top of one of the piles and unsheathed a knife he had tied to the sash at his waist. He brought the blade down, hard, on Anvit's skull. He slashed right through the top of his skull, exposing a mirky mix of blood and brain. I saw him spasm several times before he laid still. I looked back up and before I could even think to plead for my life, the beast of a man turned to me, grinned, and said 'I saw him'. He looked at the knife in his hand, still covered in Anvit's grey matter, and slit his own throat, throwing himself on the pile as he gurgled his last breaths."

My uncle's face remained stone-like as he recounted the story. It felt somewhat odd seeing someone tell of such things with a stoic face, but I reasoned it as his way of re-living such a terrifying event.

"I went over and grabbed the knife from Bishanpal's body. I took the sheath from his waist as well before I then trekked all the way back to Anvit's home in the dark. I packed the few of my things I had and came home a week early from that trip, which is why I am able to accompany you. I plan to tell everyone at the university about how wonderful everyone was, and those that follow Hinduism are delightful people. I honestly feel there's no reason for them to know about the events of what took place, and think it would be incredibly special for my nephew to take the knife instead of handing it over to some fuddy-duddy who would keep it behind a glass case."

I was dumbstruck. I had not an iota of thought on how to respond to the information I had just been told. The knife sitting in front of me had been used to slaughter an entire village.. But there was one thing that concerned me the most.

"Why would you keep such an accursed thing, Uncle?"

"Oh, multiple reasons." He seemed to be back in his normal mood, acting as if his bleakness moments ago had not happened. "First off, it was clear to me that Bishanpal was not following any of the gods that his family or his community worshiped. In the 30 years Hinduism has existed it has been confirmed that there are a near infinite amount of gods in the religion. I wanted to see if maybe there is any hint as to what this man was revering, as I am fully convinced that whatever the man was devoting his life to, may be honored by others."

"I see, simple curiosity."

"Yes, that and I felt it would be disgraceful to the men I watched die to have them lay near their murder weapon. It would also be a disgrace for such a beautiful weapon to lay in the dirt, even with its transgressions."

He paused to look me in the eyes. "Well, Absolom, now that I have given you the history of your gift, what do you think of it?"

I was excited, that was to be sure. But I felt conflicted as to accepting a gift with so much violence imbued in its blade. After a second of deliberation, I decided to settle upon excitement.

"Are you sure Uncle? It is something highly important to you."

"I know it is. But I would like it to be something important to you as well."

I tried to hide my excitement, but I decidedly failed. I accepted his gift with as calm a composure as I could muster as I inched the knife closer to my person, causing my uncle to laugh.

"I'll take that as an acceptance. I'll have to show you my collection of artifacts I've gathered from my other trips over the years. Maybe one day your collection will be as big as mine!"

"Oh I would absolutely love to see it, Uncle. Hopefully I will have the time between classes this fall." I sat expectantly, waiting for permission to be excited about the gift I had just received.

"Well," Uncle Eli said. "Are you going to take out the blade or not?"

That was what I was waiting for. I picked up the hardened leather case and felt it all over in my hands. I gingerly pulled the knife out of the sheath, revealing the jet black blade hidden inside.

"Good lord boy, were you ever allowed to be excited growing up?" My uncle said, picking fun at my subduedness. "I need to have a talk with your parents. It seems they didn't let you be a kid growing up."

"No Uncle," I retorted back without looking up from the knife, "I just try to stay calm to avoid any unwanted asthma attacks." I stared intently at the blade. The kukri had a thick back on one edge and a highly sharpened edge on the other side. Its thickness gave it a sort of axe-like quality; I could imagine the weight behind it when swung by its wielder. I had a twinge of negativity flow through me when I realized how adept this blade would have been at cleaving Anvit's head. I brushed the thought away as soon as it came. The brightest part of the knife was the dark-ashy handle, every other piece being a dark void that swallowed all the light that shone against it.

I went to test the sharpness with a finger prick before Uncle Eli grabbed my wrist. "That is the last thing you want to do, Abb. That obsidian is sharper than any knife you have ever held in your life. One wrong twitch and you'd lose your entire finger as if it were butter."

"Duly noted, Uncle." I continued observing it without getting any appendages near the blade. Towards the hilt I noticed two small notches carved into the blade.

"What might these be?"

"Those are carved into almost every kukri made. There are a couple of reasons that people have speculated on why they are there. On one hand, they are considered a survivalist knife of sorts. I overheard some gurkhas speak on how the notches allowed them to use the knife as a spile. Others say it's to keep blood from running down the handle when they get into fights. From a sacrificial perspective it might be that it is reminiscent of the cow, which is a holy animal to those who follow Hinduism. With this particular knife it is most likely that last one."

I nodded, retaining the information but still fully engrossed in the beauty of the dagger before me. It seemed as if it were carved and wrent from the cosmos itself. It was ethereal and as I gazed into it I felt lost in those cosmos. I felt the cold dark swirl around me, both hauntingly lonely and overwhelmingly serene. I felt as if I was being cradled by the unexistence as I looked into that blade. Nothing else mattered in that moment. If one looked close enough you could almost see stars swirl throughout the black of the blade, whether it be by design or trick of the eyes. The pseudo-stars rippling through the blade only helped one get lost in the beauty of it.

Through the rest of our several hours trapped on board the train together my uncle and I continued with our conversations, him telling me of all the ventures he had taken. He told me the details of the things he had collected and even told me stories of when he and father were younger. But no matter how distracted I was by our conversation, I could not help but keep the blade in the corner of my eye at all times. Something about it forced me to perceive it in some way at all times, even if I was further preoccupied. My uncle and I were still lost in our conversation as the train came to a sudden jolt, startling us both. We had arrived at our stop, much quicker than I expected.

"Ah ha!" My uncle stood upright so quickly that it seemed that there was no motion between the two positions.

"Sheathe that thing quickly and put it away, we don't want the conductor thinking that we are some sort of robbers."

I nodded, sliding the dagger back into its home. "I would be more worried about the robbers trying to take the thing." For extra precaution I slipped it into my coat pocket, making sure it was concealed from prying eyes.

"Fair point." It seemed as if the thought hadn't occurred to my uncle that others might be jealous of us owning such a blade.. It would fetch a pretty penny if one were to sell it. "We better hurry along then if that's such a worry for you."

THE NEXT MINUTES WERE simply a reverse of earlier operations: exit the cabin, collect our things, etc. We still had a few hours journey left until we made it to campus, but my uncle had arranged to have his personal buggy meet us at the train depot. I had questioned him about whether he was worried about the potential drunkard coming along and taking his belongings, but he assured me that no one would dare do such a thing. Thankfully, he was right, as both his buggy and his horses were sitting untouched near the ticket office.

Uncle waved towards a slouching man in the ticket booth while we both climbed into the buggy seats. The man nodded in return. "That is the reason I wasn't too worried about my horses being taken. Hugo is a good man" I waved at the man as well. "I see your point."

We got comfortable in our seats, then set off. For the first time on the trip it seemed that Uncle Eli and I had run out of things to say. The day so far was bustling with life and gifts, keeping me awake with the adrenaline that comes with new experiences. But that adrenaline was now quickly fading as my uncle and I rode down the dirt paths towards the university.

It was not long before I felt my eyes begin to droop. I tried to fight it continually, stubborn to keep my traveling companion company during our last few hours of journey. The early morning had caught up to me, compounded with my own inexperience to such extravagant affairs. I refused the call off rest though, hell-bent on ensuring that I would get to see the final sights of my trip. I treated my snores as an alarm, jolting myself awake each time I heard my own sleep sounds. Each time I felt myself slump I forced my posture to return to rigidity. It was only a matter of time before Uncle took notice of my struggle.

"Absolom, you should get some sleep," My uncle chided. "You've got an incredibly busy day tomorrow and should not go into it without any sort of rest."

"Are you sure, Uncle?" I protested. "Your day has been just as full as mine. Will you be okay to travel without a companion?"

"Absolom, I am a seasoned traveler. You needn't worry."

"Alright."

And with that I fell asleep.

Somnia

"See me."

It was just one voice at first, deep and growling.

Those sounds were the only thing. Nothing else existed in the moment, just the sound of a singular voice issuing that simple command. I could not ascertain where the growls came from, as it seemed to come from all directions. Sound even came up from the emptiness beneath, reverberating up from the soles of my feet into the rest of my body. There was nothing beneath that could have produced the sound, as there was nothing beneath me at all. A simple nothingness is what occupied the space around me. I felt nothing but cold in that vast space, but at the very least I could feel my own skin when I touched the tips of my fingers together. Overall, it was as if all of my senses had been eradicated and spread thin on top of the void that surrounded me.

All but sound.

"See me."

That same voice repeated itself. Over and over it repeated itself, asking me to see whatever form it had lurking in the darkness. In fact, despite the nothingness that surrounded and embraced me, I felt the presence of something in that formless dark. Something incorporeal at first that seemed to gain more and more permanence the more it demanded that I see it.

Soon the second voice began. It was more feminine this time, more inviting. It sounded more as if it were inviting me instead of commanding me. I thought for a moment that I could get used to this voice, but then it was drowned out by a third voice. Then that voice was drowned out by a fourth. Then a fifth. More and more voices joined in, until there were so many voices speaking the same phrase all at once that you could no longer understand the words they spoke. Instead, it became an incessant buzzing, undulating in tone and pitch as the different voices took stage. Then it ceased to be undulating, and became a pulse as silence could be heard in the spaces between syllables. No voices were being silenced, and instead were finding rhythm. The words began to find solidarity with each other, until the great masses chanted in unison. They all spoke the same phrase -

"See me."

Once they had found their cadence they adjusted volume, growing louder and louder, their tone becoming more and more demanding.

"See me."

Abruptly, two voices disappeared. In an instant, sounding as if it were the exact sum of the two voices that were destroyed before it, a single voice replaced the missing two. It was only two voices at first, and barely caused a glimmer of change in the cadence. Then another two suffered the same fate as the previous, being destroyed and reborn as one. An eternity passed as the voices that previously numbered infinite, solidified into one infinite voice. A booming wave of every note, chord, language, age, and emotion echoed throughout the nothing.

"See me."

I was nudged awake.

"Welcome back to the land of the living." Uncle Eli grinned down at me from his seat next me. "Sleep well?"

I rubbed my temples and grimaced."I've developed a migraine."

"Not surprising, your neck was craned the entire time. I thought about waking you, but you will need every bit of sleep you can manage, even if it is uncomfortable."

"I appreciate the thought, Uncle. The busyness of the last month has deprived me of any sort of good rest." I decided quickly not to tell my uncle about my dreams. I myself could not decipher whether or not the dream was simply my own inner machinations or something more, but the pulsing in my head caused me to dismiss the dream entirely. Everytime I tried to think deeper about the events I felt my brain swell in pain tenfold. Answers weren't worth the pain.

"Anyways, we have arrived."

I had been so groggy when I awoke that I had failed to realize the sprawling campus in front of me. We were traveling down a gravel pathway that laid in front of the entrances to the buildings that the campus was composed of. Only a few carts were on the same road, as most students had arrived the day prior and were already settled into their dorms.

The campus was not fancy in the least, nor was it big, but it was esteemed and it was sturdy. The main area had three buildings, aligned all in a row. The first building we passed was the smallest, being nothing but a one story brick rectangle with a set of wooden doors at the front. There was a thin layer of ash thick enough to see from the buggy layering the outer bricks.

"That's the old cafeteria." My uncle replied to my clear ogling of the dilapidated building. "After an unfortunate incident last year we have had to move to serving meals in the dorms. I'd advise you to stay away, as the building is wildly unstable."

I nodded in response. He was rather trite in tone as he spoke, making it clear that I should not ask anymore questions.

The largest of the three was the center building. Dark oak wood surrounded the base of the building, covering the bricks that made the foundation. After a few feet the rich wood ended, and the brick became visible. The colors of the bricks varied, creating a cacophonic mosaic that painted an incomprehensible portrait. The entire building ended with a flat roof. Jutting out of said roof was an ornate steeple made of plaster, painted to match the color of the oak wood.

"That large building is where all your classes will be held, as well as Sunday morning service. You'll also be able to find me there as well, anytime you need me, as my office is located inside."

The last building was somewhere in between the elegance and size between the last two. It was about three stories tall, being just slightly shorter than the chapel that came before it. It was also fairly squat, being not much more than a rectangle made of brick. It was a practical building that seemed to have several small outbuildings nestled out back. Among them was what seemed to be a greenhouse, a small living quarters, and a ramshackle scullery that I assumed was being used since the cafeteria was out of commission. Strangely enough, my uncle stopped before we reached the next building, apprehensive to approach it. A small gaggle of students congregated in front of this building, which I assumed to be the dormitory. My future classmates skittered in and out of the building, carrying the last of their trunks and bags into the building, rushing to assure that they could allow their family to return to the road before it became too late.

They were all finishing up their unpacking and saying their goodbyes as my uncle and I approached in the wagon; being such that by time we stopped we were the only people left outside.

My uncle and I stepped off the wagon, stretching our legs as we got prepared to unpack my belongings.

"I apologize, I will not be able to stay to help you unload." My uncle seemed uncharacteristically twitchy as he steadied the horses.

"I understand, it is late and you have to trek home. All I ask is your help unloading my things from the carriage." I began to reach for my bags. He stepped down and helped me place my belongings on the ground.

"That... and no one, other than students, are allowed in the dormitories - that includes faculty. It's a safety issue."

I had not noticed whether or not anyone else other than the students had entered, so I took my uncle at his word. I wrapped my arms around my uncle in an embrace and then watched as he boarded his wagon.

I walked into the main area of the dormitories, looked around, and walked to the front desk. At this point all of my classmates had already unloaded their things and were most likely relaxing in their rooms, so the lobby was entirely empty. The room was poorly lit with cracked wooden floors stretching across the small commons area that greeted all who entered the meager building. It was easy to tell at one point this building was fairly ornamental, though years of failed cleaning caused all the wood in the building to be coated in a thick layer of dust. It was clear that the area had been neglected.

I imagine that young men who were more preoccupied with their father's trade than their mother's house work were to blame.

In the very center of the commons area was a small booth. The desk portion was made of hardwood, much like the facade that covered the base of most of the buildings. From the surface of the desk to about midway to the ceiling was a wooden lattice, barring those on the outside from climbing over the desk. No one sat at the desk, as one would figure. There was a single key sitting on the desk which had a piece of paper which held my name and the number "302" tied to it. I pocketed the key and made my way towards my room, making sure to grab a trunk before I made my ascent. I stumbled up the dark stairways, choking on the clouds of dust that took flight each time I stepped on the mite-impacted carpet. One would think the traffic from earlier activity would have cleared the dust, but the stair ways lacked a window or any other form of ventilation. No matter where you were located in the building, there was a suffocating feeling. By the time I had reached the third floor of the dormitory my lungs were clogged with particulates, exacerbating my already sensitive lungs. I was wheezing as I approached the door to 302.

"Hello Brother! It's good to see you have finally arrived!" A man beamed at me through the door. His height was comparable to the short stature of my mother, coming to just a bit over five feet. Seeing as I got my height from my father, I stood almost an entire foot taller than him. His hair was a tad shaggy, yet still somewhat short. The color was something akin to that of a ginger cat.

I tried to respond, but managed only a wheeze. The inner walls of my lungs were still caked with dust from the trip up. He replied in kind, as if somehow understanding the language of asthmatics.

"Oh of course! I'll help you bring up the rest of your things. You'll need it if one trip is enough to make you winded. I'll go with you on the next trip down."

Once he had finished speaking I had finally cleared most of the debris from my lungs.

"Oh no it is completely fine.... I paused to wheeze. "We have only just met and there is no reason for you to help carry my things." I gurgled slightly as I tried to wave him off.

"No I insist, uhm..." He trailed off, trying to recall a name he had not yet been told.

"Absolom."

"Abbi! I insist! We're going to be living together from here on out, and I can't imagine not aiding my housemate in his time of need." He was adamant about his decision and was already entering the hallway to retrieve my things. I tried to sputter out a complaint against this nickname but he was already bounding down the corridor..

"Besides, if I allow you to finish on your own you will more than likely collapse in the stairwell, and I have never been one to not enjoy having a roommate. Let's go!"

I could not see how someone half my size would be of much help and felt that it would be impolite of me to accept the help of one I just met, but his insistence overruled my denial. I was surprised when, once we reached my things, he hoisted the two largest pieces of my luggage and lumbered towards the stairwell. The disbelief in my eye must have betrayed my attempt to remain stoic.

"Don't just loiter, Brother! Surely you aren't so frail that you can't carry any more of your own things?" He playfully jeered at me, shaking me out of my awe. I grabbed a trunk and made my way toward the stairs. By the time I made it to the door my new roommate was already entering the third-floor hallway. I, on the other hand, had barely made it halfway to the second floor. It was no different than the first trip. This dust would be the death of me.

I finally made it to our room for the second time, where my roommate was sitting on the bed waiting for me to arrive. "I think you may need to see a physician, Abbi. It is not right for someone of our age to be so easily winded."

I grimaced at him. "Must you be so quick to judge my health immediately after we have met? I understand that you are clearly much more fit than I am, despite your small stature, but to look down on me so, simply because of it? You are a rude one for sure."

James chortled at my snark towards his stature, amused by the bit of fire that was brought forth by the tribulations of the dust and stairs.

"Pretty hypocritical of you, Abbi." James claimed, a grin still plastered across his face.

"Whatever do you mean, James?"

"Well, you've made a judgment against me just as quick as you claim I have for you. We've barely even talked past our ribbing of each other."

"You are correct, and I do not know if I quite care for the fact that you are. May we engage, then, in some sort of meaningful conversation so that I may accurately judge you, brother?"

"Of course, Abbi!" James puffed out his chest and put on an accent that made him sound snobbish, then put his hand on his chest. He looked as if he were performing

"Let it be remembered then that *I* too will judge thee. I hope that *thee* will be a *worthy* roommate for someone as *great* as *I*."

A few moments of silence followed, only to be broken by the raucous howling that emitted from both James and I. We doubled over onto ourselves, lost in the cringe-inducing humor that the room was forced to behold. A minute passed before we managed to get a hold of ourselves and end our painful jubilation.

"You were correct, James. I made too quick of a judgment of you" I wiped a tear from my eyes as a smirk played across my lips. "What you are, though, is a moron."

"You are a good judge of character, Abbi!"

"It is my own special gift from God!"

James' eyes were red from the stress that comes with a hearty laugh. "Well, it seems that your gifts are rather hit or miss."

I feigned offense, "Well I have been right once in this situation! I would say that is

proof enough."

"You have made two assumptions, and only one of them has been correct. That would be a fifty percent success rate."

"Yes! Fifty percent is good!" I exclaimed.

"If you truly believe that fifty percent is a good success rate you must be as much of an imbecile as me."

I waved my hand in defeat."Alright, I concede. We are both morons. But we still do not know anything about each other other than that. So tell me, why are you here at the seminary?"

James' face muddled dark for a minute before he returned his smile.. "There's no reason for me to share that yet. Why don't you tell me your story?"

And I did as such, leaving not a single detail of my report from him. There was no need to, as I had nothing to hide. I still was curious as to his story, but I decided not to push. We had just gotten past our strange feelings and I did not want to cause them to return.

James sat on his bunk kicking his feet, clearly engrossed in my life story. I did not understand how he found it interesting, as I found my life to be incredibly dull up until that moment. He listened well, that was until he interrupted with a loud exclamation.

"Goodness! The sun has almost entirely vanished! We need to gather the rest of your things!"

The both of us had been so engrossed in my story that we both failed to notice that the dusk had turned into night. The clock read that the time was eleven o'clock. Our time to wake up was at five o'clock in the morning. We would have to hurry with the rest of the night if we wanted any semblance of sleep.

I attempted to stutter out an apology for distracting from the task at hand, but James would have none of it. "It's alright! We will go get the rest of your things together, then after you unpack your essentials I will give you a summary of tomorrow's events."

I sighed. We were back at stage one of him insisting that he help me. While I knew that his intent was not to give me any sort of judgment, as that had been ruled out, I was still incredibly uncomfortable with his help. I resigned myself to his help, as there was no way I would finish the task without keeling over.

A small hint of my mind still felt as if I could not trust James, but it would be mandatory that I remove those feelings if I lived with the man. He was kind, and I could not stand that. I had met very few truly kind people in my short life, and I had no reason to expect James to be doing anything but saving face. It was exactly what I was doing by being accepting of him, and it should be expected that he would be doing the same. That said, I still was not going to allow him to be the *only* one retrieving my luggage, so I followed him into the hallway.

By the time I had made it to the stairwell James had already entered the commons area. I was amazed at how his short legs could carry him so fast. As I reached for the door to the commons area, he burst through holding two more large pieces of luggage in his arms.

"Only one left. Will you be alright carrying it, Abbi?"

I shook my head at him in annoyance. "I am not feeble you oaf!"

"Of course you're not!" He winked as he passed me.

I rolled my eyes and walked out the door. The only thing left was my toiletries, as he very clearly left the lightest of my luggage for me to carry. I would have been much angrier if this hadn't given me a much needed reprieve, as another heavy load like the previous two would have surely caused me to suffocate. I let my insecurities go and allowed myself to appreciate the help I was being given. Once I arrived back to the room, James had again beaten me there. It seemed less as if he was walking and instead teleporting from room to room. Both of my trunks had been put on the bottom bunk of our beds, with James reclining on the top bunk.

"I hope you do not mind me taking the top bunk, Abbi. For once in my life, I get to be the tallest person in the room."

I chuckled. "No problem, James. Do let it be known that every time I bash my head against the bottom of the bunk I will be cursing your name, even if you do not hear me do it."

"Try not to hit it too hard, it may come down on top of you." James lay down and yawned. "Anyways, before I lose consciousness I must inform you about the morning. As you already know, we will be woken up at five in the morning by the bell. First class begins at six. It will be an hour in length. We will be able to retrieve our food from the front desk after class."

"Uncle had forewarned me about that, but seemed rather unwilling to explain." I replied.

"There was a fire last year...*yawn*...My brother actually witnessed it. It's a fairly long story....*yawn*... I would rather tell it another time, as I am exhausted." Each sentence was punctuated by a jaw-splitting yawn.. He was clearly beginning to doze off. "Speaking of food, there will probably come a time when you will be required to deliver the food. The students have been rotating who is in charge of delivering the meals to ease the workload on the cooks."

"Oh! That would be no problem at all. I am always willing to help."

"...Sounds.... fantastic, Abbi....." James' speaking was slowing down to a point that his words were slurred. "Anyways, I am going to sleep. You should unpack before you sleep. Things get busy around here and you do not want to live out of a suitcase for six months."

"Will do, James." Before the words even left my lips I could hear snoring coming from the top bunk. I was lucky that I had slept in the cart earlier in the day, as I still felt rested enough to distribute my belongings. I sat for a moment and took stock of the room.

It was small; I smiled to myself as I realized my mother had overpacked me. I hoped that I could fit it all in this little space. The room was rectangular in shape, with the door being on one of the longer ends of the box, with each wall being made of large bricks poorly covered with plaster and white paint. It had clearly been a good bit of time since any sort of patchwork had been done, as cracks and patches of the wall could be seen through the paint. Directly across from the door was a large window which looked out onto the cobble street that I had traveled on when I first arrived. To either side of the window were two desks, both perfectly situated so that we may receive an iota of light while we studied. Thankfully, two small light sconces were affixed above each desk and small bits of candles were burning inside. It would still be another two decades before the lightbulb would be developed, and to only be allowed to work when the sun willed would make any sort of study impossible.

Against the wall to the right of the doorway was where the bunks were located, each bed firmly fastened to each other by sheets of wood shoddily fastened together by a thick pole. It looked as if they were struggling to keep the two bunks from meeting together in a violent embrace, and I worried that I may be asleep when that fateful meeting occurs. I had taken James' earlier comment about destroying the bed by hitting my head upon it as a joke, but the longer I looked at the shoddy workmanship the more I was convinced he spoke in anything but jest.

On the other side of the room, directly across from the bed, were two closets with a sturdy dresser nestled between them. James had stacked his trunks in the closet, all half open with clothes strewn about, to the right of the dresser. It was clear that James struggled with the concept of tidiness, and I immediately resigned to being the source of any sort of cleaning in the dorm. The closet to the left was kept barren so that my clothes may take up residency. I took my time making sure that all my shirts were hung up neatly, making sure not to allow any wrinkles or creases. There was a small shelf at the top of the closet; a perfect place to store my toiletries.

By time I had unpacked my things the clock showed two-thirty in the morning. I changed into my nightwear and gingerly crawled into my bunk. I curled up on my lumpy mattress, taking care not not to jostle too much. My mind flitted about, thinking of all the high points that had occurred during the day. My mind still could not fully digest the vast amounts of information that had been inundated upon me throughout the day. That, along with the anticipation of the next day's events and my nap from earlier in the day, kept me from indulging in any extra sleep.

I laid in bed, trying my damndest to doze off into slumber again. Finally I resigned to the age old pastime of staring into one's dark bedroom until that darkness forced their eyes to close.

It was always astounding to me how different things could look when there was no light present. It's almost as if reality melts in the presence of darkness, things losing rigidity and form without the light. Almost as if they forget themselves without being able to see their own form.

It was in that formless room that I saw something.

It was a black spot, huddled into the corner of the room. Most likely a pile of clothes left lying about by my new roommate, surely nothing to be intimidated by. But I still could not help but focus on it as it swirled and morphed in my vision, seemingly undulating under the night. I, of course, was reasonable and saw it for what it was, passing it off as inconsequential.

But then the pile moved.

It stood up. It was if it had been waiting for someone to see it, sitting silently until someone had the audacity to lay eyes upon it. It turned towards me and became solid.

It saw me.

I could not see its eyes, but I also could not deny that it was now looking directly at me.

I did what any sane man would do and turned to face the wall as quietly as I could manage. Maybe if I faked being asleep this strange specter currently inhabiting the room would leave me be. It was a desperate attempt at remaining unhunted, much like someone who throws themselves on the ground in the presence of a grizzly bear. I tremored, praying to God that he may let this fiend pass over me.

When I felt it near my bunk, it was clear my prayers went unanswered. Now that it was nearby I could feel the atmosphere it carried with it. I felt swaddled by its presence; almost relaxed. It was that ethereal feeling once again, the feeling of floating through nothingness and being embraced by nonexistence. The feeling as if I were slipping away. Not into death, no, but instead into dispersal. It was as if the immortal part of my being, that part that all men have, was
fading away.

I felt myself slip into unconsciousness as my very being became much too thin to keep conjoined. My body wavered and my eyes drifted off into the finality of no longer being aware. And yet, I still could hear. I still could sense the very room around me despite me losing my grasp on my own body. I was fading into what felt like death, yet I remained ever present in the room with that being.

I heard it in my living death.

It's voice was infinite.
"You saw me."

Doctrinam

I woke in a cold sweat to the sound of a bell tolling from the academic building. It would have been difficult for anyone to not rise to the loud tolling, as even those who were hard of hearing would be awoken by the miniature earthquake the bell caused. A small chunk of plaster fell from the wall amidst the rumbles.

I rolled out of bed, groaning as I stood, and walked over to light the sconces so that the room may have some source of illumination. My head was pounding again, just like from my dream on the trip to the university. I could only reason that some deep portion of my subconscious had cracked, creating some dark phantasm that haunted my dreams and refused me any sort of rest. But again, I could not afford to dwell on it. I knew that thinking for too long about the impossible circumstances would land me with the same migraine that tormented me on the trip over. I let the dream pass from my mind and began to prepare for the day. Behind me I heard a loud thud and saw that my roommate had jumped from the top bunk, landing firmly on his feet.

"Welcome to our first day of classes!" James exclaimed while beaming bright enough to illuminate the room. I admired him greatly, but I truly wished he would slow down for just

a moment.

I yawned, trying to shake the sleep that had taken hold of my body. James was extremely energetic for someone who could barely finish a sentence through his yawns the night before.

"Our first day?" I sighed.

"I'm a freshman, too, Abbi." He said with a grin.

"Of course." I groaned.

We busied ourselves at various degrees of speed with our hygiene routines. James spoke in a solid and thoroughly rested voice,

"Oh, I must forewarn you. One of the professors, Professor Quill, is what some may say... heavy handed. My brother Peter wanted to make sure that I forewarned any that I might meet to stay as friendly with the man as possible." The tidbit of knowledge he shared was an overwhelming amount of information for my sleep-addled brain but I tried to force my mind to rouse so as to not miss anything important.

"What makes the man so terrible?" I asked, slurring my words.

"Caneings. That is just one of the many different forms of punishment he feels fit to bestow among any wretch slow enough to not avoid him."

Mental scarring was always a given with any form of higher education, but I would very much like to leave the university without any sort of physical scarring.

James and I spent the next forty-five minutes grooming ourselves, ensuring that our hygiene was up to standard so that we may avoid the ire of any of our more, staunch, professors. This was especially important as our first class was with none other than Professor Quill himself. He had been known to do breath checks. Not to check if the students had been drinking, as you might think, but instead just to make sure it did not smell. Anything short of minty would be met with a caning across the hands.

Once five forty-five arrived we were both fully ready for the morning's classes. We left our dorm and were greeted by all of our fellow classmates shuffling out into the hallways - all still groggy from a short night's rest. If one were to view us from above, we would have looked as if we were one mass undulating steadily across the gravel road. Strangely enough, there was utter silence. Everyone seemed exhausted from the day before, not even being able to muster up enough energy to talk. Travel is, afterall, a fairly exhausting experience.

We all came up to the doors and stepped inside, an audible gasp sneaking through the lips of all the freshmen. The inside was immaculate. The building was, in majority, a single room. Instead of a commons area or lobby, there was a massive sanctuary. Overall, the style and layout were what one would consider stereotypical, but the details were where the architecture truly shined. The carpets were a light brown that contracted against the dark wood of the highly detailed and carved pews. Each pew had a large dove carved onto the side, so exquisitely carved that each feather seemed to have been carved separately from the rest. The upholstery of the pews cushions were the common maroon that could be seen in almost every church that was wealthy enough to afford seating more comfortable than the bare benches of the common folk.

A large, carpeted stage was at the front with a multitude of various instruments nestled in the back. Towards the front of the stage was the pulpit, carved out of the same dark wood as the pews. One could see ornate carvings that snaked down the sides of the lectern; each delicate line was a grapevine that held bunches of its fruits, encircling biblical figures in various pious poses.

This was also carved so deeply and with such deftness that one could see the minute details of each one of the figures exhibited from across the other side of the vast chapel.

The carpet ended a foot past the outer end of each of the pews, then transitioned to a hardwood floor that was unevenly polished. Most likely a symptom of being cleaned by the same young men who cleaned the dormitory. The side walls of the building were lined with bookcases filled with antique and aging tomes filled with the musings of previous pastors and theologians. The bookshelves worked in tandem with several wooden columns that held the second

story aloft.

There were indoor latrines and a few offices that jutted off the sides of the atrium, but no other lecture halls or study rooms were to be had. There was no reason for there to be. Everyone in attendance would be at the same class at any given hour, so there was no reason to have more than one room. Along with that, any time there was any sort of chapel there would be no classes happening. The only other rooms in this building were the professors' personal offices, which could all be reached by climbing the spiral staircase that could be seen rising up behind the stage.

We all shuffled into the pews, getting ready for our first lecture. James decided to take a seat next to me. He gave me a worried look as I started wheezing.

"Are you alright, Abbi?" He leaned over and whispered to me.

"Yes James, it is incredibly dusty in here."

We relapsed back into silence. We felt as if any more words would set the bulldog of a man that was standing at the lectern at the front of the room loose upon us. I do not mean a bulldog in the sense that he was bulky, in fact he was extremely bony. I mean more of the fact that age had stretched his skin in such a manner that wrinkles and folds were the main feature of his body. He was bald, and I truly wish he had not been. While some men can pull off the aesthetic of not having any hair, the multitude of liver spots and misshapen lumps that covered his head made it a somewhat grotesque sight to behold.

This ogre was Professor Quill.

His bent over form waddled over to the pulpit and cleared his throat. It felt less like the mundane action one does to clear the phlegm, but instead to present a clear threat. Most everyone was smart enough to cut their ceaseless chatter, except for one who was idiotic enough to continue blathering. Quill attempted, again, to get the room to clear of all sound, but the one who would not stop was oblivious enough to not even cease when his conversation partner repeatedly attempted to get him to silence himself.

Finally, Quill had had enough of the disrespect. He slowly descended the stairs that separated the stage from the congregation. The movements he made were slow and methodical, almost seeming as if he were floating across the space that separated the pews. It was about two minutes before he finally reached the back pew where the rube sat. Quill loomed over the student, staring intently while waiting for the man to cease his rambling. The student had been so invested in what he had to say that he had not even noticed the old man standing over him.

"Are you a freshman?" Quill asked, borderline yelling into the student's ear.

The student jumped, almost smacking Professor Quill in the process.

"Sorry sir, I was lost in conversation."

"I best believe you should find yourself. You are here to learn, not chitter chatter with your friends." Quill seemed to deliberate for a moment, questioning what his best course of action should be.

"I think for such misbehavior, I have created just the perfect consequence."

The poor student seemed like he was about to break into tears. It was obvious he meant no harm by his transgression; his only crime was stupidity. "W-what would that be, sir?"

Quill did not respond, only walking away back towards the pulpit. The student seemed confused, but that soon faded away into a relieved expression. No punishment had come his way. Finally, after a few more minutes, Quill again reached the pulpit.

"We have an impromptu discussion for this class, which, lucky for your classmate, is on topic for the class." It was evident to everyone else other than the talkative student that he was indeed, not off the hook.

"This class is about how one should handle themselves as a pastor. Think of it as a sort of class on how you need to hold yourself as a minister."

The student had hit a moment of heightened intelligence, realizing that he was still in immense danger. There was no possible way that he would make it out of this situation without either mental or physical beatings.

"And today's first lesson is a bit of a life lesson; learning when one should and should not *speak*." Quill leaned over the pulpit, looking directly at the quivering boy. He wanted to make sure that he felt no sense of relief. The professor had no intention of allowing him to escape the situation unscathed.

"It seems that some of you all have failed to learn any sort of manners from your mothers, and as such I, *a theology professor*, will need to act in her stead. Here is the first lesson. If someone is speaking to you, *you do not speak.*"

Everyone nodded in agreement.

"As it seems one of you has not quite discovered the concept of remaining quiet, it will be required that anyone who makes a single noise in my classes again will be forced to spend the rest of the week not speaking at any given opportunity."

No one dared even cough. I was lucky enough that my asthma, for once, was behaving itself and allowing my wheezing to be somewhat soundless.

"If I discover that any of you speak while under this punishment, I will turn it from a light sentence into corporal punishment."

The hall was deathly quiet. Apparently not all of my classmates had received warning about the monster that was professor Quill. I silently thanked James for forewarning me about this beast.

"If I find out that any of you speak to or allow someone under this punishment to speak, you will *both* be caned. I am under no obligation to allow any of you to continue prattling on when you should be listening to the lecture. You are not here to speak to your friends, you are here because you are meant to be men of God."

Quill's eyes bored into the floundering student. What is your name, young man?"

The student gulped. "E-e-Emmet, s-sir."

"Emmett, as you were the inspiration behind this new law, I am extending your sentence to a month."

The nervousness left his face and was replaced with pure sorrow. The fact that he got into this situation in the first place was proof enough that he loved to talk, as some do. At the pulpit, Quill seemed to relax after giving the final verdict. "With that out of the way, it is time we start today's lecture."

Quill spoke about how a pastor needs to handle himself, paying close attention to the fact that we, as holy men, are there to listen to the needs of others. If we are hesitant to listen, our congregation will not trust us enough to confide in us. It was actually very useful information to have, and it made perfect sense to realize that a pastor should refrain his tongue so that he can listen to the needs of others. All in attendance just wished it came from the mouth of someone other than Quill.

Class ended an hour later, and we all trekked back towards the dormitories so we could eat our breakfast. The moment James and I grabbed our breakfast, lukewarm eggs and soggy toast sitting on a cheap plate, and entered our room, James burst into laughter.

"What is the matter, James? I swear if you are laughing over what happened to Emmett I may have been right about your lack of empathy."

James wiped a tear from his eyes, catching his breath. "Abbi. My brother told me about Emmett before. He does this every year."

I felt my lips twist into a confused shape as my brain tried to comprehend how someone could make this same mistake every semester.

"James, have you gone daft, or are you pulling some sort of joke? Why would Emmett attempt the same stunt every year?"

James's lip trembled as if he was trying his hardest not to break out laughing again. "You wouldn't know it, but Emmett hates to talk to others."

I sat down on my bunk so that I could begin my breakfast. It would be only an hour until our next class, and skipping a meal was not something my generally frail disposition could handle. "Then why would he be in such a deep conversation to cause him that degree of trouble?"

"That's exactly the point." James said, fully expecting me to understand the implications of this.

"You are not insinuating that Emmett allows himself to get such consequences..."

James finished my sentence for me. "On purpose. Yes, yes. Emmett is in his third semester and he has done this every year since his freshman year."

I still could not fully grasp the mind of what was most definitely a madman, but James continued to explain, much to my appreciation.

"Somehow Emmett overheard someone speak about Quill's penchant to force students into making an involuntary vow of silence and hatched a plan. You see, Emmett absolutely despises answering the professors whenever they call on him. It is not even that he is unintelligent, as the man is absolutely brilliant. He figured if he got banned from any sort of speaking, he would not have to answer any questions. He could do all of his studies while dealing with as little professor interference as possible."

"But Quill spoke as if this was the first time he created such a punishment."

"You see, that's what allows this entire plan to work."

At this point I truly wished James would get to the point. He was revealing all this information in chunks as if he were telling some sort of fireside story, hanging on every word waiting for the listeners to let out a communal gasp. I shouted in frustration.

"Out with it!"

James leaned in close, bringing his face as close to mine as he possibly could. He looked me straight in the eye, grinning with a smile that curved upwards until it looked as if he held a crescent moon in his mouth.

"The man is entirely senile."

He grinned, waiting for my response. "Abbi, Quill is 92 years old. He may seem spry and able to hold himself well, but he has absolutely no mind left to him."

I paused while processing the information. "James, are you saying the man who lectured with nary a stutter has already lost his mind?"

"Oh no, not at all! His body, his knowledge, all of that is intact. Somehow it seems that the pure cruelty that inhabits his body has managed to preserve every bit of him, save his memory and his speed." James finally followed my lead and climbed onto his bunk, devouring his food but taking care not to speak with a stuffed mouth. "Many find it's a wonder why he isn't dead yet, but it seems that he may not be able to die."

I shuddered at the thought. I was scared to think what the man may have been like in his prime. To be so mobile at the age of 92 hinted that he may have been fairly fit as a young man, and as cruel as he is, I had no urge to have known him at any younger age..

"If he ever does pass from this plane of existence," James continued, "It won't be through death, he will simply nasty away."

Not long after finishing our conversation we both finished our meals. It would soon be time for us to reconvene at our next class. Much like earlier, the bell tolled and we all began to exit our rooms again, this time with more vigor than when we first had awakened this morning. Since the sleep had been eradicated from our systems and we were well fed, everyone chatted away with their peers as we went down the trek to the academic hall. In the back of the line was Emmett, keeping to himself and smirking as if he had outwitted the whole university.

This time, instead of sitting through one lecture as we did with Quill, we would instead be sitting through back to back orations. The first was, admittedly mundane, being on Abrahamic Tradition. This was taught by Professor Stoneheart, who one could consider average in every way, save the fact that he could never been seen without a piece of rye bread in his hand. He ate during the entire lecture, pulling out another piece of rye each time he finished the previous. It made the dull drone of his voice somewhat bearable, as one cannot help but find humor in the concept of a middle aged man with a rye addiction.

The class that followed was a study of other religions. The university I attended was fairly progressive when it came to its beliefs on theology, and claimed that the students would benefit from learning about what it called "competing beliefs."

This class was taught by none other than Professor Eli Teendyth..

The moment Uncle Eli took to the stage, I noticed a visible change in James' behavior. While he had been fairly nonchalant about the previous two lectures, he showed nothing but intense interest in every word my uncle spoke.

There was little introduction to the class. Instead, my uncle launched immediately into the content of whatever he felt necessary to teach us. Today, he felt it was important that he tell us about the formation of the Hindu faith. He lectured about all manners of things that had to do with the religion. He relayed all the information about the religion he had already told to me on the train ride up here, making the first half of the lecture fairly dull to say the least.

He continued on for the rest of the hour, delving into rabbit trails that almost led to him overreaching his time limit. As soon as we were dismissed, James made his way towards the front of the lecture hall instead of heading to the dorms for lunch. I decided to follow suit, as I would take any chance I could get to speak with my uncle. As we got close he looked up from the papers on the lectern and grinned warmly at us.

"Absolom! It seems you've managed to make a friend already! What might your name be, young man?"

James looked at me, giving me a strange look as if to ask why a professor I should have only just met, was greeting me as if he knew me his whole life.

"Abbi... how is it that Professor Teendyth knows you already?"

Before I even had the chance to respond Uncle Eli ushered a retort. "Absolom, are you embarrassed of your uncle? Why didn't you tell your friend that you and I were related?"

James stared at me dumbfounded for a moment, gears turning violently inside his mind. When it clicked an expression of pride filled his face and emanated throughout his body.

"Yes! Why didn't you tell me!"

I shrugged slightly. "I just felt it was not that important."

James stuck his bottom lip out in an exaggerated pout. "Abbi, you have to tell me these things! All the conversation we had last night and you made not one mention of this!?"

"Why? I mean, I truly do not see why it would be such an imperative."

"Your uncle is nothing more than a celebrity on campus! Most every student adores him! Well, that's mostly what my brothers say anyhow." James exclaimed.

My uncle blushed. "Well I wouldn't go so far as to say that..." His voice trailed off, easily swayed by the praise of one of his pupils.

"But Professor, I would say it's true."

"Thank you for the compliment then." My uncle changed the topic in an attempt to not succumb to flattery. "Anyhow, what did you think of the lecture? I hope you found

it interesting?"

James and I both nodded excitedly. That lecture had indeed been engaging. Even with a religion as young as Hinduism my uncle managed to keep all the given information up to date as it was not uncommon for theologians to be a decade or two behind what was currently happening.

"Of course, Uncle!" I chimed in. "Much better than being berated by Quill."

My uncle let out a humored exhale. "Well, that's not difficult. Most would prefer watching dust settle than being screamed at by that old porcupine. Besides your classes, how are you fairing Absolom? Is James treating you alright?"

He shot a pleasant smile at my roommate.

"He is a tad of an annoyance at times, but not enough for me to complain about. I feel as if he would get along well with Mother. They have quite similar temperaments."

A slight grin spread across James face. "I would not mind meeting your mother."

Uncle Eli nodded, then spoke to James with a chuckle. "What about you James? I hope my nephew isn't too quiet for your liking."

"No no, not at all Professor! Other than him feeling the need to lie to me about his identity..." He shot a short, sarcastically venomous glance at me. "...Things have been going swimmingly."

Uncle Eli stood there a moment, clearly happy that his nephew and his roommate got along so well. It was then that something clicked behind his eyes. "You said your brothers spoke highly of me. Who might they be?"

"Oh most of the Alludy men have attended this seminary, but your most recent student would have been Peter Alludy." James had already proven in our short time together that he held a certain melancholy for his family and his history. That melancholy was not present in the way he said Peter's name.

"Ah."

On the other hand, it was a name that apparently had not sat well with my uncle. "Well, I need to get back to my work, as should you two. My door is always open if you have any questions or want to know more about one of my many rabbit trails."

He quickly stashed his papers into his bag and trudged off towards his office.

We gathered our things as well and made headway towards the dorms, as our hour lunch had already been shortened by our need to ingratiate ourselves with the campus faculty. We rushed as quickly as we could, walking briskly to our room. Neither of us said anything, but a sheepish grin could be seen creeping across James' face.

THE REST OF THE DAY was uneventful. It was fairly clear as to why the students found my uncle to be their favored professor, as the rest were fairly mundane. I mean yes, the content was interesting enough, but there was a certain draw my uncle had when he spoke that kept all those watching interested. It was no wonder why he had succeeded so exceptionally in his field.

As the night came to an end I had decided to finish unpacking my things. James had already fallen asleep at this point, curling up in the top bunk muttering nonsense to himself in his sleep. He was not a fitful sleeper, but not a gentle one either. It would take one screaming at him to wake him up. It was by some sort of miracle that he managed to awaken to the sound of the bell tolling.

Even so, I tried my hardest to keep my volume low as I rummaged through my belongings, sorting them into their respective drawers. The ride on the way to the university caused my clothes to unfold themselves, meaning I had to redo all of my laundry as I transferred it into my drawers. I shuffled through each pair of britches, hung each shirt up at the closet, and put any toiletries on the shelf in my closet.

The adrenaline that came from a day of being accompanied by James was wearing off, and I felt the dread of the previous night come back to haunt me. The room gave me such intense unease at this point that I felt the need to strap my new kukri to my hip. If the strange creature decided to return I would at least have some way to maim it if it were to decide to bring me harm. I took it out of my luggage and pulled it out of its sheath looking deep into the abyss colored blade that was so gracefully forged into existence. I looked deep into the volcanic glass, hoping to see my reflection mirrored in the blade.

And yet, there was nothing to be seen. Instead of the crystal sheen that should have been present in the blade, there was deep nothingness. It was almost painful to perceive; a deep hole that led into endless black. I shook my head, breaking myself away from the blade's gaze. Even after breaking myself away, I still felt as if something was peering at me from the internal walls of the blade's surface. I wondered if, just perchance, the blade was just as much a threat as the figure that had taken up residency in my dorm.

Thankfully James broke the tension, muttering the name "Eli" to himself in his sleep. I had not the foggiest idea as to why James would be murmuring about my uncle in his sleep, but I did not think much about it. It truly was of no importance to me, and I was happy to have been broken out of the dark trance that I had been laid in.

I expected to find it just as difficult to sleep that night as I had the night before, and had the night gone without James sleep talking, I very much would not have received any semblance of sleep. His presence had become comforting in the short time I had known him; a comfort that gifted me an almost restful night's sleep, something that would quickly become a rarity.

Secretum

My friendship with James slowly turned into brotherhood over the following months. Despite our rough and argumentative beginning, it quickly became clear that James and I were awful for each other in the best of ways. James had a troublesome streak, to say the least, which was something that contrasted my more reserved and rule-oriented ideals. As the fall came and went, we grew closer and I began to notice the change he brought about in me. He would force me out of the comfortable situations that I found myself to enjoy, and instead made it so I joined him on his misadventures. It was never anything so severe as to cause problems with the law, but we did indulge in the more-than-occasional prank against our professors and peers. I, in turn, ensured that he never took anything quite too far. Any mischievous behavior he wanted to enact would always be vetted through me, as I had learned how to push the boundaries of others without breaking them. We were soon known as menaces across the campus to some, yet were nothing more than boys playing innocent pranks to others.

It was not just me looking out for him, though. He ensured that I no longer allowed others to trample me as they had for my entire life. I was still timid under his tutelage, but I felt a fire grow inside me every day I spent with him. I felt myself becoming more and more of what my father would have called a "smart-ass," and I did not feel a bit of conviction against it. We truly did play beautifully against each other.

It became a tradition that we would sit in adjacent seats during our classes, close enough that we only took the space of one student. We spent most of our class time making jokes at the expense of peers and professors, all save of course Uncle Eli. James was skilled at making the callus that had formed over me melt away. We were a distraction towards each other; a distraction that was very welcome.

The thing that spoke to me my first night at the seminary continued to haunt me. I never saw that dark form again, but I knew without a doubt that it was always present somewhere within my presence. It was watching from every dark corner that I walked passed, ensuring that I always sped quickly by anything that lacked illumination.

I could feel its presence stronger in some places than others. The remnants of the cafeteria held the feeling of being looked at in extreme concentrations. Every moment I ventured near that dilapidated building I felt as if something was peering at me from in between the pieces of wood that had been burned away. Over time my brisk step stopped being nonchalant. The constant feeling of observation caused my nerves to break down more and more until I could not help but sprint from location to location whenever I was not in the presence of James. Thankfully he held no animosity against my newfound propensity of keeping the lanterns in our room burning throughout the night. He could sleep in any situation whether it be noise, light, or class.

But even in that light I felt those eyes looking at me through the dark of our windows. I felt the presence of something covetous peering through the cracks of that damned cafeteria. No matter what it was, I could not escape its gaze. For some reason or another, it wanted me.

James made me forget about the thing that craved me in the dark. Even as others began to notice my growing paranoia and distanced themselves from my person, he still continued to act as my brother despite my concerning behavior. Even as I shut myself away from the outside, he continued to stay by my side. With him, I could ignore the thing that was watching me and enjoy our time together.

The only problem in this arrangement was the fact that our ignoring our work had not gone unnoticed. I could not focus enough on schoolwork with the waves of fear consistently washing over me, so I spent most of my days ignoring the reality of my fears with James. He, on the other hand, had no real wish to do any of the work given to him purely because of his disinterest in most of the topics spoken upon. Only one problem continued to arise in our daily goings-on:

Professor Quill.

Even when I did not feel my fear of the darkness ruling over me, the concerns of facing any sort of consequences from the old man haunted my thoughts. Our peers had faced plenty of them: rearranging the seats in the lecture hall for no reason, alphabetizing the bookshelves, scrubbing floors, and the like were among the punishments he dealt out. Yet we, somehow, managed to skirt punishment. It was not as if we were innocent from any misbehavior, either.

Admittedly, we had played our fair share of practical jokes against the decrepit man, though none of them could fully be tied back to us. That did not mean that he did not know it was us. In fact, after a particularly misjudged attempt at a prank involving letting a skunk into the dormitory we knew that he was certain it was us. James smelt too strongly of the odor for him to be innocent.

Thankfully, the other professors did not mind enduring our chicanery. Most found it humorous and only cared that we received good marks on our work, and while we put forth little effort, we still received at least average responses to what little work we did put forward.

It would have gone to stand that he could have just forced us not to sit together. He could even go so far as to force us to change our housing situation, but it seemed that that was too simple a punishment for him. Instead, strangely enough, he held back. He seemed to be plotting something, either that or building up our transgressions until he could enforce some overarching rule that would be enforced on the whole class. That build up continued until the final straw was broken.

James had fallen asleep in our early morning class, as was common, and I had nudged him awake. I *attempted* to wake him anyway. He was especially unconscious this time, and it would be only another moment before the snoring started. At that moment, I nudged a little too hard and he partly fell out of his seat.

James woke up screaming. "I'M UP!"

"ABSOLOM TEENDYTH!" Quill screeched from the lectern.

I was startled, and added into the screaming. "SORRY SIR."

Quill shuffled off his podium towards me, limping all the way. It was still astounding how a man of his age could move so quickly. Once he reached my location, he committed the worst act of violence against a student I had seen as of yet. Despite yelling at me, he smacked James against the back of his head with his cane, echoing the loud thud across the hall.

I tried to squeak out a response as I watched the professor glare at my roommate.

"Why did you yell at me sir? James was the one who decided now was a good time to take a nap."

James shot me a glare while he rubbed the back of his head. I would apologize later.

"Absolom, are you aware that I am the one in charge of making sure the students receive their amenities?" Quill asked with a very loud whisper.

"No Reverend Quill, I did not know that."

"That includes any sort of fuel for lights." He stared pointedly at me.

"What does that have to do with me, sir?"

"I do not know what you are doing at all hours of the night, Absolom. I do not fault poor James for falling asleep in my class, as it is very clear that you have been keeping him up at all hours of the night." I began to sweat profusely. I had no idea what it was that Quill had in store for me, but a sadist such as him taking notice of my new found phobia was not something that boded well for me.

James broke in. "Reverend Quill, I've been the one using all the fuel. When night hits I struggle to sleep so I instead use my time to study." James very clearly wished to save me from whatever fate befell me, but the smirk he gave me made it clear he did not do this out of care, but rather to make me feel guilty for trying to pass off Quill's wrath.

"James, we'll speak on your lying habit later. Though all men are sinful you seem to have an especially difficult time with it."

James snarled at his words, but did not fight Quill's comments.

"It is pretty clear that your friend Absolom has developed a fear of the dark."

"I am sor-"

Quill would not even hear my plight. "I really do not care how this came about or whether you have always had it. The simple truth is that you are not only acting as a stumbling block for your peers, but also siphoning away the school's funds."

"So, what are you going to do to me then, Quill?" I had resigned myself to my fate and dropped any sort of effort to show respect. I just hoped that whatever he had chosen as punishment wasn't too severe.

Quill rubbed the stubble on his face.

"Overnight in the cafeteria tonight."

I felt the color drain from my face.

"But sir, there has not been any progress on its restoration! I cannot stay there overnight, it will not be safe!"

"Come now Absolom, you are an adult now. Do not try and get out of your consequences. Besides, this is a light sentence compared to the disturbance you have caused in my class this morning." Quill had a smirk across his face.

I shuddered. "Can I at least take a light with me?"

Quill thought for a moment then reached out a shaky hand. It was cold from poor blood flow and was rough from age. He grabbed my hand, opened it, and placed a small lighter inside.

"Here, you can use this tonight."

"Qu..Quill, I will not be able to see with something this small." I could feel the panic begin to build up in my throat. Even in the well lit room I felt that craving thing staring into me.

"Well Absolom, maybe you will learn to get over this little fear of yours. It is unbecoming of a man, let alone a pastor, to be so ruled over by his fears." There was a twisted look that curled on his face whenever he was distributing punishment. It was clear he took enjoyment from it.

James spoke up again. "Sir, why am *I* not being punished for falling asleep in class? Is it not a bit unfair that I am the one who had such an outburst but am not being punished?"

Quill turned to look at James. "Do you feel guilty for the fact that your friend is suffering the punishment and not you?"

"Of course I do sir! It's unjust that I can be free from punishment." James was very good at playing the role of a paragon. Yes, he may have been the least likely to follow rules. In fact it seemed at times that he would go out of his way to break these rules. But that did not change the fact that the man had one of the purest hearts I had ever experienced.

Quill brought his face close to James'. A look of disgust spread across his face at the smell of Quill's breath.

"Good."

At that Quill perked back up and shuffled back to his podium. "Well, that is it for the lecture today. Sadly we are unable to finish the topic due to the outburst of your peers. We'll continue tomorrow."

We all scrambled out of our seats as quickly as we possibly could. There was no reason to stay where we could be further harassed by that vitriolic old man. We had food waiting for us back at the dorm and we would much rather eat that then be chewed out further for some other inane reason. It would be unsurprising to get a caning for loitering around the lecture hall
too long.

While we walked down the sidewalk I heard a small voice speak up from next to me. "I'm sorry, Abbi. Had I not been so careless you wouldn't have-"

"You have nothing to worry about James, and absolutely no reason to apologize." The need to comfort James momentarily snapped me out of my panic. "Quill is an extremely unreasonable man. There is no reason for you to shoulder the blame. That is what he wants from you, afterall."

"You're right, Abbi. I just worry about you. I try not to think about how you'll handle the dark of the cafeteria, let alone the dust." James spent a lot of time worrying about my disposition. He may not have shown it, but his experience with my asthma attack on my first day had given him quite the fright.

"I will be fine, I promise."

He didn't seem convinced, but he dropped the subject. He seemed ready to move on from the events of the morning.

AFTER WE HAD DEVOURED our breakfasts we returned back for the rest of our classes. Stonehart was boring as usual, though my panic worsened the experience. Even my uncle's class that followed was dull. He was speaking on Hinduism, *again*.

Knowing everything made time pass by swiftly, thankfully. James was not paying close attention either, as he was still very much engrossed in his depression. It was taking a bit for him to bounce back. I could always sense when he was bothered, as his hand would subconsciously drift onto my knee. I was happy that he found me comforting but I always moved his hand back to his own lap. I always did this as people who were less accepting and those who did not understand our brotherly relationship might think negatively of both him and myself.

Once class passed by we made our way up to my uncle's office. He had arranged that our lunches would be delivered to his offices and we would eat with him. James was most definitely my uncle's favorite student, something that may have exacerbated James' apparent admiration. I, on the other hand, was his beloved nephew. He figured it would be a great chance for us to converse together and learn more about his expeditions.

It had become a tradition at this point.

The moment we walked through the door Eli could tell there was a problem. A look of concern crossed his face and he wrapped us both in his arms and patted James on the head.

"What happened? James, you look as if a loved one died! And Abbs, you look

positively shaken!"

James looked at the ground while I stood rigid beside him, trying to keep from trembling in anxiety.

"Quill." We both said in unison.

"Ah. Of course."

That was all the explanation Uncle Eli needed. Almost all the professors currently employed by the university had been taught by Quill at some point. It was almost a rite of passage to be abused by him. "I apologize on his behalf. It seems as if he's taken a slight vendetta against you Abbs. Whenever I speak with him he says some sort of vile comment about you, nephew."

We continued to stand at the door's entrance, entranced by negative emotion. Uncle Eli ushered us further into his office and sat us both down. "Both of you eat. It's beans and cornbread today."

Both of those were a personal favorite of both James and I, so needless to say it didn't take much convincing. After a bit my nerves had finally calmed enough to tell Uncle Eli about the early morning events.

"I see." He looked concerned. "The cafeteria would be highly unsafe for someone of your disposition. The dust alone would cause your chest to seize. Not even taking into account the cold air, *and* mold from water damage."

"Exactly why I'm so worried." I made no mention of my phobia or the thing lurking in the dark. My uncle would have assuredly reported to my parents about it, and I would be pulled from my courses at my mother's insistence.

"I hate to think how much the things in there might affect my health."

James spoke up. "Professor Eli, is there any way you can overstep Quill? Surely Absolom doesn't have to carry out this punishment.

Uncle Eli looked solemn. "There really is no way. It's dangerous to overstep Quill. He is a very wealthy man who has poured a lot of funds into this place. Any sort of overstep may cause him to cease his funding."

"Oh it surely can't be that much." I chimed in.

"About 80% of our funding comes from the Quill household."

"Ah."

Both James and I returned to looking defeated. There was no way out of the situation.

My uncle let out a large sigh. It seemed he wished there was a way out of the situation as well.

"I hate to admit this, but you are going to just have to rough through it. It is a very unfortunate circumstance, but it seems that we are stuck with Quill's decisions."

"I guess I really have no option other than to just accept the punishment."

We finished lunch in silence.

NIGHT CAME QUICKLY, bringing a deep chill. Quill didn't even stay late to ensure I slept in the cafeteria. He knew I wouldn't dare not face my consequences. Knowing how much of an influence Quill had over the university, I would not even be surprised if he used my disobedience as a means to punish my uncle for some unknown reason as well.

That night the sky had decided it was the perfect time to storm, sending a nasty mixture of rain and snow causing the ground to turn into an icy mess. I swear it was as if Quill planned for it. I would not be surprised if that demon of a man found a way to bring the bad weather as a means to spite me. I felt my feet slip on the thin sheet of ice that covered everything as I made my way to the broken down building. After falling many times I finally found myself standing outside the large wooden door to the old dining hall. They were similar in design to the doors to the dormitory and lecture hall, yet the thinner areas of the door had turned black and at some places were entirely missing from the very apparent fire damage.

The moment I stomped through the threshold of the cafeteria the scent of mildew accosted my nose. There was no possible way for me to ignore the dust that was flitting through the air. Heaps of moist ash coated the ground, making a soft carpet over the hardwood flooring that used to be visible. Thankfully I had thought to grab a scarf from my belongings so that I could cover my mouth and nose.

I tied the scarf over my mouth, lit the lighter Quill had so graciously given to me, and set off to find a place that I could lay down comfortably.

Thankfully, that lighter was not the only source of light but it was still the strongest. Pieces of the roof had crumbled away from damage so that the moonlight was able to stream through when it peeked between the moving clouds. In that light I was almost able to see the whole of the building's interior. Small icicles formed in the holes in the ceiling further adding to the moist atmosphere of the building. Thankfully humidity didn't bother me as much as dust.

There was still plenty of that in here.

The interior of the building was nothing more than a great empty hall when you walked in. Tables and chairs were strewn around the area. In the back was an opened door whose gaping maw led way to the actual kitchen.

I felt the cold air that breezed throughout the cavernous dining hall brush against my back. The settling wood did not help the fact that the moment I entered the building, that feeling of being watched returned. I reasoned that every noise and bump I heard was just the rot of the walls setting in or a creaky floorboard. Every chitter was nothing more than some large rodent.

"Must be an opossum." I reasoned to myself. "I would not want to disturb one of those. Even worse, it might be a raccoon."

But worse than all of these things was that incessant feeling of being watched. There is nothing quite like the feeling of being perceived. That little unexplainable phenomena where a human of any age, gender, or race can always feel within almost certainty. And I felt it in the dark, just like I had in every shadowed area. But for once I could ascertain where that watching was coming from. I felt it stare at me through that vacuous blackness leading into the kitchen.

Like any sane man, I decided to check the main dining area for a place to rest first. I wanted to ignore that darkness on the other side of that door, so I ignored it and searched for a place to rest. Once I got to know my surroundings it was made clear that nothing in the area could support me to rest on. Almost all of the tables were blackened and spongy from fire damage and exposure to the elements. Most of them were barely able to support themselves, let alone a grown man on top of them. The chairs were in similar shape, if not worse, as the upholstery had molded. I continued searching the area, hoping that maybe one of the tables had stayed stable enough to support my weight. I was about to give up hope and use the floor when I heard it.

A click.

The door had closed.

I sped around, bringing my eyes back to what was once the dark and gaping maw of the kitchen. I stared for a moment. Maybe I had misremembered. Maybe that door had never been open. But I knew I heard the click, and I knew that I had just seen the open mouth of the door frame open and waiting to devour whomever would step inside.

Normally I would have fled, much as I had for months now. But something ate away at me, telling me that I should investigate whatever had closed the door. I thought, maybe, I could put these foolish fears to rest. Surely those unseen eyes I had felt gazing at me were some sort of animal. Maybe, just maybe, it was a raccoon. Maybe it was the skunk we had used to torment Quill. We had found it on campus after all, so it would not be so far-fetched to believe that it had always been in the tattered walls of the cafeteria. Maybe even just a gust of wind, or maybe something fell and caused it to shut. There had to be some plausible reason for the sudden click.

But inside me I knew that all of those were simply me wishing that my fears were unfounded. If it was something so simple, I would no longer have to flee from the thing that was stalking me. I hoped deep down for a natural answer, but I knew that my hopes were unfounded. The doors were too heavy for an animal to have closed it. Too much ash had built up and created a natural doorstop around all the doors, which would have given the wind little hope of closing it. I would have heard the clatter of something knocking it shut. And none of these could explain that cursed thing that spoke to me my first night on campus. It would not explain the dreams that had haunted me since my arrival.

I held my lighter out in front of me and tread towards the door, stepping over wet ash and small patches of snow to avoid having it seep into my shoes. There were no prints that may have suggested any sort of animal. I could not even feel the wind blow near the door. No loose wood was present, either. I leaned down and pressed my ear against the door. I prayed that I would hear the scuttling of racoons or rats on the other side. But I heard nothing, and stayed for a moment hoping that I would hear some sort of movement.

And eventually, I did. But it was far from the noises that I wished to hear. Instead of the scuttling of paws and nails, I heard footsteps. Heavy ones. Footsteps that asked to be heard. Footsteps that were walking towards the door I was leaning against. When the footsteps stopped the creak of leather began. The distinct sound of someone bending down. Then the sound of breathing. Labored breathing. Not just vaguely on the other side of the door, either. The breathing was directly in my ear. Despite the door being thick between us, I could feel the hot breath creep down my ear canal. It wheezed, the breath of a man who did not know what it meant to get a deep breath.

"Tell Him you see Him."

At that, the door slammed open.

I fell to my knees, clutching my chest as it beat hard inside of my chest. I felt myself begin to weep. My horrors had not been unfounded, and had just increased tenfold.

But this time, it was not the kitchen door that flung open. Instead, the front door was now wide open. Wind and snow rushed in as debris flooded into the area. Standing in the maw was a figure holding both a lantern and blankets.

"Abbi! What happened? Are you okay?"

I could not respond. I felt as if I was choking, the air being shoved out my lungs as dread took its place. I could only reply in stifled sobs.

He did not push the matter, instead running towards me and wrapping blankets around my body.

"Shhh, I'm here. I knew you feared the dark, but I did not know it was this bad..." He said as he tried to comfort me. I shook my head no, trying to convey that it was much more than the dark that frightened me. He did nothing but try to comfort me. We stayed in that dark until my sobs stifled and I could regain my composure. Even then, we stayed silent for another moment. James then broke the silence.

"I am so sorry for letting you out of my sight. I truly did not know your affliction was
this bad."

"I-it was not just the dark, James" I huffed, the air still not fully occupying my lungs.

"Then what happened?" James asked.

I told him about the door, as well as the footsteps and the sound of the heavy breathing behind the door. I did not find it important to tell him about the voice's message though.

"Abbi, if you intend to prank me at least remember to set up the joke." He said in an angry tone of voice. "You had me worried, and all for a joke I might add."

"What do you mean, James?" I gave him a puzzled look.

"The joke doesn't work if the door is open, Abbi." He said flatly.

I turned around, being met with the open maw leading to the kitchen. The new light from the lantern illuminated the inside showing no signs of life.

"On the bright side, it seems as if the roof is intact in there. Seems like it should be dry."

James got up and walked into the kitchen. It seems he had already forgotten his anger towards me.

"Oh! The oven is even intact! Seems as if there's some wood in here that we could use too!" James tossed some wood into the brick stove, then opened the lantern and tossed the ignited fuel inside. Immediately the bright light filled the room and illuminated the kitchen.

Strangely enough, the kitchen seemed untouched from the carnage in the other room. Yes, there was still burn damage from whatever fire had happened. The counters were slightly charred, and any wooden utensils were most definitely no longer intact. But the piles of ash were all but nonexistent. Any fire damage to the ceiling was minimal.

"You would think a fire that started in the kitchen would have caused more damage."

I mused.

"Oh, the fire wasn't started in here." James corrected me.

"What do you mean? I mean it would make sense for a kitchen accident..."

"That's your first problem, it wasn't an accident."

James seemed to be knowledgeable on the event.

"Well, if you know so much, why not enlighten me?"

James began to recount his knowledge on the event. "The damage happened last year when my older brother attended. It caused the entire campus to lock down for a while. A student that was rambling about betrayal broke into the cafeteria one night and lit the whole

place ablaze."

"He sounds like a quack. Was he a strange man?" My curiosity was piqued

"Not really. In fact he was a star student. Pretty close with your uncle, even had lunch with him on the regular like we do."

"Huh. Wait, do you think there is any chance he may still be hiding here? Maybe the thing on the other side of the door was him. He might have been hiding in the cafeteria all this time."

"Oh, no way. He used himself as the fuel. He doused himself in gasoline and lit himself up." James said matter of factly.

"Oh, and how did your brother learn of this?"

"He followed him to the cafeteria. Saw him lurking around in the dark and was concerned. My brother saw him through the window as he threw the lantern on himself. He even was going to follow him inside, but he was so glad he didn't. They weren't able to put the fire out before making the building irreparable."

James' story left me with one question: Why had my uncle not just told me the true story outright? I reasoned to myself that perhaps he had just not known the details.

That led me to another question. Though related to the story, it was separate from my other concerns. "How did your brother handle it?"

"Oh he handled it fine. He struggled with it for a bit afterwards, but he wasn't all that close to the student. He's fine now."

"You have not told me much about your family, James. Up until now I assumed you were an only child." I pushed a little. I hadn't broached the subject since the first time I asked him. I wanted to avoid the regression I experienced when we first met. I braced myself for the same situation to occur a second time.

But instead he let out a deep breath and steeled himself.

"I come from a preacher's family, much like you Abbi."

"That does not surprise me. Most students here are. These students really like to follow in their father's footsteps."

"You see," He sighed again, questioning whether he truly wanted to reveal any information about himself. "I didn't. I wanted to go into scholastics. Yes, theology interested me, but I had always preferred the more secular areas of knowledge."

"What is the reason you came here to study then?"

James' eyes cast down to the ashen floor of the kitchen. The flames licked across his face and glinted off the tears building in his eyes.

"My father figured this would be the best way to fix me."

I gave him a sort of confuddled look, trying to piece it all together. "I do not think I can find any part of you that is broken, James."

"Don't play dumb, you know exactly what it is I mean."

"I... I do not, James."

"The day my father saw me making eyes at a deacon's son was the same day he decided to ship me here. I also received quite the beating." He stopped and regained his composure when he felt his breaths become shaky.

"My mom tried to defend me. He moved on to her once he was done with me. This wasn't the first time he's beaten me, or her. He has done worse for less."

"Your father's congregation must be rather small if he behaves like that..."

"On the contrary! Almost every person who lives in our small village attends. They love him."

"Oh."

"But that's all in the past now. I'm here, and I cannot deny I've met some lovely people at this university. Almost makes father's abuse worth the people I've had the chance to meet. Though I fully expect to lose one of those now." He braced himself, seemingly ready for me to scold him like his father had.

"I am not going anywhere James. Thank you for telling me." My comment did little to cheer him up. He continued to stare dejectedly at the floor.

"May I ask you a question though? I promise no matter the answer I will not

abandon you."

"What would that be?"

"Do you feel that way for me, James?"

"I love you more than any others, Abbi."

"I love you too, James."

"I don't think you mean that in the same way I do." James brought his knees into himself and buried his face in between them.

"I am not sure how I mean it."

Confractus

It wasn't long after that I found myself in that pitch black again. I had the dream so many times at this point that I knew I was asleep. It was the same darkness every time. And it was the same thing leering at me from the dark each time as well.

"See me."

It always asked the same thing. Every time it was that damned thing telling me to see it. This time though, the dream played out differently.

I followed the advice of the voice behind the door. Somehow I knew that that disembodied voice was not the same as the voice I had heard in my dreams. The shadow that had decided to make me its prey was without a doubt not the same thing in the dark in my dreams. The thing from my dreams felt too vast to be the shadow, and that shadow too familiar to be the thing of my dreams. All the same, I could not say that they were fully separate. Almost as if they were different iterations of the same being, as the same hunger that wanted ownership of me pervaded both of them.

I waited for the multitude of voices to appear and conform into another. I waited until the loud booming voice screeched its request to me. I waited until the very crescendo of the thunderous voices. I waited until I thought they could get no louder still.

I let the thing say it's piece.

"I see you."

It was barely a whisper from my lips, yet it echoed throughout the blackness as the overwhelming siren from the thing in the blackness silenced and heard my response. We both stood in the darkness. I felt a multitude of consciousness fixate on me, staring me down in the nothingness we both inhabited.

And then the darkness was no more.

There was no longer blindness, no more the overwhelming sound of downpour.

An overpowering violet light washed over me, giving form to the nothing. It was still empty - save two things. One was a building, familiar in shape. The modest steeple rising from the front betrayed it as the obvious: my fathers church. If one were to measure its distance from myself it would be a little over a mile, yet it was clear what the building was to me.

Above the church was what could be described as a cloud at first glance. The first thing that betrayed it as something else was the color. It was neither light and airy like the cloud on a summer day, nor was it morose and thick like a storm cloud. It was sickly instead, being the chromatic hue of polluted water.

It didn't move like a cloud either. Instead of drifting on the wind that would guide it, it stayed in place. That would not be strange, taking into account the lack of a breeze in the nothingness we shared. What did make it strange was the motion that it underwent. It folded in on itself repeatedly, expanding and collapsing in on itself. It was impossible to see an edge on the mass, as it was constantly creating new borders for itself.

Then was the contents of its downpour. The drops that formed underneath it were too large to be water and the sound too heavy for it to be sleet. The shapes that fell from this polluted cloud were too distinct from one another.

"Come closer."

I was drawn forward, feeling the luminous call of the entity that stood in the nothing. I began to move forward, trudging over the vast nothing so that I may reach that thing that stood as a lighthouse in the inky black.

The building and cloud both seemed close, just a short walk away. Yet no matter how much I traveled it stayed the same distance away. But it was no matter, I would reach it eventually.

Hours passed and I still walked, drudging through the open air. I felt the draw continue to call me closer. I continued to walk no matter how much my legs began to ache. I continued to walk even as blisters appeared on my feet. I continued to walk as those blisters became open sores, and I continued to walk as I felt my hunger begin to dissolve the lining of my stomach.

I eventually got close enough to the structure and the cloud to perceive them correctly. The building was my father's church, and the things that fell from the undulating mass above were deceased birds.

Doves.

They fell in droves.

Any that didn't hit the church continued to fall into the nothingness beneath us. The ones that did fall onto the church caused large dents to form in the roofing. Small holes had begun to appear in places that could not handle the stress.

I continued to move forward. The decreasing distance did nothing to the perceived size of the church. Even standing right outside the storm of doves it looked the same as it had when I was a mile away. I could no longer walk straight from the pain that pervaded my body.

I steeled myself and continued to walk forward the best I could. I stumbled forward endlessly, until finally, I reached the border of the storm. I braced expectantly, fully ready to be stricken down by the deceased birds that fell above me. I continued forward, relieved that the birds somehow evaded me. Every time one would be about to crash into me, the bird would regain life anew, fly a few meters, then regain its position in death and continue falling into the nothingness.

Again, I continued further even more, deafened by the roaring of the solid rain passing by my ears. I opened the doors of my father's church and stepped inside.

There were no lights to brighten the interior, but the all encompassing violet glow that seemed to be emanating from the cloud. I opened the next set of doors to the sanctuary. I was met with the sight of every pew being filled by those who were present at the town meeting. Some were there in full form. Others were distorted, as if they were being viewed through a stained glass. At the front of the chapel were three figures. Next to where the pulpit would be placed stood my father to the left, with my uncle to the right.

But the pulpit was not standing. Instead, it lay shattered between them. Standing behind it was another figure. It was featureless, as if it had been redacted from existence. No, not featureless in the sense that it had no eyes or mouth, but instead as if it had been cut out of existence entirely. It left nothing but a tall, man shaped hole in space.

I was greeted at the door of the chapel by two figures, one clearly being James and the other being that of a woman I did not recognize. Standing next to James was a calf, not much more than six months old. On the woman's shoulder sat a dove, quietly cooing into her ear.

They both took an arm and led me down the center aisle. Everything felt as if it had been prepared for my arrival. It felt as if they expected me. All present watched carefully as I walked past, tears in their eyes as if they were about to experience a celebration of matrimony.

We reached the pulpit, calf and dove in tow. I was encouraged to step onto the altar, in front of the broken pulpit. I found myself opposite of the rigid shadow. My father and uncle stood before me, both staring as if in some sort of daze. They brandished a small knife each, clearly the retaining knives of the Kukri I had been gifted.

I stood there, expectantly. I was unsure of what it was I was currently witnessing. I felt it was my duty to ensure it came to completion, but I was unsure of how to officiate. The void stood unmoving as well, waiting for the ceremony to proceed.

My uncle and father both stooped towards James and the woman, took their prospective animals, and brought them forth to me. They looked up, almost looking for approval, then swiftly slit the throats of both the dove and the calf.

Both were torn to pieces

Piece after piece was thrown at my feet. Not just meat, but bones, offal, nerves, tendon, skin. All of them were laid before me. The shadow came around and kneeling beside me, began to devour the pile of fleshy things in front of us, gorging itself. It looked up at me expectantly, then continued to feast. I felt my knees become heavy, dragging me down to kneel next to the void. Once I reached him, I continued on in the same manner he did. I could not think of anything other than the meal that was being laid before me.

I shoved everything that I could into my being, digesting and enjoying every piece that the animals had given up. It was clear to me that I was eating the fruits of a sacrifice. Whether the sacrifice was to me or the void thing beside me I did not know.

But what I did know was that I was meant to partake. Those in the church knew I was starving. This was my sustenance.

I continued to consume, feeling the bloodied meat drip from my chin and bones crunch between my teeth. The salty fat of marrow filled my gullet as it slid down my esophagus. The more I ate the more I realized how famished I had been. No matter how much I consumed, I could not eat my fill. My stomach ached as more and more dropped into it, slamming against my raw belly that had been stripped of its lining from hunger. The thudding against the roof became louder in contrast. I could not find a way for me to satiate the hunger. Fat popped between my teeth. The roof was beaten even harder.

The bodies of the animals that had been sacrificed shimmered for a moment.

I paid no mind to when the roof caved in from the force of the birds collapsing into the chapel. I paid no mind when the birds crashed into the congregation, crushing their skulls much like the roof. It did not faze me when the figure disappeared from the corner of my eye, nor when I felt the heavy weight of a blade attached to my hip. I was too busy enjoying my meal. I devoured each tooth as a tiny morsel. I felt strong again. Stronger than I had before the journey to grasp the distant void in this familiar church.

When I finally finished what had been prepared for me, I was finally able to take in the fullness of the scene that was laid bare before me. The slumped over bodies of the attendees had been eviscerated by the falling doves. I looked at my feet, expecting to see at the very least small remnants of the calf and dove that I had devoured, but was met with a much more grizzly sight.

Instead, two contorted bodies lay at my feet. They were almost unrecognizable due to the sheer amount of mass torn from them, yet I still knew.

The corpses of James and the mysterious woman faded out of view as I awoke.

I AWAKENED IN A COLD sweat. I was still in the kitchen of the cafeteria, James beginning to stir beside me. He didn't ask me if I was alright as it was commonplace for this to be the state I began the day with.

"Dreams again?" He muttered to me groggily.

"Of course." I responded in turn.

I stood up and dusted the ash off myself. "Well, class begins soon. You should head back to the dormitory and collect your things. It's dark enough out that you should be able to go

about unseen."

James groggily rose to his feet and began to pack up his blanket and lantern. "Smart idea. You can handle yourself now, right?" He asked as he winked at me.

"I mean I could have handled myself the whole night just fine."

"Right." He chuckled as he moved towards the door to leave. "See you in class, Abbi."

I was alone in the cafeteria again. I would not be allowed to enter the dorm until lunch, so I was stuck with just what I had on my person, meaning the shaggy clothes I would wear to bed would be my attire for the day. My breath would most likely be atrocious throughout the day. I propped open the door to the outer cafeteria, grabbed my lighter, and stamped out the hearth. It would be better to not allow Quill to know that I had more light than just what was given.

After I had been assured the embers were out was when I had heard the bells that signaled our first class tolling. I shuffled out to the commons and joined everyone who trudged towards the lecture hall. After finding my place in line next to James, we both lumbered towards our usual seats and sat. Both of us were careful not to mention the night before.

Classes went quickly. Quill went uninterrupted, everyone was scared of his display the day before. In fact, all classes went smoothly. James stayed alert throughout even the most boring lectures, and I managed to keep my mouth shut. Although poor James seemed to still be blaming himself for my punishment.

Lunch came before we knew it, and we both went to Uncle Eli's office so that we could spend our time together. We both sat at his desk, quiet and still.

"Well Abb, how did last night go? How did you fare?" He inquired.

"I did fine, all things considered. It was in more disrepair than expected. It is no surprise they cannot manage the funds to repair it." I was eager to discover why there were discrepancies between the stories I had been told about the cafeteria. "James, you should tell Uncle Eli the story you told to me."

My uncle raised an eyebrow.

James concentrated for a second, questioning whatever story he may have told me. Then a look of epiphany crossed his face.

"Oh that's right! Professor Eli, did you know that my older brother was the one who reported that the fire had started?"

Uncle's face twisted for a minute. "Oh my! Well if it had not been for him, the fire might have spread to the lecture hall. Worst yet, the dormitories could have been affected as well. At least the *accident* had been contained." Sweat glistened on my uncle's forehead.

"Oh! I'm surprised you didn't know, Professor!" James remained aloof to how clear it was that Uncle Eli knew it wasn't an accident. "According to my brother, the student who started it was actually fairly close to you. I'd say just as close as we are to you."

"I mean, yes he was. He had been messing with things he should not have and ended up setting fire to the whole of the cafeteria. Poor boy got lost in that fire as well. I try not to think of it." A moment of silence filled the room as my uncle held an impromptu wake for the deceased student. "Ah, but it's no good to dwell on such depressing things. I have mourned and will mourn again, but right now I'm in the presence of the living."

James seemed satisfied with that answer. I was somewhat uneasy with it still, but before I could protest any further the topic was changed.

"Oh, apologies for the change, but I received a telegram for you, Abb."

"Must be something from Mother. I would be surprised if Father found the time to write."

"You should be even more surprised. It's from Charles Willith."

A look of disdain spread across my face.

"Who's Charles Willith?" James interjected.

"He is an old windbag of a deacon that serves under my father. He has a bit of a vendetta against the Teendyth's because we try to curb his thievery." You could hear the venom drip from my lips. "What does he want?"

"He wants you to come home, actually. Seems that they broke their promise and installed whoever "his Benji" is."

"As was to be expected." To think that they would actually honor the deal between my father and them was laughable. "I'm guessing they want me to return so that they can gloat?"

"No. It seems that they highly regret it. It sounds like the town went to hambles since they instated him. He even went so far as to include that Benji was "the biggest disappointment for a son a man could receive."

I knew then that Willith was serious. That man would never even dare to use those words in any sort of lie. It took something drastic for Willith to say such things about his precious son.

My uncle continued. "They haven't even been able to hold communion for months. He continually drinks the wine."

"What of my father? Could they not just reinstate him until I finished my schooling?"

"Willith does not make mention of that. He insists that you are the only one prepared for the task."

I paused to think for a moment."Well, it seems that I will be returning home early." I saw James' countenance drop immediately. "Oh do not worry James! I am sure you can come and visit! Maybe even stay for winter break! My mother would adore you."

Uncle Eli joined in to console James. "Oh most definitely. In fact, strangely enough you remind me of Abb's mother. You even look similar."

James chuckled to himself, warming up to the thought of visiting me at my home. "It does sound quite strange that someone who looks like Abbi could have a mother that looks akin to me. You must be lying to me."

"Oh no, Uncle Eli is right. You are both even of similar heights. I reached out and patted James on the shoulder. "Similar countenances, too."

"Well, I guess I'll have to come and see for myself."

My uncle interjected. "Anyway boys, I hate to cut lunch short but I have some pertinent business to attend to today. You both might as well return to your dorm for lunch."

And at that, we both gathered up our lunches and made our way back to our dormitory.

LUNCH CONTINUED AS usual, at first. Mostly the both of us sitting there conversing about our previous interaction with my uncle.

"He really did seem rather eaten up over that student's death. I wonder if we caused him any damage by reminding him of it." James pondered, empathetic as usual.

"I find it strange." I added. "He was never one to shy away from a gruesome story. Did I ever tell you about how he received the blade he gifted to me?"

"I don't think so." James replied.

I went to retrieve it from underneath my pillow, but was interrupted by a vengeful wrapping against our door. A chill ran down our spines when we heard the angry voice of Quill on the other side.

"You damned brats! Open this door this instant!"

James put on the friendliest grin he could muster and greeted Quill at the door. Refusing him entry would only cause more trouble.

"Hello Professor Quill! What can I do for you this fine afternoon?"

Quill's face looked even more demented than usual, his wrinkled scowl puckering in on itself in rage. Without saying a word he raised his cane above James, then proceeded to bring it down swiftly against his head, repeatedly. James cried out in pain and tried to plead with Quill.

"Professor, whatever is the reason for this, I assure you we can talk..."

"You and I both know why this is happening, James!" Quill said as he planted a hand against James' sternum and pushed him backwards, knocking him towards the ground. Quill's strength was formidable, even in his old age. Had James been prepared, he may have been able to brace himself, but Quill was fueled by the adrenaline of his hatred.

Quill stood over James, bludgeoning him with his cane repeatedly. Blood began to pool underneath James. His skin rapidly took on the sickly purple hue of a bruise. I saw him as I saw him in my dreams, and the guilt of inaction flooded my veins again. I would not refuse to act this time. I slipped off my bed and walked over to Quill, who was still enthralled with the violence he was enacting. He said nothing, lips pursed. As he swung his arm down, I caught it in my hand and held it still. I stared down into his face, the vessels in his eyes bursting in rage.

"Absolom, you will get yours in turn. Get your damned hands off of me this instant!"

I did not hear him.

A thudding pervaded my ears. A low downpour that only I could hear. I noticed every wrinkle in his face. Every spot that had formed with age. Every skin tag. He truly was an ugly man, both internally and externally.

He had started to get louder in his protesting. Threats of violence. Something about never leaving the dorm again. I felt my grip on his forearm get tighter. I felt the strands of his muscle part under my grip. I was lost in the increasing rush of the downpour and the disgust I felt towards this man.

Tighter.

I was grasping his arm with both hands now, one at the wrist and one towards his elbow. His arm grew white and cold as his already poor blood flow stopped. I could see panic spreading throughout his face, desperate to get free from my hands. He may have been spry for his age, but he was still an old man. Although I was sickly, I could breathe freely for once.

I could feel tension as I began to bend Quill's forearm in opposing directions. The rushing was too loud now. I could not even infer what he was saying. His eyes had become devoid of hatred and were only pleading with me to cease my actions.

People began rushing into the room and grabbing both Quill and I, trying to separate the both of us. None of them succeeded. It was almost as if they were not even truly interacting with us. Instead of being present in the room with us, they were merely watching it all play out. Quill's arm stopped denying its intended path and began to give reprieve. Quill's eyes grew wide with pain as I felt the popping of shattering bone inside his arm.

Quill's arm hung at a strange angle as he looked into my eyes, nothing but fear present for a swift moment. He did not scream. He did not curse. He merely whimpered as shock took hold of his body. Those watching in the hall wrenched him from my grasp. The jostling caused him to snap into reality, and the anger that was so ingrained in the man returned. His cursing returned, swearing threats of harm upon me.

I did not care. I simply returned to bed and fell asleep.

IT WAS MORE AKIN TO unconsciousness than sleep, and for once I felt some sort of rest without the dreams that had plagued me for the past few months. As my eyes fluttered open I saw a blackness outside of the window, indicating that I had slept until the late hours of the night.

The room was still illuminated though, and in that light sat a figure. I jumped, startled by the stranger in my lodging. The sudden jump caused me to bludgeon my head against the bottom of the bunk.

"Oh I didn't mean to startle you!" The strange man seemed kind enough, reaching out to me as if to make sure I had not concussed. "I didn't even think to ensure I wouldn't startle you. I hope you aren't h-"

I swung my legs off the side of my bunk and charged towards the man, fully ready to evict another strange person from my room if necessary. I was stronger than I ever had been, though my breath was just as ragged as it always was. Even then, I knew I could defend against this stranger. I had enough of these intrusions and was exasperated by others' inability to leave James and I alone. No amount of mischief warranted the sheer amount of harassment that James and I had endured. I pulled my arm back, just about to strike the man in the jaw, until I was interrupted.

"Peter, is that you?" James muttered from his bunk.

The both of us turned to look at him, sitting up in his bed.

The stranger let out a hearty laugh. "Yes James. Can you please tell your friend not to hit me?"

James jumped down from his bed and rushed the man in a display that showed the most energy I had ever witnessed from him immediately after waking.

"What are you doing here? It's such a joy to see you!"

I looked on in confusion, still unsure of who this man was. I took a closer look at his features. The thick red beard. The hair that was the same hue, yet much better kept. The same cherub-esque cheeks. While he was a good bit taller than James, which was not a difficult feat, he was still considerably shorter than most.

"Abbi," James said, his face still buried in the man's shoulder. "This is my brother Peter!"

"Ah, I must apologize then for trying to assault you, Peter. I have been under immense stress recently." I pleaded my case, hoping that he would understand.

He let out another hearty chuckle. "I've heard. Word spreads fast."

"Is that why you're here, Peter?" James asked. "I'm in awe of how quickly you arrived."

"No, I was already here to have a meeting with Professor Stoneheart. We had planned on doing some collaborative research together. He was also insistent that I try his new rye recipes, but that is besides the matter." He explained.

"And you weren't going to tell me?" James scolded.

"I was going to surprise you, but I saw a commotion and a doctor rush into the dormitory. Think of the surprise when I entered to see my little brother lying unconscious on the floor."

"Wait, a doctor was in the dormitory?" I interrupted.

Both James and Peter gave me a peculiar look.

"I mean, yes? He needed to be in order to treat both Quill and James. Why are you surprised?" Peter replied.

"I just find it strange. First Quill, then the doctor, and now you. The security rules they have put in place seem to be ill-enforced."

Their faces contorted even further. "What security rules?"

"The one about only students being allowed into the dormitory." I said. Perhaps these were newly in effect and they had not been informed. "My uncle informed me about them. That was why he could not help me bring my luggage into the dorm, and why James had to help me."

"I think your uncle must be misinformed." Peter replied.

"I would think it would be a safety concern to bar *everyone* other than students from entering the dorms. I mean in the rooms might be moderately understandable, but to go so far as not even allow them in the lobby would be ridiculous." James added.

"Are you sure you are not mistaken?" I asked.

The both of them nodded in unison.

"That's not the first thing your uncle has gotten wrong. I wonder if he's doing alright. He may be having some sort of mental break. Perhaps the stress of work is getting to him?" James pondered.

"Wait. Absolom, who is your uncle?" Peter inquired.

"Professor Eli Teendyth."

Peter seemed to wince at the name.

"What is the matter? James, I thought you said your brothers enjoyed my uncle's teachings?"

"I said *most* of my brothers." He replied.

"You two really should be avoiding that man. I do not trust him a single bit. He's not nearly as godly as he claims to be." Peter cautioned us as a darkness spread across his eyes. "What other *things* has he been getting wrong?"

"Well, he was strangely dismissive of the student that was killed in the cafeteria fire. Almost as if he needed to be reminded of his existence. We just assumed he didn't want to speak about it." James answered.

"He did not even claim it was any sort of arson when he first spoke to me. Simply claimed it was an accident." I added.

"HA." Peter let out a laugh that could only be described as triumphant. "I can tell you that you are both being lied to by that man.

Now James and I shared the same confused look that he and Peter had shared previously.

"What is he lying about?" James asked.

"There is no way on God's earth that he could forget about the events that happened that night *because he was there.*"

"Explain." I demanded.

"That night I heard a quarrel in my neighboring dorm and only two voices were present in the scuffle. My neighbor's and your uncle's."

"That does not prove anything" I added, indignantly. "Just that he got into a tussle with
a student."

"I would agree, but once one of them burst from their door into the hallway and I heard the other sprint behind them. I decided to follow. I couldn't catch up fast enough to see who was chasing whom, but I never once lost their trail."

"So you saw the fire happen?" James asked.

"I saw more than that. By time I caught up to them the building had already started smoking. My peer had already lit himself ablaze." He paused for a moment. "I saw a shadow standing in the fire light."

I thought back to the shadow that stalked me ever since I arrived on campus. Could it be that this student had a shadow following him too? I just hoped that it had not been my uncle that Peter saw that night, and instead that his peer simply had been followed by the same apparition that I had, or at the least a kin of it. There had to have been some sort of explanation. I rested my hopes on something more supernatural being at play the night of the fire, but my faith was dashed as Peter continued.

"The shadow walked towards me with a gait that was way too calm for something that had just watched a student burn to death. He met my eyes in the darkness and walked closer, never once blinking. When he came up next to me, he placed a hand on my shoulder and spoke in your uncle's voice, "No one will believe you," he said."

We sat in silence for a moment. I could not try and claim that some apparition was the one to have caused the fire now that Peter confirmed that he had spoken to my uncle that night. Of course, there was always the chance that Peter was lying, but I felt that he had no need to. My uncle also had now been caught in several lies at this point, so I was not entirely sure what I could believe that came from him.

"It makes me wonder if the seminary is really worth all the awful things that seem to reside here. Quill is already bad enough, are you truly saying that my uncle could be worse?" I asked.

"I wouldn't let a few bad people ruin your experience. I can fully claim that my experience at this seminary was nothing short of life changing, experiences with some of the professors aside." Peter replied.

"Also, don't count your uncle as one of those evils yet either. I still believe there might be some explanation." James added. "Nothing else to do but to ask him about it tomorrow at lunch."

"I would agree." I added. "We can question him about the situation tomorrow."

Peter interjected at that thought. "Won't be possible. Quill has put you in lockdown and you're not allowed out of the dorm at this point."

"Did he put that into effect, or was that simply his angry yelling?" I asked.

"Technically just angry yelling, but I wouldn't risk the consequences. You're already in enough trouble."

"Well, I'll go and talk to him myself." James said. "No reason to fear the man."

"I'm not sure if that's the best idea. Even if he is innocent I still do not trust him."

Peter replied.

"I could take him in a fight."

"Fair point, you are scrappy."

The conversation paused, signifying the end of the conversation.

"By the way, Peter. How was it you knew my name?" I inquired.

"James talks in his sleep."

THAT NIGHT WAS QUIET. No dreams were forced upon me that night, and the pitch black of my eyes was the only thing my mind perceived. It was bright when I awoke. There was no reason to wake up with the bell. I had no plans to attend any classes. With the ever looming threat of consequences, as well as the fact that I would not be finishing my schooling after all, it made no good reason to go out of my way.

I took the opportunity to begin packing. I had amassed a great deal of things over my short tenure at university, meaning that I had a great deal more to stow away for the journey. James had absolutely lavished me with gifts when he learned my birthday had only been a few weeks before the semester started. Turns out, his family was fairly wealthy for those of pastoral lineage. It made me feel a twinge of disgust to learn that his family was more akin to the Williths than my own. It made me wonder if Benjamin had any sort of trauma akin to James. Then I remembered the hell that the Willith spawn had always been so willing to abuse me with and brushed the compassionate thought from my mind.

What James and I had in common was trauma. It seemed as if there were two different sects of people in existence. Those who suffer and those who cause the suffering. James and I both belonged to those who suffered, as did my father and my mother. On the other hand, the Williths, Quill, and the like, were those in the ilk of causing suffering. My uncle was becoming more and more debatable on where he lied. It was a clear cut scenario, a harsh truth to have learned at such a young age as James and I did: the wicked flourished and the corrupt caused suffering. Suffering belonged to the righteous.

I thought about these things, as well as the lies of my uncle as I ransacked my room to find what belonged in each neatly organized box. As I checked beneath my pillow for any spare laundry that may have snuck its way into my bed, I felt my hand rest upon something tucked away beneath my pillow and suddenly remembered the existence of my knife. I decided to admire it, so I sat on my bunk and unsheathed it. The sunlight glinted off the black blade, only letting a few streams of light into itself. Those few streams illuminated the interior of the blade, causing swirls of chromatic light to intertwine and dance throughout the edge.

The more I looked the more the colors took the shape of the shifting faces that I remembered from my dream. The vicious, the lustful, the wanting. All could be seen in those swirls that flowed through the blade, making a graven image of the accursed cloud in the blade. I could almost hear the rushing sounds of falling doves as the swirls passed through my vision. That dark and egregious cloud came to my mind again and again as I replayed the dream where I first saw it. The sacrifices, the bodies shimmering in the crowd, even the familiar splotch of dark that had lurked behind me in the dark.

But where my recollection of my dream began was not where the visions stopped. What I first thought were simply memories of that damnable dream, twisted, taking shape to new horrors. That perverted ordination same gave way to scenes of abject gluttony. I saw visions of the most luxurious of mansions, only to see men and women in chains operating the ins and outs. I saw spreads of magnificent food, enough to feed entire towns of people. At the head of the table sat one man who devoured it all. I saw love give way to obsession. I saw oppression change to hatred. Then I saw the hatred change to action, and that action to love.

The scenes overlapped each other, thousands of events played out. Each had one thing in common with the last:

perversion. Each event had started out with some other intention, yet quickly evolved into a demented version of itself. Kind men became prideful due to their praise. I saw the faces of scholars grin at the thought of discovery, only to become sullen with the knowledge they had gained. I saw Quill as a young child, happy and full of life. Then I saw him crumble and harden at a father's harsh hand. The sound of downpour continued.

Yet not all of this perversion was truly evil. I saw lies, taken out of their natural context of misdeeds instead used to beautifully delude the downtrodden. I saw thievery, twisted instead as a means to give to those less fortunate. I saw the best of intentions crumble away into nothing but villainy, yet I saw the worst of deeds done in the name of love.

Then lastly I saw one final perversion. I saw a door; the door to my uncle's office. The downpour broke, and I could hear the voices of James, Eli, and myself clamored throughout the hall. We laughed and deliberated over my uncle's stories, calling him out on embellishments and lies that at one point seemed so very innocent. Then the door opened, and I left, leaving Uncle Eli and James by themselves in the office. The door closed. The laughter continued, but slowly and surely got quieter and quieter. Then it vanished all together. Hushed whispers filled the room, one voice slightly panicked and the other trying its best to be soothing.

James' voice became more and more panicked, trying to remain firm.

My Uncle's voice remained insistent.

And then, a yelp of pain.

And then muffled sobs.

And then the torrent continued.

I regained my mind.

It seemed that I had become overly engrossed in the visions the knife had shown me, as the sun had already set after a full day of absolutely nothing.

James had yet to return from his classes. He had not even stopped by during the
lunch break.

I shrugged it off at first. Perhaps he was still spending time with Peter. He was leaving for home in the morning, so it would be of no surprise that he would gravitate towards him for the little bit that Peter was here. But even then, he would have told me. Sure, I had been entranced for the past few hours, but he would have at the very least left a note.

I decided the best course of action would be to ask our peers if they had seen him on campus. Yes, it would be a bit of a risk due to my treatment of Quill and it went completely against my better judgment to speak to those who may have come to see me as a monster, but my worry was quickly becoming a panic. Most of my peers seemed unbothered by my treatment of our elderly professor, as their receiving of me was surprisingly normal despite my outburst. A few thanked me for the service I had done for the seminary. That's not to say all of them treated me warmly, but those who treated me coldly had done so before the day's events.

Not a single one of them could place where James might have been. Last they recalled seeing him was just before the lunch break as he trekked up to my uncle's office for lunch. The thought scared me. Those lies of his had culminated, and

I no longer could trust if my uncle was a safe man or not. I thought again to the dream I had. I thought back to his hands as it slit the neck of the calf. That, compounded with the awful sights I had seen in the gleam of my blade, gave way to an intense dread that weighed down my chest.

I eventually grew tired of anxiously waiting for James to return. I put on my coat and ignored my gloves as I ripped the lantern off the wall, lit it, and strapping my blade to my side, set out in the middle of the night to search for him, even though curfew had begun hours ago.

Despite Peter's warning I truly did not have any intent on following my punishment.

I decided to search the buildings closest to the dorms first. I skirted around the back of the building, making way to the outbuildings that dotted the otherwise empty area. He was nowhere to be found in the greenhouse, nor was he near the small lodgings that had been built for the groundskeeper. The scullery was empty save a few articles of clothes that had been left and some dishes that had not been cleaned from the night's meal.

Next, the lecture hall, as it was on route to the cafeteria. I need to be careful to not be caught, as I was still fully breaking several rules that had been enforced over me. Any extraneous travel could inhibit my search for James. Thankfully, they always kept the front doors of the lecture hall unlocked, so it was no issue to enter so I may search. It was unlikely that he would still be in the hall, but I figured I would give the building a once over. I started at the lower hall, which was assuredly empty. I then moved on to the upper floor where the professors' offices were located. Most were dark and locked, except for one.

A thin beam of light shone from the door of my uncle's office. I crept closer, hoping that I may find James still just sitting in the office holding a conversation with my uncle. I got as close as I could yet heard nothing from the inside. It was then that a floor board betrayed me, alerting my uncle.

"Hello? Who's there?" He barked into the darkness.

I had no escape. The moment he opened the door the entire hallway would be illuminated, and there was no way I could run fast enough to enter any sort of cover. I stepped inside his office.

"Hello, Uncle."

A look of genuine shock spread across my uncle's face, surely surprised to see his nephew skulking around in the dark.

"Oh Absolom! What are you doing out so late? It's past curfew. And you especially shouldn't be out after Quill ord-"

"Uncle, where is James?" I interrupted coldly.

"Ah yes," my uncle replied. He shifted from side to side. "Last I saw him was at lunch. Why do you ask?"

"He never returned." I said, a hint of accusation in my tone.

"Strange. Do you think he may be with Peter? It would make sense that he would be spending the day with his brother before he left."

"You see Uncle, I thought the same thing, But I know for a fact that James would have informed me as such." I replied.

"Maybe you do not know James as well as you think, *Abbi*." He retorted. For a moment, I could have sworn he was mocking me.

"I know James perfectly." I replied. "I think it may be you who I do not truly know."

"What could you mean by that?" He growled. He was slipping, showing more anger every time I challenged him.

"I know you lied about the fire, Uncle. I also know that he has not been seen since he spoke to you about it at lunch."

A calm washed over him, as if he suddenly became aware of how he could regain control of the situation. "Ah yes, that. I must apologize. I have not been entirely truthful to you about that situation. You see, I was there. The boy who set himself alight was a close pupil of mine, and he was becoming more and more troublesome. Even went so far as to make several allegations against me, though all of them were dismissed as nonsense. It was a rather traumatic experience that I did not wish to relive. I told the same to James as well, and he seemed understanding. Now really, I would suggest you go find Peter. It really is the most logical conclusion, even if you think otherwise."

Normally, I would have believed him. But something in his words betrayed something in himself. It was not just the lies he had told, but even now in truth it felt as if he were carefully choosing which details he would include in the story he was concocting. His eyes glared at me expectantly, as if trying to gauge how he would form his response.

"Uncle, I would just like to find James. I would rather not listen to any more of your drivel." His stature changed, seemingly forcing itself to be larger. He felt threatened by something, but remained composed in his verbiage.

"I am not entirely sure where he might be located at this very moment." He replied in a statuesque manner. My triteness had not been the response he was searching for.

"But wherever he may be, if you find him, give him this." He outstretched his hand and placed a belt into my open palm. A cold, leathery strip was laid into my hand. But even once he handed the thing over, he still kept a firm grasp on my hand. "James forgot his belt in my office."

"Why would James leave his belt in your office?"

His stare held, looking directly into my eyes. We were almost of the exact same height, yet he looked down on me. The happy-go-lucky man who had so warmly conversed with both James and I was gone. Whoever this man in front of me was, was not the same man.

Why was it again that my mother hated him so much?

Ah.

That was right.

My mother, in all her fiery nature, was never one to show fear. It was not in her nature to quiver and cry and worry. Instead, she summoned all of that fear and turned it into passive aggression. Had she been more physically apt, she would have been a much more

violent woman.

As I stared into my uncle's eyes, for the first time I did not see with my father's eyes. I did not see the love my father always had for his brother. I saw with the eyes of my mother. I felt her fear. His hand slid away from mine, his face stern for the first time in my life. His eyes still held- cold and unwavering.

He did not blink.

"You know, Deacon Willith will be here to collect you this weekend."

I struggled to respond. This was the first time I had seen this side of my uncle in such a manner, and I dare not fail to respond. I was standing in the presence of an angered stranger, and it would be better to not anger them further.

"O-oh, so soon? I figured it would be at least until the end of the first semester."

"I think it would be best for everyone involved that you refrain from causing any
more trouble."

"Yes sir."

"You may take your leave."

"Yes sir."

I left without hesitation, not wanting to further be in the building with the stranger named Eli Teendyth. I tried to remain composed until I left the lecture hall. The moment the cold night air hit my face I found myself springing in the direction of the cafeteria. I still had to find James, and it seemed the last logical place he may be.

The moment I entered the cafeteria my suspicions were proved correct, as I heard muffled sobs leaking out from a dimly lit kitchen. Those sobs were all too familiar, a sign of a James that needed some sort of consoling. As I entered the kitchen, I was greeted to the sight of James curled up on the dilapidated floor, curling around himself in a fetal position.

"It's okay, James. I'm here." I said as I lifted him into a sitting position and embraced him. "Tell me what happened."

He tried to speak, but the sobs came out even harder. My usual tricks did not work, so I sat there with my arms wrapped around him. Our love for each other may have assuredly been of different breeds but that did not change that I cared for him, nor did that change that I was the best suited to comfort him in his time of need. He laid there, curled into me and sobbing for almost an hour. My coat was soaked with a viscous mixture of mucous and tears that flowed freely from James. Eventually he stopped long enough for me to pull him to his feet.

"Let's get you back to the dorm. It's cold here and unsafe." He did not protest. He did not say anything. He simply nodded and trudged along as I pulled him towards the exit of the cafeteria. As I opened the door I saw the shadow of my uncle walk past in the distance, seemingly heading towards his carriage so that he may leave for the night. I did not know why he had not left for the comforts of his home yet, but did not have the capacity to confront him on James' state. Getting my friend to comfort was much more important than whatever excuses my uncle would make for the night's events. I felt that it would be best to let him pass by, especially for James' sake.

After a few minutes we exited the structure, making sure that Eli was out of sight. James mindlessly trailed behind me, only moving because of me guiding him by the hand. Once we reached the dormitory room, he slid his hand out of mine, climbed his bunk, and fell asleep. Tiny sobs could still be heard from the top bunk as we both drifted off to sleep.

Transitum

I was awoken by bright light and shuffling, a sure sign that James was awake. Hopefully he had received some semblance of sleep the night before.

"Good morning James," I greeted him. "How are you feeling this morning?"

"I'm doing alright. Tired, but that's not something terribly uncommon."

I sat up in my bed, noticing that James had been shoving things into his duffle bag. He seemed to be packing.

"What are you doing?" I inquired.

"I'm going home with Peter today."

"Oh." I responded, downtrodden. It was only a few more days before I would be leaving to return to Afton. James' impromptu departure meant that he would not be present for when I made my leave and it was unlikely I would see him again after I left. I felt a dread that I would no longer be able to care for him, and I worried how he would survive the world without me. He was the gentlest of men, and feared for what he might have to face on his own.

"Yes, I know that you will be leaving on Saturday." He responded, very clearly, and just as equally sullen. "But Peter has to return this afternoon and he cannot postpone."

"Is this about what happened last night, James?"

"I will get a hold of your address and I'll make sure to write." He ignored the question. "Maybe I'll even make the trip and visit."

I did not insist on continuing the conversation. When James did not answer the question it meant that he had absolutely no intention of answering it. It would be better to leave well enough alone. I decided to get out of bed and join him in packing my own things. As I got up I knocked over my knife, which had been propped up against my bunk. I grunted.

"What is it?" James asked.

I picked up the knife and inspected it. "It seems one of the retaining knives to my blade got knocked out just now." I got out of bed and began searching under the bed for the missing piece.

"I'm sure you will find it." James soddenly said, but he made no effort to help me look.

"It is probably somewhere in the room, I must have just misplaced it." I said from the floor.

We both meandered around the room completing our morning hygiene. It seems that James had no intention of appearing for class either, as he spent the entire day packing. We both took a break from our packing and ate lunch when it was delivered to us. We did not speak as we ate. We did not speak as we resumed packing. The few times that James uttered a word seemed to be filled with trepidation. Even after we completed our packing he said nothing. He would not look up from his feet.

As the sun began to set James stood up. He still would not look up from his feet.

"Absolom, have you figured out how you love me yet?" He said, his voice quiet. It saddened me to hear him call me by my full name. He had refused to call me by my pet name since last night. I wished deeply that he would call me that again, as I did not want it to be tainted by Eli.

"I love you more than anyone I have ever had the pleasure of meeting, James." I moved forward to wrap him in my arms, something that was always certain to return him to his senses.

He winced.

I pulled back.

"That is good enough for me, Absolom." He began to pick up his things, as it had come time for him to leave. I decided to follow suit and attempted to grab a piece of his luggage

as well.

"Oh no no, Absolom." James stopped me before I exited the door. "I hate to ask, but I would rather you stay here. I am downright awful at goodbyes and I would rather not extend this one."

"Alright, I will stay put," I conceded. "But remember, this isn't goodbye. We will see each other again soon, I promise."

"Of course we will, Absolom."

And with that, James left the room carrying the whole of his belongings on his back, just as he had with my luggage when we first met. I had wished that he could have stayed even just a short while longer until I left, but it was important that he return home before he was forced to endure worse than he already had.

THE REST OF THE DAY passed swiftly. Once the weekend arrived I would be leaving to return home. And so I continued to pack. I had plenty of time, so I decided to be as methodical as possible simply to waste time. I folded every shirt as neatly as I possibly could, same with the pants. I packed my books away in boxes, stacked away in alphabetical order.

But even with my slow and intentionally tedious method, it was still only mid way through Friday afternoon when I had finally packed away all my belongings. Everything had been accounted for, sorted, and taped away.

Except for one thing: the small retaining knife that belonged with my kukri. I searched the entirety of the room, high and low, yet could not seem to find it. Yes, it was small, but not small enough to simply evaporate as some small items did.

There was a positive though, as it created a new distraction. Now that all my belongings had been stowed away for travel I had nothing to keep me from thinking how dull things were without James to accompany me. So I filled my time with sleeping and searching for the knife. I figured I would find it in an afternoon, but that quickly turned to a whole night. Once Saturday came I still could not find it. I had resigned to the fact that I may not find the remaining part of the set. The time was nearing that I would be leaving campus to return home, as I was expecting to be collected sometime in the afternoon as my collectors would arrive on the noon train.

I gave up searching for it after lunch and decided that I should begin to move my luggage to the curb so that the process of loading my belongings would take as little time as possible. I could not move all my things in one load like James could. Thankfully, my newfound strength made the process of moving much easier than it would have been several months ago when I first arrived.

I considered it a blessing.

As I finished moving the last of my luggage I saw a familiar face. It may have been familiar, but it was rather out of place.

"Peter!" I called out.

Peter waved in response and came rushing over. "Ahah! Perfect, just the person I was looking for." He seemed slightly panicked, as his breath was rapid and he wiped sweaty palms on his trousers as he stood before me

"What is it?"

"Do you know the whereabouts of James?" He asked, barely holding himself together.

"What do you mean? I thought he, and you, were supposed to have been home by now."

"He was. He never met me where he was supposed to. Did he ever return to the dorm?"

I felt something tingle in the back of my mind.

"No. I was under the impression that he was with you."

It was then that a wagon appeared at the curb. Once it fully stopped, Deacon Willith, Mr. Sterling, and Uncle Eli all climbed out. Mr. Sterling immediately began scooping up arm-fulls of luggage and began packing them into the back of the wagon.

The moment I saw uncle my panic was replaced with rage. Before I could even think I felt myself rush forward, grabbing Eli by the collar of his shirt.

"WHERE IS JAMES!?" I demanded.

He stuttered over himself, clearly not wanting to reveal the persona he had shown to me the previous night in front of those who could be considered to be his peers.

"W-what is it you mean, Abb?"

"Peter just informed me that he has not seen James in several days. Neither have I. We both know that James is not the type to simply disappear without a word."

"I have absolutely no clue either, Absolom. I would ask that you remove your hands
from me."

I removed my hands. It was not simply due to his request. In fact, his insistence that he had control of the situation was starting to no longer intimidate me, but instead had become a source of annoyance.

"Thank you. Now, let's talk abou-"

"No. You stay put, because I am not done talking to you. Peter, I know where your brother is." I took off sprinting in the direction of the cafeteria. The moment I found James I would wrap him in my arms. What was he thinking, vanishing without a trace? Maybe he felt safer in that kitchen.

When I entered the large doors of the cafeteria it was clear that my assumptions were right, as all of James' things were sitting outside the closed kitchen door, stacked neatly in a pile.

"What would he be doing here?" Peter asked as he picked his way across the dining hall.

"It is a place that is special to the both of us." I responded. "Especially the kitchen. He is most likely inside. I found him here before, the night before you were supposed to leave."

Peter and I stood next to each other as we both pushed upon the door. For a moment we stood together, taking in the view of the kitchen. Just as I assumed, James was laying in the center of the kitchen. He was very clearly asleep. I was beginning to think that was his main way of dealing with his problems.

Peter seemed relieved to have found his brother. Tears of relief curled in the corner of his eyes as he ran into the kitchen to embrace his brother. He seemed to have yelled something as he ran through the door, but for some reason I could not comprehend what it was.

Peter dropped to the ground and scooped James up in his arms, the strange brown substance that was covering the floor staining his trousers. A look of panic spread across his face, his lips moving in a frantic scream that produced no noise.

I heard none of the thudding that had accompanied this feeling in the past.

"Are you alright, Peter? I cannot seem to understand what you are saying."

He continued to yell in a soundless voice as his face became more and more frantic. I did not see why he was worried. Chances are, James had fallen asleep in the kitchen and did not awake in time to meet Peter to leave. It would not have been out of character for him to do as such, and it was not unlike him to sleep as heavily as he was now. There really was no reason for Peter to respond as poorly as he had been.

What truly was peculiar though was the strange stain that covered the floor. It had not been here the night before; its vastness would have made it impossible to miss. I bent down to investigate it further. It was slightly tacky, dry in most spots save where the substance had been its thickest. Even stranger was its scent; it was both metallic and sweet simultaneously.

It was blood.

Sound rushed back into my life. Not gently, but with force and violence. Sound as a whole was so enraged that I dare ignore it. Peter screamed in between his sobs, trying his best to form coherent sentences. And it was then that I noticed the one sound that was not present.

Snoring.

"ABSOLOM! WHY ARE YOU JUST STANDING THERE? GET SOMEONE!!"

It felt in that moment as if it were the first time I had ever heard any sound. It was a frightening thing that stunned me from responding to Peter's demands. Finally Peter got exasperated and ran out of the kitchen to find help. James' body was left laying on the
cold ground.

I took the opportunity to get closer. A small fraction of me hoped that he would stir as I got closer to him, but I knew otherwise. There was too much blood on the ground for him to simply be sleeping.

"It is okay James, I am here." I cooed to him. "Let us see what is the matter."

I gave his body a once over as I felt small droplets of tears form in the corner of my eyes. I could not let myself break yet. I had to be there for him, even if I could not save him. Overall his body was spotless with no sign of harm. That was until I got sight of his wrists, ever so gently covered by the blood soaked sleeves of his sweater. Long gashes stretched down the length of his forearms, the clear source of his exsanguination. Stranger still, there were burn marks that traced the outline of each cut. It seemed as if he had tried to cauterize his own wounds.

"Oh James, you foolish boy." I said to him, my tears becoming even harder to hold back.

His hands were wrapped tight around something. I stooped down and peeled apart his fingers. They gave off several sickening cracks as I unfurled them. Inside was a little letter wrapped around a small object. When I unfurled the note, a small knife clattered to the floor.

A small knife made of obsidian.

The fullness of emotion was beginning to come upon me. I felt the tears roll down my cheeks as I read the letter that James had been clutching:

Dear Absolom,

I expect you to be the one to find this letter. If not,
I assume it will

somehow reach you eventually.

Firstly, I am sorry for hurting you this way. I know it's cruel of me to leave

you in such a violent manner, and even crueler to do it with something dear to you.

But, I had to make this decision.

In my life I have only truly loved one person the way that I have loved you. I know you will never love me the same way, but knowing you at least loved me as a brother was enough for me.

There was only one man that I thought of as my mentor, and that was your uncle. Eli Teendyth was a brilliant man. I admired and looked up to him, even loved him, for that. To me, he was just a more wisened version of you. He reminded me so deeply of you in almost everything: appearance, mannerism.... voice.

I see him now in everything you do, and it is torturing me. You are a beautiful person, but I also see the vileness of your uncle in you, and I cannot handle it. It scares me to think that you will turn out just like him when you are older.

Eli Teendyth is a vile, disgusting man. I only wish that he had been in this damned cafeteria when his last victim set it alight. If he had been, I would not be here, doing the same thing as that poor wretch.

And that is why I can no longer bear living.

I love you, Absolom. Even in death.

Goodbye.

Tears fully rolled down my face. The overwhelming feeling of loss overtook me as I read the letter.

But then I reached the final paragraph and the sadness vacated my body.

In its place, hate arrived. I had thought that I had known hate. I thought I had hated Quill. Surely I must have, I harmed him.

"Do as you must." A voice said through the sound of storms drumming in my ears.

Peter arrived, this time with both Eli and Mr. Sterling in tow. Eli rushed forward and tried to wrap his arms around me in an attempt to comfort me.

"Oh Abb, I am so sorry..."

I shoved him away from me, following up with a swift right hook to the jaw. There was no need to blame my violence on some sort of fugue state or a call from the beyond. I needed no excuse. The surprise hit sent him backwards, almost knocking him off his feet. He gathered himself and immediately charged forward to retaliate, screaming more profanities than a man of God never should.

Right before Eli reached me, Mr. Sterling stepped in between us and blocked Eli from striking me. He then promptly swept me up and hoisted me on his shoulder, keeping me from harm's way. I was not a small man by any means, but Mr. Sterling always stood about a foot taller than the tallest person in a room at any time. He gave a disdainful glare to Eli as he scolded him.

"No sir! No way are you hitting a man who just lost his best friend. Especially

not Absolom."

Eli returned the hateful glare in kind. "He struck me first," he growled in petulance. His facade crumbled as the defiance he met grew.

Mr. Sterling's eyes narrowed. "I'm pretty sure pastors are supposed to turn the

other cheek."

If my uncle had said anything more, Mr. Sterling did not acknowledge it. He continued to stand around with me hoisted over his shoulder. Peter regained his position holding James' corpse. He did nothing but sob, a broken heap cradling a sibling that he should have never had to watch die.

Deacon Willith entered the cafeteria, shouting about being late for the train. I cannot blame him for being so cold hearted, as he did not know of the scene taking place in the kitchen. Thankfully, he gave pause when he saw Peter mourning, but that did not stop him from his usual uncouthness.

"Let's get going Sterling, we have a train to catch."

Sterling sighed in response to Willith's inability to feel empathy, yet trudged along in response. To say I went willingly was not entirely true, as I kicked and punched Mr.

Sterling like a petulant child, begging him to let me hit Eli. Mr. Sterling was too strong and I could not break through his grasp no matter how much adrenaline was coursing through my veins. He only released me once we were on the wagon to ensure I did not run off to assault my uncle.

I SPENT THE MAJORITY of the trip in the wagon bed mourning. Once the rage and hatred wore off, all that was left was the bitter truth that I would not be seeing James again. I would not be sending him letters and he would not be telling me stories about him and his brothers.

He was gone, and I would never encounter him in life again. I found myself staring into his note throughout the trip home, mulling over his words, trying to decipher what monstrous act my uncle had done. The more I pondered the more I found myself separated from my own consciousness. I no longer read the page as we rambled on, merely staring at the paper itself.

Time passed swiftly, as I do not even recall boarding the train, then departing and reboarding another wagon. All that mattered was the paper with the scrawled notes of my deceased friend. And the more I stared, the more the letters shifted and danced. No matter how hard I tried, the page swum and swirled with my tears. Eventually, all the letters had left their original places, and had begun to spell out new things that my brain could not comprehend, yet somehow, still knew they were words. A mass of letters I somehow understood conjoined in the center.

"You know what happened."

"I!" I said way too loudly.

I stopped and corrected my volume, as I had no wish to alert Sterling and Deacon Willith to the fact that I was talking to a piece of paper.

"I have no clue. I ask that you enlighten me."

The letters started to shift again, opting to spell out a scene instead of words. They shifted until I saw the view of my uncle's office as if I were looking through the doorway. There was no color or texture, just the simple black and white of pen and ink. The outline of a man sat at the desk, I presumed it was my uncle. He waved at someone who was not yet depicted on the paper. As the second figure began to form out of the letters, much smaller and much angrier. It was clearly James. He waved his arms furiously, berating my uncle for some unheard reason.

This was it.

I was watching the day James confronted my uncle. Though I could see neither face, James' anger was palpable and Eli remained in his normal unfazed composure that he held around people he felt as lesser.

I watched as Eli stood from his desk and wrapped his arms around James. A new set of words joined at the center of the page.

"It's okay James, I know you are confused."

James tried to push himself away from my uncle, but his almost supernatural strength he had was null when it was compared to someone so much larger. Eli's grip got tighter around James, sealing away any hope James had of escape.

The heads of each letter-amalgamation seemed to fuse into one another, a sickening misinterpretation of an embrace.

"You remind me of someone else I know, James."

The sound of muffled sobs started somewhere in the back of the carriage. I think they may have been mine, but I am not entirely sure. They may have been James'.

"I hope you do not mind that I call you by her name."

"P-please, Professor Teendyth you're hurting me."

"Please, call me Eli, Margaret."

I felt myself become sick at the mention of my mother's name. I swallowed to keep myself from losing control of my stomach.

The page remained blank for a moment, then the words reappeared.

"I love you, Margaret."

The picture returned into view. James hurriedly rushed out of the room, attempting to keep his trousers from falling down. Eli picked up a long piece of leather and wrapped it around his fist as the scene faded away again.

"You are no fool." The paper replied.

I nodded through my sobs, confirming. There would be no other reason why the belt would be left behind. I did not want to admit it. I wanted my uncle to be innocent, even if I treated him with contempt. I wanted to find a reality where I did not have to hate him. It was wrong to hate.

"You hate him."

No. I could not hate him. There was never an excuse for hate. It was a concept ingrained in my body that there was absolutely no reason to ever hold hatred for someone. It was unchristlike. But that did not mean that I did not feel it leaking into my psyche; I wished nothing more than to inflict the same thing upon my uncle that he inflicted on James. Was that hate or was it justice?

"It is just."

"Could it possibly be just to hate?"

"Praise be the Putrid Cloud."

At that, the wagon shuddered to a stop. The back canvas lifted, streaks of light flooding into the wagon past the hulking figure of Mr. Sterling.

"Hey kid, we're back in Afton." He said, trying to be as gentle as possible. He seemed to be empathetic to my fresh loss, not holding me to any sort of responsibility to my outbursts. Willith, on the other hand, was a stark contrast.

"Hurry along, Absolom. The quicker we can make your presence home known the better." I looked up at them and groaned, my eyes puffy and sore. A sneer crossed Willith's face.

"And I suggest you stop sniveling before the people see you. It's unbecoming."

I dried my eyes as I pocketed the note. As I glimpsed the contents, they had seemingly returned to their original state. I grabbed a few of my things and climbed out of the rear of the wagon. Forcing myself to right my mind, I asked Willith to clarify the situation.

"So remind me why you brought me back so early again? All I recall you saying in the telegram was that you had done exactly what you said you would not do, and instated Benjamin anyways." We grabbed my things and started towards the church. Willith grimaced a response.

"Things have, admittedly, not gone according to plan."

"And you expected otherwise?" I retorted. I heard a chuckle come from Sterling.

"I mean, to an extent I expected my son to continue to be troublesome, but I didn't expect him to be so disrespectful towards the faith."

Willith went on to explain. "Not long after we instated him his behavior worsened. Sterling had to outright ban him from the tavern." Sterling nodded and confirmed. "He started going out of his way to start fights. He even tried to kill someone. If it had been just my word, he would probably still show up every night to get drunk. But all my other patrons made it well known that if he or any of his compatriots tried to enter the bar again, they would make him leave with more holes than what he walked in with."

"What a crude way to put it." Willith sighed at the obvious inferiority that both Sterling and I had compared to him. "Not long after, people stopped going to Sunday service. They said they did not want to hear anything that Benji had to preach about. With nobody coming to service he converted the church into a sort of, clubhouse, for himself and his friends. Even went so far as to set up a distillery. The local whores have even had the audacity to perform their services in the sanctuary."

"Don't act like those women are agreeing to any of it. I doubt your boy is even paying them." Sterling interject.

I shook my head at the news."Did it ever occur to you that you should just reinstate my father until I returned from at least a single semester of Seminary? And why does this matter to you in the first place? You have never once actually cared for this congregation or town, let alone your faith."

Sterling answered for him. "No one is tithing."

"Ah, of course."

Willith had turned crimson at our mocking. "Absolom, I am not fond of this attitude you have developed during your absence. This must be the influence of that dead boy that corrupted you."

I stopped and reached out, grasping the back of his neck, and squeezed. His greasy neck folds tried to slide out of my grasp. "Maybe you should have my father handle this instead."

He squirmed under my hands, somewhat in shock at the amount of force a man he once considered weak, produced.

"That will be the absolute last thing I will ever do." He growled.

"Why?"

He slightly turned to me with a dumbfounded look, one that was downright bewildered by the fact that I did not know why he despised my father so much. "N-now is not the time

for that."

I gave a slightly tighter squeeze, but released my grip when I felt Mr. Sterling's hand on my shoulder. "Calm down kid, he's not worth it." I nodded and directed my attention to Mr. Sterling as we finished the trek of delivering my things to the front of the church. He seemed to be curious as to how I was no longer easily winded. He chuckled when I told him that getting into a fight somehow realigned my health.

ONE COULD TELL THAT the church had been abused before even entering. Beer bottles were piled in the snow leading to the steps of the front door. The once beautiful wooden door had been stained with a myriad of colors, each clearly from different bodily fluids that I cared not to identify. A repetitive thumping shook the front porch. Muffled cries could be heard if one listened closely, yet they were mostly drowned out by raucous cheers.

I brushed some glass bottles off of the stoop and set down my things. Willith and Mr. Sterling followed suit. I unlatched one of my cases and pulled out the sheath. I then pulled the small retaining knife out of my pocket, still stained with James' blood, and returned it to its

rightful place.

Willith seemed to panic for a moment. "I asked you to take his place, not kill him!"

My patience for dealing with perverts was becoming extremely limited, and I brushed him off. "I do not plan on it, but they will be more likely to listen if I have a knife."

Mr. Sterling shrugged. "Kid's got a point."

"Alright. Just please, I do still love him." Willith begged.

"Of course."

I threw open the doors to the church and entered. Rotting food and chipped paint littered the floor of the small foyer. One man lay passed out on one of the chairs. I continued deeper into the sanctuary. Nobody paid me any mind as I entered. Pews had been pushed to the side and hay mattresses were scattered across the floor. More rotten food was here, tainting the air with the rancid smell of decaying meat. In one corner was a group of rusted metal canisters with several tubes running throughout them, clearly the aforementioned distillery.

Worst of all was the large huddle of men standing around on the front stage, each and every one of them were naked. Muffled sobs came from the center of the crowd, a clear indication of what was currently occurring.

"You all are disgusting."

"What was that?" One of the men peeked up from the crowd.

"I SAID."

I raised my voice to be heard over their debauchery.

"YOU ALL ARE DISGUSTING!"

At that point I had gotten all of their attention. The crowd all turned towards me. All of them had a sickly yellow hue to their skin, a sure sign of their alcoholism. Benjamin stepped forward. He reminded me so very much of the Eli I had seen in the paper. So assured that he was wanted sexually that he was blind to any rejection.

"Well hello, Junior! Glad to see that you made it home safe. Would you like to join us?" He grabbed the woman that had been servicing them by the hair. "This one always did have an eye for you. Wouldn't stop going on about how handsome you were even after ya left."

She seemed vaguely familiar, most likely one of the local prostitutes. My father helped minister to them fairly often, so it was most likely that I had seen her at one point or another. She was bruised, clearly marking this was not the first time they had abused her.

"I think I would rather not, Benjamin. I actually think I would prefer that you leave."

Benjamin chortled. "Alright, let me finish up with the hedge-creeper over here and I'll get on my way. I'll be back after you finish cleaning."

"No, Benjamin, I want you to leave now."

Benjamin broke off from the group and walked over towards the distillery and began filling a large jug of moonshine. "Junior, I have to tell you. You're extremely important to me. You remind me on a daily basis just how annoying sober people are."

"Now, Benjamin."

Benjamin let out a long sigh and gestured at one of the other nude men. He was large, standing just below Mr. Sterling's height. Unlike Mr. Sterling, this man did not have an ounce of muscle on his body. Flabs of skin hung from his body, cascading as if they were sickly curtains. I did not recognize him. It seems that Benjamin had started accumulating drunkards from neighboring towns, as no one from Afton was sane enough to befriend him. It was clear there was only one way I could get them to leave.

I gave them one last warning. "Benjamin, I really suggest that you leave. Even your father wishes for it."

"Oh yeah? And what are you going to do?" He asked, swilling his moonshine.

I lifted my blade, showing it to Benjamin.

He chuckled in response, clearly not taking the threat seriously. "You're bluffing."

The tall man started lumbering towards me, his holy poker fully on display. He had clear intent on bringing me harm, something of which I had no intention of letting come to pass. I had suffered enough in this lifetime and had no wish to leave this event a laughingstock.

In one quick motion I slipped my blade out and sliced it across the tall man's groin, cutting off his glory. A scream shredded through the sanctuary as blood began pooling underneath him.

"I have long forgotten how to bluff, Benjamin!" I shouted.

"How dare you! He wanted to be a father!" Benjamin cried out.

His other underlings began to cry and flee, stumbling over themselves. Had they not been so inebriated, or had been an angry drunk like Benjamin, they would have realized they could have easily stopped me. It was clear that Benjamin wanted to avoid having anyone who might threaten his leadership counted among his disciples, as the only one that might have given him any trouble was now currently clutching his groin, doubled over in pain.

"Maybe he should have thought of that before displaying himself so proudly to the world!" I retorted. Some of the men were brave enough to hoist the tall man out of the sanctuary. Benjamin sauntered over to me, unaffected by the terror that pervaded his followers.

"Fine. I'll leave and give you this precious den of yours back. You'll never get the stains out, anyways." He pushed past me, a jug of moonshine still tightly grasped in his hand. Deacon Willith followed him out the building, pleading with him the entire way. It was evident that Benjamin still could not do wrong, and all was clearly forgiven once the problem of tithe was solved.

"Please Benji! Forgive me for what I've done against you."

Benjamin did not respond as he walked out of the church, clothes forgotten as the moonshine warmed his body against the cold day.

I walked up to the stage, the only remaining person being the prostitute who had been so brutally beaten. I grabbed her by the hand, then called out to Mr. Sterling.

"Mr. Sterling! Would you mind bringing my luggage into the church?"

Not even a second later he entered the room with my things. "Are you feeling alright, Martha? Looks like they did a number on you." He asked the woman.

"I'm alright, thanks for asking." She responded in kind.

I opened my luggage and began rummaging, looking for a pair of clothes I could spare. Once I found a pair, I handed them over to Martha. "I cannot imagine that those clothes of yours are in any state to be worn. You may borrow some of mine." She hurried off to get changed, leaving just Mr. Sterling and I in the room.

"They made quite a mess in here. It will take at least a month to fix it all."

Mr. Sterling nodded in response. "It should be no problem. I'm more worried about the people. Benjamin ran rampant while you were away I don't think the women will ever be able to feel clean again."

"Did my father do anything to help? If it was as bad as you say, surely he must have made an attempt to stop things."

He went sheepish, clearly not wanting to admit the truth.

"He must have done *something*."

He shook his head. "He seemed almost pleased to be done with it all."

"That... does not sound like my father. I guess I will have to have a few words
with him."

It must have been something Willith had said to him. My father was always devout, putting extreme pride in his vocation. There was nothing more important to my father than his and the Teendyth family's position.

Mr. Sterling let out a soft chuckle. "You'll have to tell me what he says."

A minute later Martha came back clad in clothes that were incredibly ill fitting. The pants were cuffed, wrapped over themselves multiple times. Even then, they were too long, seeing as Martha was only slightly taller than my mother. She had taken a piece of rope and used it to cinch the waist tight. The shirt poofed out awkwardly, looking more like a bed sheet than a piece of clothing. She had rolled up the sleeves in a manner similar to the pant legs. Her hair, which was medium length and brown in color, frizzed due to the stress of her assault.

"Thanks for saving me, Abbi!" She stood up on her toes and gave me a peck on the cheek, then wrapped her arms around my side. "What do you need our help with? There is no way you're gonna be able to clean all this by yourself..."

"I would adore the assistance, but I must ask if you would allow me some time to clean by myself. It has been a long day and I need to think about some things."

Martha gave me a concerned look, then looked at Sterling.

"I will tell you about it once we leave." Sterling said to her.

She nodded, then released me and followed Sterling out the door..

"Martha!" I shouted after her.

"What is it, Abbi?" She called back.

"You're a very pretty woman."

She blushed and ran out the door. Mr. Sterling let out a laugh. "You have no clue how long she's wanted you to hear that come from you. See you later, kid."

WITH THE QUIET THAT I was now surrounded by, the loss of my friend came to the forefront of my mind. I could not help but feel the scene of my uncle forcing himself upon James replaying in my head. I could not help but imagine his cries.

I was almost thankful for the events with Benjamin, as it allowed me some reprieve from the onslaught of trauma that would be forced upon me every time I was alone. Every time I thought of the way that my uncle said my mother's name I felt an urge to vomit.

And what of my father?

Why had he not fought harder for the people of the town? He had always sworn that he adored them, yet when under attack by such a satanic influence as Benjamin he simply *allowed* it to happen. It was something quite unlike my father, a man who devoted himself to his duties. A man who let his family go so far as to suffer for his faith. To seem relieved when the position was taken from him, was uncharacteristic of him

I thought of the dream and the sacrifices both my father and uncle took on my behalf. The symbolism was clear to me, and I was beginning to become concerned that my father would make that "sacrifice" for me as well. It was becoming clear that speaking to him was an imperative. His change of personality did not bode well.

After a few lonesome hours of cleaning the church on my own, a cacophony of voices could be heard outside. I wrapped my fingers around the hilt of my blade, fully expecting another gaggle of Benjamin's friends to burst through the door to reclaim what they thought was rightfully theirs.

Instead, a small woman with brown hair burst through the door.

"We're back, Abbi!" Martha called out as she ran towards me, burying her face in my shirt. "I'm so sorry about your friend. I can't believe he would take his own life like that."

I looked down at her and saw tears streaming down her cheeks. It was apparent that Mr. Sterling had told her the day's earlier events, at least to the extent he knew about.

"I am okay, Martha. I promise you that I am okay."

Mr. Sterling followed through the door next, hollering back at the crowd outside. "Hold on! Don't all rush inside, now! You'll overwhelm the kid, it's been a hard enough day for him

as is!"

Martha beamed at him and waved at him excitedly.

Her energy reminded me of James.

"Hi Mr. Sterling. What's with all the commotion?" I asked as I looked up from

Martha's face.

"Felt like it would be wrong for us to just let you mope and pick up this place on your lonesome. Will take long enough as is."

"Thank you, Mr. Sterling. It's very much appreciated."

He lurched forward and wrapped his arms around both Martha and me, embracing us in a hug so tight there would be no chance of escape. "Of course! Also, I have to admit that I didn't think you'd have yourself a girley friend so quickly."

A blush went across both mine and Martha's faces. I tried to argue otherwise. Martha did not. Mr. Sterling gave a hearty chuckle and dropped the both of us. "Leave it to a Teendyth man to make an honest woman out of a prostitute."

Martha kicked Mr. Sterling. "Watch your mouth, Jonathan. You're gonna make me

hate you."

Mr. Sterling started laughing even harder. Once he regained his composure, he shouted for everyone to enter the room. A flood of people that I recognized as his regular patrons all flooded in. He patted me on the shoulder and reassured me. "I made sure all of them sobered up. I wouldn't trust any of these drunks to hold a single thing in this church."

"Why would you invite them then?" I asked.

"Well they ain't drunk right now. Fair amount of very talented people in this crowd."

"Seeing as you know these people more than I do, would you mind delegating?"

He did a sort of mock curtsey, something comical coming from such a large man.

"Of course, Reverend. Leave it to me. You should go get some rest, especially because we may be able to have this place up and going by next Sunday, meaning you'll have to start prepping for your sermons."

I let out a heavy sigh. "Ah. That sounds nice. I am going to go rest for a bit, but first I would like to get a survey of the damage."

"You're the boss."

And with that, he entered the fray and started barking orders to the crowd. Somewhere during our conversation Martha seemed to have run off somewhere, most likely chatting with her fellow coworkers that had appeared with the crowd.

I stood on the stage, staring down at all the carnage. Some of the pews had been entirely broken, others their upholstery ripped and stained from being used for purposes that a pew should never be used for. A large blood stain now marred the center of the sanctuary. I then surveyed the altar, which was in an equally harsh state. Not only was the carpet scuffed and torn, all manner of instruments that had been used for worship were beaten and bent. Worst of all was the pulpit itself. When I saw the state of it, I felt a strong sense of dread flood through

my body.

The pulpit lay broken in two.

I felt myself begin to hyperventilate, all control of my breathing being lost in panic. The chatter of the people began to become more and more raucous until nothing but the sound of downpour remained. I looked through one of the windows and could have sworn that I saw something large and black fall from the sky. I scurried to the very back of the stage, coming upon a hatch that I had not opened in a long while. A small rope ladder fell from the hatch and I climbed in, finding myself in the church's small wooden steeple. It was large enough for maybe two or three people to fit safely, though they would have to be extremely close.

I sat and curled my arms around my legs as I tried to steady my breathing. The comfort of the small space backfired, though, as the calmness and familiarity felt reminiscent of those nights in the kitchen with James. My body began to break down even further, the full impact of the day finally coming to fruition. I tried to stifle the sobs, yet they could not stop. I had not only lost a best friend, I had lost an uncle that I had loved dearly. I had the over looming threat of whatever my dreams had decided to make me privy to. Even worse, I still had that nagging feeling in the back of my mind that something that was not the God I loved was controlling

my life.

That damned cloud.

"The Putrid Cloud" it had called itself, or the paper called it, or that dark figure called it. I had no clue if those were all one in the same. What I did know was that "Putrid" was an accurate descriptor. I did not know why it felt the need to show me such horrendous things, but I did know I wished that it would cease. The scene of my uncle assaulting James would not leave my head. It replayed, looping ceaselessly from beginning to end. The only solace being that those demented letters refrained from showing their faces. Seeing the look of pain upon James' face would be enough to have broken me then and there.

I tried to stifle my tears as I heard the creak of ropes, but any attempt was ill fated. Embarrassment was added to my sorrow when I noticed that it was Martha.

But instead of shaming me like most would, she simply pulled up the ladder and closed the hatch. "It's okay, Abbi. I won't judge you for anything." She cooed. I couldn't reply with anything more than more choked sobs. She forcefully unclasped my hands from around my knees and pulled my legs flat against the ground. I do not know if it was due to my exhaustion or if she had secretly been that brutish of a woman, but there was not a struggle for me to move.

Instead I did exactly as she guided me to do. She then laid next to me, curling herself around my arm and whispered comforts into my ear. She continued as my sobs began to waver, and then ceased entirely. She expected nothing in return. She just laid next to me, offering her presence as more comfort. When I was entirely silent was when she expected something from me, and it was nothing more than an answer to a question.

"Would you like to tell me about what happened?"

"I would rather not burden you with it." I replied.

"You'll have to tell me eventually." She responded in kind.

"Will I?"

"It won't even be your decision. It will just spill out. People can't keep things held in for long. Especially something terrible."

"Ah, so Mr. Sterling did tell you about James."

"Of course."

"Well then I would think you do not need me to recount the events then." I rebutted.

"I would still like to hear."

I began to outpour the trauma that I had been dealt in the previous months in a vomitous stream of words. I did not know what it was about Martha, but she felt so incredibly safe. She felt familiar, and that brought me peace.

I started from the day I first met James. How overbearing he was in insisting that he help a man he just met carry his luggage. How James was right, at that point I would not have been able to carry things on my own. I told her of how he freed me from my stoicism that had been so deeply ingrained in me. I told her of all the mischief we got into. I even went so far to tell her of the dreams I felt so harshly descend upon me ever since I first appeared at that damned school, as well as the terror that the dark had brought upon me.

"Abbi! It's fairly dark here, are you going to be ok?" She exclaimed as she looked around in a panic at our small quarters

"Yes, I have moved past that thankfully."

"Are you sure?. I want to be certain, I don't want you to be frightened.."

"Thank you for your concern, I am fine, Martha."

She nodded and motioned for me to continue. I had reached the moment where it felt as if existence began to fall. The week leading up to my departure, starting with that fateful night. I told her of the night James and I spent by the fire in the kitchen and the confession that James gave to me that night. Finally, I reached the events of his death.

"Why would he do such a thing?" She asked. "You said that he could not bear to love you because of your uncle. What could your uncle have done that would have caused him to do something so... serious?"

"He..." I choked on my words. I had not yet said what that paper had shown me. Saying it aloud seemed almost as an admission of James' death.

"He r-r..." Tears started to build in the corner of my eyes as I felt panic build inside myself. The guilt at the thought that I might have been able to prevent it, if only I had taken my mother more seriously in her disdain for my uncle. I could have stopped it. I doubled over, cradling myself while trying to shush myself. I could have stopped it.

No.

Him.

I could have stopped him.

Very quickly I felt her arms wrap around my being, a gentle cooing being hushed directly into my ear. "It's alright, Abbi. I'm here."

I could not escape the trance. Unlike my previous experiences with feeling out of control of my body, this had nothing to do with that looming presence. This was simply the result of the trauma that had been dealt to me. I found myself muttering the same thing repeatedly, unable to finish the simple three word sentence. Each time I stuttered I restarted the phrase again, searching within myself any attempt to speak the damnable phrase. A phrase that caused the death of someone beloved to me.

Finally it came to me.

"Eli raped him."

Almost immediately my sobs devolved into a series of shrieks and apologies. I had finally given acknowledgement to that heinous act that had taken my friend's life. I could not get the sight of that bloody knife out my head, a knife that he had gotten from me. I tried to mutter apologies and admissions of guilt, yet they only left my throat as guttural sounds that barely resembled syllables, let alone words. Martha wrapped her arms around me tighter.

"You're a brave man. You have done nothing wrong." She whispered repeatedly in response to my sobs.

Eventually I began to tire and my panic began to subside as my emotions made quick work of dulling themselves. "How do you know I am brave?" I responded as I finally took a steady breath. "This is the first time we have ever held any sort of conversation. I had not even known your name until several hours ago."

"I don't need to know you deeply to know how brave you are, you've shown that enough today alone." She blushed as she spoke.

"Today was merely something I had to do. In fact, I may have gone overboard. Resorting to violence was not really something a pastor should do. I think I may have been simply enacting what I wanted to do to my uncle in those moments." I explained.

"I guess that makes you a much better person than me. If I ever meet your uncle I'd kill
him myself."

I hoarsely chuckled, relaxing my body and laying down in the full length of the steeple's small room. "I appreciate that immensely. I think I would like to do that myself."

"Can you end Benjamin as well? I think that would be much appreciated."

"I think his old man would die of heartbreak." I said. No matter how many people despised Benjamin, his father always supported him in whatever he did.

"I think it would be the first time in his life. Maybe it would teach him some empathy."

I could not help but wonder if maybe Martha was right. Suffering is something that all men experience in their lives, whether it be when they are young or old. I had to question if Willith had experienced that suffering yet.

"I do not think it would be possible for him to feel anything other than disgust for someone else." I retorted. "I have known that man since I was child. I've experienced him take the food directly out of someone's mouth and proceed to eat it himself. He's a very sick man."

I heard Mr. Sterling's voice call for us in the chapel below.

I began to get up from my reclining position. "Well, I guess we should be heading down to rejoin the others. I think we have been up here longer than intend-"

Martha pushed me back down and climbed on top of me. "They can wait for another minute. Now that you're feeling better, I don't think I've properly thanked you for rescuing me." She said seductively. She rested her weight on me, straddling my torso.

I began to feel an entirely different sense of panic. I struggled to push her off, but she was insistent on staying put. She leaned over me and put her lips to my ear.

"I'm gonna make you my husband, Absolom Teendyth. I swear by it." She whispered in a loving tone. With that, she gave me a peck on the cheek, jumped off of me, and opened the hatch.

"What do you want Jonathan?" She yelled down the ladder.

I followed suit, climbing down behind her.

"You need to be down here helping us all clean the sanctuary." He scolded her. "What were you even doing in the stee-"

He cut short when he saw that I was following down behind her on the ladder. A mischievous smile spread across his face.

"I swear it is not what you think." I responded, my eyes still very clearly puffy

from crying.

"So good you cried, huh?" Mr. Sterling teased as he jabbed his elbow into me with more force than he intended. "Well I can tell you you definitely made her dreams come true."

"Mr. Sterling, I have absolutely not the slightest clue what you are talking about." I huffed out.

He let out a hearty laugh. "Let's just say she's been trying to get your attention for a while now, but you've been too busy being sick that you haven't noticed."

I felt a perplexed look cross my face.

Mr. Sterling responded in kind. "I'll tell you the whole story sometime later. Right now it's late and I need to get these people home. They've done hard work." Most of the crowd had already left, meaning that by "these people" Mr. Sterling meant himself.

I surveyed the sanctuary. They really had done a phenomenal job in the few hours they had been at work. The women had gone through and sewn patches into the ripped fabric of the pews. The intact pews had been rearranged back into their normal positions. The ones that had been cracked were surrounded by all sorts of wood scrap, clearly in the process of being mended together. The instruments on stage were sadly beyond repair, but at the very least they had been gathered and stacked in a pile of rubbish. The pulpit was still cloven in two.

I reached for Mr. Sterling's hand. "I must seriously thank you for your help, Mr. Sterling. You all have made things so much easier."

He shook my hand in return. "Of course. Can't have the church run down for our brand new pastor." He reached over and gave me a hefty pat on the shoulder. "I'm incredibly proud of you, kid. I gotta get home to the wife. Would you like me to make sure you get home safe?"

"I am going to stay behind a bit longer. I still need to think about, everything."

"Understandable. Make sure you get some rest. And be careful, Martha might be just around the corner waiting to jump you."

He walked out the door and I was alone in the sanctuary.

Being back in solitude did not bode well for my mind, which very quickly devolved into mulling over the things that the cloud had said to me through the paper.

I really had no proof that the paper and the cloud were one in the same, yet I just felt as if that was the only logical conclusion. They both held the same authority.

I continued to clean the chapel until the wee hours of the morning, brushing away grime that I hoped would also brush away the trauma of the past months. Instead I found myself thinking about James and how we found his body. I felt my mind crumble when I realized the purpose of the burn marks on his arms.

Perhaps I could have saved him, but I had no real reason to doubt the information he had given me. If only I had been more skeptical. Hell, if I had only paid closer attention to my things. But nothing I could do would bring him back now, and no sort of vengeance against my uncle would bring him back either.

It was a few hours from dawn when I finally freed myself from cleaning. I placed a few of my things into the church to keep them safe, grabbed the luggage with my essentials, and began to make the short trek to my parents home.

The back alleys were as familiar as ever, a very welcoming sight in the ever changing times. In the comfort of those back alleys I found myself thinking about Martha and how very much she reminded me of James. There's a certain quality that those who are victimized share. A sad wisdom that pervades through them, as if they were forced to come to understand something that mankind should not.

I felt conflicted at what I felt for Martha. I had only just lost James, who I still could not fully sort out what my feelings for him could be described as. At the front of my mind I thought of him as a brother, yet that pervading thought of how he thought of me made me question if brotherhood was the only thing I felt for him. Even if I had not felt the same feelings for James as he had for me, I wondered if to so quickly fawn over another was a sort of betrayal.

More so, I questioned if the feelings I felt for either of them were simply a response to being cared for. Pure gentleness and kindness were not things that were granted to me often as a child, as it was something only granted to me by my mother. Sadly though, the care of one person does not always feel as if it is enough. Could it be that I was simply falling for them due to them falling for me?

Most of all, I could not shake the feeling of how very similar the two of them were. Sadly, I could not just storm in and remove James from harm like I had with Martha. It was too late for any heroics with James.

As I trekked through the snowy alleys, thinking of how Martha seemed to be a different iteration of James, I found myself face to face with a man who was in a similar situation. A man, who in all intents and purposes, could be considered a different iteration of my uncle.

Laying on his side against the wall was none other than Benjamin Willith. He was unconscious, clearly from drinking the day away. When I saw him I felt such rage flow through my body. The same rage I felt when I had struck my uncle earlier. A rage that bordered on the line of hatred.

It was wrong.

"But it is just."

I remembered the words the cloud had said to me through the note. And even Martha seemed to agree, even if it was in a joking way. I thought of all the things Benjamin had forced the people of Afton to suffer through. The assault, the violence, and the downright cruelty that had been allowed to happen by Deacon Willith and his putrid spawn.

It was just to hate both of them, I assured myself.

No, no. It was not just to hate anyone. That is what I was raised to believe. That is what the church taught me to believe.

But even then, did God not strike down those who threatened his people?

And that was exactly what the Willith's had been doing. They were ransacking those who were hurt. They were the sole proprietors of any and all suffering that happened in the town. It was in such a state of disrepair when I arrived.

Everyone seemed as if they were so downtrodden when I returned.

I saw the hope return to their eyes when they looked upon me.

I was that hope.

I was their hero.

But still, to take it so far as hate was wrong.

"It is still just."

As I looked down at the man laying on the road, I saw a man who had done nothing but cause the suffering of the people who my family had always taken great care to love. I also saw my Uncle Eli.

I turned him onto his back and continued home.

Tranquilla

Benjamin's death was a bit of a blessing for the community. It seemed that no one truly realized the stress that his presence put on the town's people, as he was the reason for many to indulge in their vices.

In fact, the only person who seemed too terribly affected was Deacon Willith himself. I cannot say that his sentiments were shared by his wife. I never learned why she seemed so relieved, but it never really occurred to me to care. Benjamin was the type of person who deserved to be disdained by his mother in death.

The following months were filled with that trauma being lifted from the town with an increasing disinterest in the lechery the town so loved since I was a child. The change actually began with Martha. She stopped her work and swore off allowing men to have her services. She claimed that now that I had her attention she wanted me to be the only man she gave herself to.

I began to use my earnings from the church to ensure she could survive. I even ensured that she would have something heavier to wear, as the rags she owned would do nothing against the bitter cold.

A good amount of Martha's co-workers followed suit, claiming that they too wanted to make a change for the better. Soon, the newly reupholstered pews were full of women who had never stepped foot in the sanctuary in their years of existence.

It took the men a little longer to let go of their vices. In fact, they doubled down in their alcoholism for a short time now that the women who they spent their nights in the arms of had sworn off their profession. I had a good amount of angry complaints from several drunk men claiming I had "stolen away all the whores".

Soon enough, one of the men realized that they were becoming more and more like the deceased Benjamin. The moment they had the realization they swore off any and all alcohol, and soon after the other men followed the example of the women. By the time the church had been put back into its original state, almost every single resident of Afton could be seen in the pews of the church. A revival had taken place in the town, one that reinvigorated the very core. They were even present for the Christmas service.

Only two persons seemed somewhat disgruntled with the new found faith of the town. The first of which, which should be somewhat obvious, was Deacon Willith. The loss of his son had shattered the man so intensely that he seemed that he did not care that he would be making more through the church's increased donations. His eyes had become sunken through the mourning process. His jowls had begun to diminish rather quickly, clearly neglecting to feed himself. He still made an effort to appear to Sunday services once the chapel was back in operating order, still making an effort to loom in the back pews, but the overbearing presence I had been so accustomed to was nowhere to be found.

Strangely enough, my father had been the other who was not too keen on the new air of the town. He was a tad harder to read the intent of, as the take was not something that would have been expected of him. He was not vocal about his disdain, but he became even more stoic and trite in his behavior. Of course, he had always been a tad cold, and was distant from the very moment I returned. But that coldness had evolved with the change and became an incessant need to avoid me. He did not even attend the Christmas service that I led.

I could not help but wonder if had seen me that night in the alley, but truth be told it did not matter. I felt no shame nor guilt for my actions, let alone any fear that I would be caught.

Even those who upheld the law of Afton were elated by the death of Benjamin.

No, it had to be something else entirely.

Perhaps it had been my relationship with Martha. Her and I had become increasingly close, stealing away quiet moments in the church's steeple on a regular occurrence. They had started out simply as a way for her to comfort me in the trauma I had developed. Soon enough I managed to get her to share with me her plights. Having been the child of a prostitute with an unknown father left her in a position where it was nothing short of impossible for her to not follow in her mother's footsteps. Mr. Sterling had been the closest she had to a father figure. He was sufficient enough, but the negative influence from her mother did nothing to help give her a positive future.

Knowing her story made me even more inclined to want to care for her. While not all of her peers and coworkers shared the same sentiment, she craved the ability to not have to continue with her profession. As such, I offered her the ability to step away from it all. It was becoming increasingly clear that her prediction of me being her husband would most likely come true, and I was increasingly alright with the concept. We would both steal away as much time as we could together, holding each other close in the church steeple while exchanging small pecks on the lips. I found her company even more important than the tradition I held with my mother, as I felt it more pertinent to spend my time with Martha.

I thought this might have been the reason for my father's coldness. Perhaps some sort of feeling that his son was being corrupted by a wayward woman. He may have thought we were engaging in more intimate activities than the occasional kiss. Others in the town thought the same, but they did not seem to care. Mother swore that my father's stoic behavior did not have any sort of connection to me, but instead was a reaction to adjusting to no longer being a pastor. That could have been a fairly reasonable excuse as well.

I was coming to terms with my father's distance. I had done so when I was younger, but I had not yet fully grasped his struggle to connect with his family. Thankfully, I could be assured of one thing. My father, despite his struggles, was still a good man. I had seen the countless sacrifices he had made for others, and while they were sometimes to the detriment of the family, they were always with good intention. Even if he believed that my courting of Martha was the cause for my behavior, it would be soon enough that he felt otherwise.

Martha had nothing to do with my sour behavior, of course.

Neither did the death of Benjamin.

The true cause was the newfound torrent of dreams and messages from that thing that was speaking to me. The same dream of that perverted sacrifice played through my mind every night. I was forced to watch as James and the woman I could not make out were brutally slaughtered by a man I hated and one who seemed to regret my birth. I felt the same onslaught of guilt every morning, not the guilt of devouring their corpses, but instead the guilt of not feeling any guilt for it.

Those visions played through the back of my eyes during the waking hours. The cloud was no longer locked away to the night time, as I found myself entering fugue states where those awful visions replayed through my mind.

I started to feel as if I would lose control of my body during the waking hours. I still had that urgency that all humans do, as several quirks began developing in the back of my mind. I no longer walked without my blade by my side. It was not any sort of sense of insecurity that caused it, but instead a growing obsession with the connection the knife gave me to my dreams. The few times that obsession failed and I left the knife behind, it would not be long before I felt it strapped to my side again. It refused to leave my side.

Rough storms began to be a regular and strange occurrence. The dark clouds reminded me of the cacophonous torrent from my dreams and struck a strange fear into my body. Yet all the same they seemed to excite me as well. It felt as if maybe something would ride into Afton amongst those clouds.

That foreboding, yet exciting, obsession is what drew me to stare at the clouds on stormy days. It is what forced me to feel as if I had to carry that blade with me everywhere as a token of my appreciation. That cloud was something I had begun to care for, and in a sense I felt as if it cared for me.

And without the preparation that its foresight granted me, I would not have been able to grant the town the care it needed. Ever since I had returned to Afton I had been showered with praise and admiration for my act of saving the townspeople. Everything I said was listened to with baited breath and every man, woman, and child could be seen in the pews when I preached.

That fear that had crept through my muscles was slowly overshadowed by the new found fire that I had discovered.

AS WITH ALL THINGS, peace must end. I had returned to the town of Afton in early December. We had passed through our harsh winter and were again on the cusp of the warmer season, as the beginning of April was about to occur. The ground had just begun to thaw, leaving massive muddy puddles at the lowest points of the town. The church was located on one of those lower points. The drainage began to collect and seep through the foundation, leaving massive water stains on the church's carpet. At spots the crimson carpet had turned a dirty brown from the collected water.

I had been spending my nights at the church at this point, trying my damndest to steer clear of my father. I felt that I would rather avoid any "consequences" my father may have had for me after the events with my uncle. The church was my sanctuary. So, I spent my days tending to the church's carpet when I was not fraternizing with Martha. Today, she was spending time tidying up her home, as I would be spending dinner with her.

I meandered throughout the sanctuary, laying down tattered rags on every spot of moisture that began to peer through the carpeting. The room was silent save my own breath, that was until a loud and raspy cough echoed throughout the chapel. A man whose skin hung way too low stood at the door, the form of the now emaciated figure of Deacon Willith darkening
its frame.

"Hello, Willith!" I called out from my position near the altar. I did not mind his intrusion. He had not been a bother for months and I refused to let him take away my peace.

"Hello Absolom." He wheezed out. His health had plummeted since the loss of his son.

"I have a letter for you."

"Oh really?" I inquired. "Who is it from, and why do you of all people have it?"

"Your mother is in poor health today. She asked me to deliver it for her." He explained.

Deacon Willith had grown closer to my mother ever since the loss of his son. Mrs. Willith took his grief as a sign of weakness and was very prompt in assuring him that she would not be tolerating any "depressing behavior." It was not long after that he was on our doorstep, apologizing to my mother for the way he treated us all those years. He made it clear he blamed himself for his son's death. My mother, who was never one to let the downtrodden go uncomforted, made sure that he had someone to care for him. I cannot deny that seeing him defanged brought me immense joy.

"Well that was awful sweet of you, Willith. You still have yet to tell me who the letter

is from."

He handed me a small piece of paper and clarified. "Peter, that young boy's brother."

I snatched the paper from his hand and began to ingest the material in front of me.

> Your attendance is requested at the funeral of our beloved James Alludy. It is to be held on April 5th at 5pm in his hometown of
>
> North Elmira.
>
> Please respond to this telegram if you will be attending.
>
> P.S. Absolom, I will arrive to pick you up on April 3rd. You need not RSVP. Peter.

I felt a tear come to my eye. It was no wonder that they had to wait until the spring thaw to bury his body. I would have to hurry to prepare my things, as the third was only two days away.

"It truly is difficult to lose someone close to you." Willith tried to comfort me in my grief.

I let out a small sneer in response.

"What??" He asked

"Deacon Willith, do you not remember how you treated me the day James took his life?"

"Yes, I regret it every day, Absolom."

"I would hope you would, Willith."

"I truly am sorry. It was downright unchristlike of me to treat you in such a manner. I know it was no excuse, but had I known how it felt sooner..." His demeanor was small, physically begging me to accept his forgiveness. But it was far too late for that. The wounds of his treatment had reopened. He may have changed but he was still the same man who stole from almost every family in the town. The same man who mocked me my entire childhood. The same man who raised that mooncalf of a son.

"That is NO excuse, Charles. How is it such a foreign concept that you do not have to feel something to comfort those that do?" I barked at him.

"I know, I know. I was acting very poorly. I hope that one day we ca-"

I turned on him."And how DARE you even think to compare my James to that unholy bastard that was your son! If anything, something should have been done sooner about him!"

I felt all the pent up emotion leaving me. I only wished my uncle had been there as well. He deserved an equal lashing. Honestly, had my uncle been present my treatment of Willith might have been less harsh.

"I know. I spared the rod and I should not have."

"Your son is burning in Hell, Charles Willith."

The presence was back. That damnable spiritual aura that Willith had lost came rushing back. The snap behind his eyes was audible.

"Absolom." He growled at me.

"Yes, *Charles*?" I replied with a smirk on my face.

"You were always such a judgemental child."

"*I* was judgemental? Because your damned brat that went out of his way to make me suffer was the paragon of unbiasedness." I stood over him. He was much shorter than he had been when the fat layered his heels.

"Yes. You were judgmental. Even before my son spoke to you, he always recalled you walking up to him and directly addressing his weight."

"I mean of course, he was a fat bastard and he deserved it."

"Ah, and you still judge and refuse to listen to the point. Before he had even spoken to you *once* you began to harass him for his weight. I remember the exact day. Now I will never deny that I should have disciplined him better and his treatment of you was

much worse."

"And how are you sure that my harassment of him predated his behavior?"

"Do you know why he began to drink?" Willith inquired.

"No, nor do I care."

"He heard it helped those who drank to lose weight."

"Well that's rather pitiful of him, is it not?"

"FINE! DO YOU THINK VICES ARE ONLY FOR THE WEAK?" He yelled.

"Of course."

"Do you know where your father is at this moment?!"

"Probably somewhere ministering to the people." I felt so smug as I said that.

I was so sure.

"He's at the brothel in Jericho"

> "It is disgusting of you to make up lies, Charles." I sneered at him.

"That is always where he has been. Either that or at my house rutting my wife. Or any of the other deacon's wives for that matter."

"And how do you know this?" A certain confidence pervaded me. There was no way the accusations were true.

"I HAVE ALWAYS KNOWN ABSOLOM." He shouted so loudly that the walls of the chapel shook. "How do you think I had ALL OF THE DAMNED MONEY THAT THIS CHURCH BROUGHT IN. I was BLACKMAILING HIM you FOOL!."

I paused to look into his eyes before I replied. "You mean to tell me that I should believe that you did not just steal it?"

I felt a waver in my confidence.

"Why do you think he was always missing from your home? He was too busy spending his time at mine. Or Deacon Tyndale's. Or Deacon Schmidt's. Ask ANY ONE

OF THEM!" He was animated now, the sweat dripping from his face, his hands waving wildly.

"And why did they not say anything?"

"Your father is a very convincing man with many connections, Absolom, just as you are. He had ways of keeping them silent." He took a breath and closed his hands to steady them.

"I do not believe you."

"Of course you don't. You've already judged your father innocent." His words were envenomed.

"Well, Deacon Willith, as long as we are airing our 'truths' I have one to inform you of." I replied with twice the potency.

"Tell me. Tell me about whatever grave secret you have."

I leaned down into Willith's ear and spoke into it with hushed tones. As I stood there, bent down beside him, I caressed the side of his neck with my fingers, then wrapped each one around his windpipe. Months ago this would have been impossible, but thankfully his grief had made threatening him much easier.

"Benjamin's death was no accident, Charles."

His breathing became ragged as he processed the information I had given him. That aura of his disappeared in an instant as he realized he was sharing a room with the reason for his son's death. "W-why would you tell me this..."

"If this information you just gave me was true, you told me just to hurt me. I felt as if I should do the same." I hissed.

"I-I just wanted to clear my conscience..."

"Well now I have as well, Charles." I retorted. "Let it be known that almost everyone in this town supports my culling of your son. Any attempt at 'clearing your conscience' will only affect you."

He frantically shook his head, rattling his brain against his skull.

"I am going to have a word with my father. If I find out that you are lying to me I will ensure you die in the same alley as your son."

He gulped and nodded again.

"I hope you know I fully expect that you are lying to me. In fact, I suggest you make your relationship with God right."

"I already have." He replied.

"I find that debateable."

I unwrapped my fingers from Willith's throat. He slumped forward as I released him, as he no longer had me holding up his body weight. I pushed past him out the door, focused on clearing my father's name.

I WALKED THROUGH THE door to my parent's home and called out for my father.

"He's not home right now, dear. What do you need him for?" My mother called out from the sitting area.

"I need to talk to him about some nonsense Willith decided to try and spread to me."

"Oh what was he on about now?" She inquired. "I thought he had given up trying to cause problems?"

"Apparently not."

"Oh goodness. What did he say?"

"He tried to claim that Father was an adulterer."

My mother's face went pale as she heard what I said.

"Absolom..." She said the name quietly, almost inaudibly.

I leaned against the doorframe. "I know. What a downright atrocious claim, especially for a man like Father." I continued, still assured in my own beliefs.

My mother let out a small sob. "Absolom, please listen..."

"What is it, Mother?"

She cast down her eyes and refused to look at me. "He wasn't lying."

I heard a thud against the window as a bird hit the glass.

"This has to be some cruel joke, Mother..." I pleaded. "Why would you make such a joke? Are you in league with Willith to make up some fun against me?"

"Your father has been fornicating behind my back for years."

"No, Mother. He was too busy ministering to the people!" I felt my voice crack.

"He was." She assured me. "At least, sometimes he was."

"And how long have you known..."

"Since the beginning."

"And how long has that been?"

The moment I asked my father came walking through the kitchen door. He still had the stoic expression across his face, the face that I had convinced myself for years had some sort of care in it.

"What is going on in here?" He asked as he saw the tears streaming down my mother's face.

I looked at him for the first time with hatred. No, it was not just the simple disdain that one feels when they are an insubordinate teenager, but instead the feeling one gets when looking at a pile of vomit. He had the same face as his brother. It made hating him easier.

"Ah, I see." He said matter of factly.

"How dare you?" I asked him firmly. Another bird hit the window, dying instantly.

"How dare *I*?" My father retorted. "I have done nothing wrong in the least, Son."

"You cheated on Mother!" I screamed at him.

He rested his hand on the back of a chair."Biblically, those who have been cheated on hold the right to do the same for their spouse. Eye for an eye and all that." He retorted.

"Father, I refuse to believe that Mother, *of all people,* cheated on you. It was difficult enough hearing the same of you."

"Oh, she forgot to tell you of her little romp with your uncle?" He held such hatred in his voice. I began to wonder if his stoicism was merely an attempt at hiding how truly hateful he was.

"I find it difficult to believe that she consented to anything from him."

He shifted to stand in front of me."Oh she could have prevented it. She was far too friendly to him. It was only a matter of time before he got the wrong message." My father did not seem to comprehend how unfair of an accusation it was. I heard my mother's sobs become heavier.

"And that makes it alright for you to commit adultery." I stated, matter of factly.

"Yes."

"Incredible."

"I would not expect you to understand, son."

"I need not understand anything other than that you are a downright hypocrite. I highly doubt God will accept *you* in the courts of Heaven." I lashed out. I wanted my words to make him show some sort of emotion and break the blank face he still held.

I succeeded.

He rushed forward and grabbed me by the neck. His eyes became red as the blood vessels popped from his sudden tenseness. "I find that judgment ironic coming from someone who fraternizes with sodomites and whores!" He barked in my ear.

I stood defiantly against his grasp. "Excuse me? I feel as if you should refrain from referring to my loved ones in such a manner." I choked out.

"I will refer to them however I damn well please. Your uncle has made it very clear how the relationship with that James boy went on."

"You have not the faintest idea."

"Oh I don't? Which of you gave and which one of you received? And to think now you're carousing with that Martha whore. I'd be astounded if you weren't crawling with diseases." He sneered, his breath crawling across my face. "I did not raise you in such a manner. Absolutely disgusting." He glared into my face and I returned the stare.

"Well, I think you did raise me to behave in such a manner."

He tightened his hands around my neck as he screamed. "THEY ARE DIFFERENT!"

I continued to hold my composure as he berated me. He wasn't worth the trouble. But still, he was my father. He was a man I had loved and admired ever since I was a child.

The things he said still stung.

"If anything I am better *in spite* of your rearing." I replied. "I never treated James or Martha as tools to relieve my desires, unlike how you treat every woman you interact with."

He struck me.

"Don't even ATTEMPT to lie to me. And then striking your uncle? How dare you treat your family with such disdain."

I gripped his arm. "You treated your family just the same."

He struck me again with enough force to give me pause in any response I may have given.

"My vice was GOD GIVEN. I did not seek out to have a whore for a wife, and I do not even know if you're my child! You've always looked like my brother. To think that I may be living in the house with my brother's bastard was downright *destructive* on my mind. The Lord gave me those women to cope!"

His hand loosened just a small amount as he spoke, allowing me to respond.

"Why is it Mother's fault for what Eli did, and not his?"

"Your uncle always had his proclivities. She should not have been so seductive to him."

"You disgust me, hypocrite." I spat at him.

I saw his teeth grind right before he struck me again. He began to bashing his fist into the side of my head, aiming directly for my temple. I felt a few steady cracks as the weak point in my skull was hit. Right before I felt as if it were to give way, he pushed me onto the ground and began to stomp my chest. His foot falls were heavy. I felt my ribs crack as he sat himself on my chest and wrapped his hands around my neck. Right before I felt the air begin to leave my lungs he was pushed off me. He hit his head against the floor with a thunk and laid still for a moment.

My mother stood behind him holding a broom, a panicked look on her face. She kneeled beside me and touched me on the cheek. "I'll handle him. I've learned how to soothe him."

"Has he laid hands on you before, Mother?" I croaked out.

She gave a gentle nod, affirming my suspicions. "I just made sure to hide it for your sake. I'd say I was pretty good at it, seeing as you never found out."

My father began to get his bearings as he struggled to his feet. He snarled at me. "Leave now. Go anywhere but here. I think it's best you don't come see us again."

I coughed blood in agreement, got up from the ground, and hobbled back to

the church.

I CRUMBLED THROUGH the front doors, body throbbing from my father's assault. It was terrifying to see the true side of him. He had always seemed so calm, so loving; I wondered how often Mother had to hide his violent nature.

I collapsed on the floor of the sanctuary, right at the altar steps. I felt an outpouring of emotion flood throughout my body. I began weeping for the family I lost. Both my uncle and father had been perversions of themselves, twisted versions of the people I thought I had known. Yet I was the one who suffered for it. I was the one who had to deal with the consequences of their actions. I was given absolutely no justice. It felt as if God had barred me from any sort of happiness. Every time I felt any uplifting times they were soon met with the utmost tragedy.

If God had control of all things, why did He do this to me?

"GOD! WHY DO YOU PUNISH ME? WHY ARE YOU DOING THIS TO ME!?"

"I have done nothing." An all too familiar sound of downpour replied in my head.

I sneered, disgusted that the being from my dreams had the audacity to speak to me again. "Now I truly know you are the devil, as nothing else would try and claim to be God.

"If that is what you think." It replied, somewhat dismissive of my comment.

I continued to rant against the thing that had decided to make me its prey. "It is what I think! I think that you are some pitiful creature that has decided to make me a target! I think that you are trying to make an example of me; I think you are trying to make me a modern-day Job!"

"It may be so."

"To think you would even try to make ME think that you were the voice of God disgusts me. I know better." It enraged me to think that some sort of demon believed I was foolish enough to fall for its tricks.

"Do you?"

"Of course I know better!" I screamed, angry that it would dare question the extent of my faith. "I have heard His voice."

"Have you? What does it sound like?" Not once did the thing sound as if it were mocking me. Instead, it sounded curious. It wanted to know how I would reply.

"It sounds like... well it does not sound like you, that is for certain."

"If you insist."

"God would not torture me the way you have. You have done nothing but take from me, and that is how I know you are of the devil. But I am stronger than that. I will not fall to your demented test and I will stand firm in my faith. Yes, I cannot tell you the exact dialect that God uses but that does not mean that I do not know him. I know God more than anything else in this life."

"As well as your father?"

I chose to ignore its snide remark, continuing to verbally flay it with the best insults I could muster. "I doubt you are even able to perform miracles. It would be asinine to believe that you could do something as meaningless as turn water into wine!"

"I have done many."

"OH YOU HAVE!?" I screamed. "THEN BRING BACK JAMES!"

"It is not my will."

"WHY NOT!? PUNISH MY FATHER AND MY UNCLE THEN! GIVE

ME SOLACE!!" My screams became punctuated by sobs.

"It is not my will."

"THEN MAKE IT YOUR WILL!"

"You can enact these things yourself."

"I AM JUST A MAN WHO GOD WILL NOT SPEAK TO! HOW AM I TO ENFORCE THAT JAMES MAY NEVER SUFFER THE COMPANY OF THOSE WHO HARM HIM? I DO NOT KEEP THE BOOK OF LIFE! I DO NOT CONTROL THE FLOW OF THE AFTERLIFE. HOW AM I TO KEEP HIS SOUL SAFE!?"

"Embrace me."

The doors to the front of the church creaked open and Martha stepped through. The downpour of voices ceased, as did the conversation. She rushed in and wrapped her arms around me. She was smiling at first, until she saw that my face had bruises and a trickle of blood coming from my temple. She took a step back to look at me fully.

"What happened, Abbi?" She asked.

I told her about my father.

Her countenance dropped as she touched the red marks on the sides of my neck. They felt raw. I felt her breathing become ragged as an intense anger filled her, until she finally looked me in the eyes and proclaimed:

"I'm gonna kill him."

"No, no Martha. That would be wrong."

"He tried to kill you!" She yelled.

"Even the same, we should not take it upon ourselves to judge him ourselves." I was lying through my teeth. The god that spoke to me was right. I should take initiative myself. I was always taught that God had given mankind sovereignty as his children. Why should I not be the one to decide his fate?

But that is where the truth lied.

I did not want Martha to abstain from violence for my father's sake. I wanted her to abstain because I wished to bring about that justice. God had chosen me to bring about whatever justice was due to my father, he told me as such directly.

Thankfully, I do not think Martha had any true intention of violence. I put my good arm around her and whispered a simple "I need you" into her ear and felt her entire body relax.

"I do not need you to take action against him, I just need you. I love you, Martha." I said to her, her face growing warm against my chest. She looked up at me with a gaze

of adoration.

I loved feeling adored. I still felt a pang of guilt at our relationship. I felt the ever looming presence of James whenever I showed any affection to Martha. I still had not reasoned the type of love I felt for James, but that was long past mattering.

What did matter was that I showed love to Martha. I needed her pacified.

Her face had always felt so familiar.

"Can we go spend some time in the steeple together?" She asked.

I nodded and led her to the ladder. I needed some time to think as well, so the simple comfort of laying together was extremely inviting. We climbed in and did nothing but rest at first, simply laying against each other. I couldn't help but think on those things that the voice spoke to me about, before Martha had interrupted.

Its true intent had only ever been to protect me from misfortunes to come.

At that moment I decided. I would kill both of them. If God was truly against them, I could be assured that they would be separated from his glory. I could be ensured that they would be cut from Heaven. I did not know how, but I would kill them.

I felt relief wash over me.

"Are you alright, Abbi?" Martha asked me.

"Yes, very much so."

We both fell asleep in the steeple that night, curled into each other's arms. The dream was different this time. I was not greeted with that pitch black. I was instead standing at the front pulpit, every townsperson sitting and facing me. Two bodies laid in front me, taking the place of those sacrificial animals that had been there before. My father and uncle stood next to them. I woke up as I was handing each of them a small blade.

I was startled awake by someone shouting my name. I clambered down the rope with Martha behind me and was greeted by the grim face of Peter. He seemed bedraggled from the months of mourning.

Apparently, in the hustle of the previous week's events I had entirely gotten the date wrong, thinking the day after would be the 3rd. I was extremely ill packed, yet thankfully all of my belongings were stored in the church.

I walked over and gingerly embraced Peter. He blushed when he saw Martha climb down from the rafters behind me. She had chosen to wear the clothes I had given her, making Peter misread the situation. I did not argue against it.

"How are you doing Peter? Are you faring well?" I asked him.

His glum expression did not waver. "Not entirely." Peter, unlike Willith, deserved to mourn. Anyone would have endless reason to mourn someone as great as James.

I stepped back from the embrace. "I apologize, I seem to have gotten my days mixed up and am not quite packed yet. Give me a moment and I will be prepared."

Martha gave a confused look.

"Ah, sorry I forgot to tell you with all the bustle of yesterday. I am heading to North Elmira for James' funeral. This is Peter, James' brother."

"Oh hello!." She said as she reached out her hand to shake Peter's.

He blushed for a moment, thinking again of what he thought we were doing only moments before, then shyly took a hold of her hand. It was strange to see Peter so quiet.

Loss had changed him, much like it had Willith. Sadly, I do not think Peter's change was a positive one.

Peter sat quietly in the pews while I shoved my clothes in a trunk. His eyes were no longer cheerful. They had looked almost exactly like James' before his passing. It could be said that they still resemble James', just as they were after he took his own life.

They were cold.

He said nothing as he sat in the pews, he just watched as I hastily packed.

Martha attempted to make conversation to no avail. He would only respond in single words or blush and shy away from her. He was no longer Peter, just his flesh walking about.

The moment I stored all my belongings away I walked over to Peter and dragged him to his feet. Had I not, I do not think he would have ever gotten up.

"Everything is set. Let us make haste, Peter." I said.

"Alright." Peter responded.

I kissed Martha and headed towards the wagon. Peter grabbed the reins as I stowed my luggage. He did not say a word.

Spiritus Mortem

Peter barely spoke on the journey towards North Elmira. His body remained rigid the entire journey, only moving when he needed to steer the horses another direction. Not once did a hint of the old Peter return. At one point I did try to comfort him.

"I know it is hard, but one day we will all be reunited with the Lord. We will all see him again." He merely responded with a sad smile and a nod.

As I sat in silence I was able to fully see the toll James' death had taken on Peter. He had lost weight. It was much thinner than he was months ago. His rosy cheeks that were clearly a common trait amongst James' family had all but disappeared, leaving his face gaunt and shallow. His hair, which was a fiery red before, had begun to grey. He had somehow seemed to shrink in height as he carried himself in a manner that made him seem small. It seemed he wanted to hide.

Admittedly, I was probably a tad more energetic than what should have been appropriate with the subject matter of my visit. I could not ignore the freedom that I had felt with the permission given to me by my God. I had not even recognized how desperately the feeling of helplessness was eating away at me since my uncle's betrayal, yet now that I was granted the means for justice, I felt free. I cannot imagine how difficult it was for Peter to be sitting next to me who seemed borderline elated that they were going to attend a funeral. I tried to adjust my mood accordingly.

A DAY LATER WE ARRIVED at the Aludy family home. A small gaggle of people, all short in stature and with fiery red hair, were gathered outside of their home. They frolicked in the front fields of the family's large home, children playing in the grasses and making mud pies. The house itself was small, situated on top of a steep hill that was only just shy of being considered a mountain. We disembarked the carriage and made our way up the steep climb, entirely bypassing the house and making our way to the very spacious backyard.

It encompassed the whole of the hilltop, trees dotted around the landscape. In one corner was a good sized shack that had piles upon piles of logs for fuel. A small creek cut through the land, giving a clear cut threshold from the house to the acres of property. The only way over that creek was to cross over a small piece of corrugated roof. Most of the men were either chasing after their children or relaxing on the back patio enjoying a smoke.

It was clear who among them was the patriarch, just as clear as it was who James' father was. Especially since they were the same person. Whilebeveryone on the property were almost identical in their appearance, one of them was almost the exact image of James. That was, save for the much portlier stature. He sat with a certain air to him, a certain melancholy that is reserved for those who are responsible, yet he still had a smile across his face at almost all times.

It was James' smile.

I went to greet him as a short and stout woman came rushing at me from over the hilltop.

"It's so good to finally meet you, Absolom!" She exclaimed.

She had the same red hair as the rest of the family. Tiny freckles dotted her nose, a trait that she had passed down to her sons. A pinkish hue washed over her arms, a clear indication that she had been out in the sun much too long for her complexion. She wrapped her arms around me and let out a delighted squeal, a strange sound to come from a woman that was most likely on the cusp of fifty. It would have been much stranger if she were able to be considered anything outside of "cute."

She was followed by her husband, the same patriarch who was not long before sitting on the patio. The smell of freshly burnt tobacco followed behind him. "Sarah, lay off the poor boy, he just got here."

"Can't I be excited to be able to meet him finally? I heard so much about him from-"

"No, you can't." He growled.

"Fine." She pouted in an over-exaggerated manner.

"Now get." James' father gave her a swift slap on the rear end as he said it, his wife giving out a yelp that did not seem entirely adverse to his actions. She quickly scuttled off.

"Damn I love that woman..." He said under his breath. "Apologies, my wife loves
meeting people. "Anyways, nice to meet you Absolom. I'm the Right Reverend Alludy."

"The pleasure is mine, Revere-"

"It's Right Reverend." He interrupted.

"Apologies. It's a pleasure to meet you, Right Reverend." I found the term confusing. I had never heard someone refer to themselves as "Right Reverend" before. A look of confusion spread across my face as I responded.

"Ah, you must be Protestant." The Right Reverend Alludy replied with a
slight chuckle.

"I mean, yes. Pentecostal to be specific."

The Right Reverend Alludy's eyes rolled upwards as he let out a slight chuckle. "I guess Peter never told you that the Alludy family is Anglican."

"Not a single mention." I concurred. "James never said anything either."

A strange look spread across The Right Reverend's face, a clear distaste for my mention of his son. I assumed that it was nothing but the fact that his death was still fresh. Even I still struggled to process his death. The only thing that brought me solace was that I would one day be able to hold him again in Heaven.

The Right Reverend left the conversation, not even uttering a single word of closing.

I stood in the same spot for a moment, trying to process the strange interaction I had just had. After that point, no one approached me to ask about my relation to James.

Nobody even asked to question who I was and why I was loitering on the front lawn of their home. I was left completely alone in a foreign place.

Peter seemed to be in a state of disarray as well, sitting quietly underneath an apple tree that was on the far corner of the property. Nobody seemed to be keen on bothering him either. I went against the crowd and went to speak with him. I thought I would ask if there was any way I could view James' body.

"That shouldn't be a problem," James replied to my inquiry. "We have a cow that's about to give birth any moment as well. Barn is in the same clearing as the graveyard, so I need to visit there either way."

"Thank you for being willing, Peter."

"I'm more willing than most here, it only makes sense that I would take you."

"Understandable. Your father seems to be taking it especially hard."

"Yes."

He said nothing more and gestured for me to follow him to the graveyard. We passed over the top of the hill and began making our ascent through increasingly dense trees. We made the trek in silence. I was glad that I received the blessing I had, as I would not have been able to make the trek in my asthmatic state from a year prior. Peter seemed much more adept at making the trek, as even with the healing that God bestowed upon me I was not able to properly handle the exertion.

Eventually we reached a clearing. Towards the entrance was a small barn which emanated loud lows from the cow that was inside. Past the barn was what was clearly the family graveyard. A decorative metal fence encircled a small plot of land. Only a few tombstones dotted the plot, a clear indication that the family had not been in the new world for an overly long period of time. There were only six gravestones, one of them placed in front of an open maw in the ground.

James' spot.

A grave marker solidified its intended occupant; a simple stone slab that said nothing but "James." It lacked any sort of "in memoriam" phrase, nor did it have his birth and death year. I assumed they had not completed it yet.

His casket was sat directly next to the grave; a simple wooden box with no ornamentation. Nature had taken it's duty though, and spots of moisture and mildew spotted the casket from the outside, making it clear that it had been sitting in this exact spot for the entirety of the bitter winter. I opened the lid, Peter standing silently beside me. His breath was ragged, and not from the trek.

I laid eyes upon James' body.

He was as beautiful as I had left him.

They had clearly embalmed him, as he was almost entirely intact. With the addition of the preserving cold, he looked almost exactly as he had the day I had found him. We both stood in James presence, the only sound being of the bawling. I felt tears run down my cheeks as I stood in awe of him.

"I'll leave you alone for a minute so you can say your goodbyes." Peter said. "I need to check on the cow."

I stooped down, pulling out a small sheet of paper. Bending over his body, I slipped the note he had written when he took his life back into his pocket.

I began to tell him everything that had happened since he passed. Everything I had told Martha. And everything I had not told her. I assured him she was keeping me safe. I told him how much he would have loved her, and how much she would have loved him. I knew they would have, because they both loved me so deeply. I apologized that I was never able to give him the love he desired from me. I did more than apologize. I begged him, pleaded with him that he would forgive me. I told him about my father, how he was no different than my uncle. Both of them being downright perverted men in so many unimaginable ways. I told him I understood his fear of me as he died, as I was beginning to fear myself. I was my father's son. I was like both of them, and I saw in my heart so many different ways I could hurt those around me.

I also told him about God. Not the things he already knew, but the things I had learned. I told him about the way my mind was beginning to fold in on itself. I felt so enfeebled from the things I was seeing and being informed on. The God in my ears may have healed my body, yet my mind was the weakest it had ever been.

To those outside, I told him, I was powerful. I was a good pastor. I was a good leader. But I wanted nothing more than a way to ensure justice, and I felt that there were only miniscule ways I could bring it about. I told him about how depressed it made me.

Finally, I told him that I was going to protect him. I told him he was safe. There was no way that he would ever come across my father and uncle in the afterlife, as I would ensure that they never would step foot into God's presence. They were too corrupt, too evil. The God in my ears, that Putrid Cloud, had assured me they never would be allowed in Their presence.

As I ranted and raved I felt tears fall from my cheeks onto his suit's breast pocket. The sleeves on his jacket were too short. As I caught a glimpse of the still opened wounds on his wrist and I asked myself why they had not healed.

The dead do not heal.

I kissed him on the forehead, swept the hair out of his eyes, and closed his casket.

I stood in silence for a moment, then made my way to the barn where Peter was tending to that cow. He was bent over a small body, sobbing. The cries of the mother cow were harsher, more akin to wailing than lowing.

When Peter felt my presence he stood up from his position, wiping the tears from his eyes. The cow laid on her side, panting heavily. A the body of a stillborn calf laid still by

her side.

"She'll be okay. She seemed to handle the birth fine." He said, shakily. "The calf was too weak. Why can't things just be strong enough to live?"

I was about to give him some sort of comfort, but I was interrupted before being able to give a reply.

"It's no matter. It's just the way things are."

And with that, he walked out of the barn and made his way back towards the house, giving the mother cow time to mourn. We walked through the dense trees with the wailing of a bereaved mother at our backs.

WHEN WE RETURNED I sought out a place on the patio and watched as children muddied their clothes against their parents wishes. The Right Reverend stood around with three men who looked almost exactly like him, just at different stages of life. Most likely his brothers. Of course, I could not be fully sure as almost all the men present look like copies of each other. Peter was an exception, being much more gaunt than any of the other members of his family. I would not claim that James fit the general description either, as most of the men present were extremely portly while James was stout and muscular. Had he lived to their age he may have looked more like them, though not as eerily similar as all the men present looked.

And that was not a small number of men, either. With all the children taken into account there were about three men to every woman. To have almost every man present be of the same build and stature was a borderline supernatural feat. It was surreal experiencing the hours pass as I watched as indiscernible copies of the same man romp around the front yard with their children, who were themselves just smaller copies of the same man. As hours passed my ability to tell them apart began to blur.

"All are the same." A familiar voice said in my ear.

I did not respond.

For a while I thought I had a grasp on who was who, noting a small birthmark on one man that I did not notice on another; that was until I noticed the same birth mark on another man. Soon, even the women began to look like unbearded versions of the men.

Even worse was, at times, I thought I could see James walking amongst them, a tiny calf walking next to him. At one point I looked out into the greenery to see James, frollicking happily with the small calf at his side, only to quickly realize it was nothing but a child and the farm dog that took up residency with the Alludy family.

He had that grin on his face, that look as if he were about to get the both of us in trouble. There was also love in that look.

Then a chime rang, snapping me out of the illusion. I could discern them again.

"Supper is on!" Yelled Mrs. Alludy. I had completely missed that she had disappeared from the lawn, taking refuge in the house to prepare food. We all shuffled in
for dinner.

While I did not expect to be seated at the head of the table, I also did not expect to be forced to sit with the children. I do not think that they held any grudge against me, but it was becoming more and more evident that my inclusion to the event was merely by
Peter's insistence.

Dinner was some sort of soup that I could not place the ingredients of. I refrained from eating, as the consistency felt foul in my mouth. Most of the food shared the same texture;

a mealy slop that could hardly be called gruel. I would have choked the mixture down, had it not been for the unceasing shifting of the forms around me. The moment something as gelatinous as Mrs. Alludy's food touched my lips I would have vomited the entirety of my stomach's contents onto the table. It worried me that the Alludy family claimed it was the best thing they had ever tasted.

After everyone had finished their meals, we sat around the house and held shallow conversation. I could not remember their names at any point. Some would saunter pass, not taking care to speak to me, yet others would pry into my deepest life points. I was less of a kin in mourning and more of some sort of spectacle to be observed. Those who spoke to me wanted to know little more than the life of the strange man that their little wayward sheep met at seminary. I wondered what Peter had told them about me that made me so foreign to them. Perhaps it was the fact that I was from a different denomination.

Even worse yet were the multitude of children who had not yet learned the concept of having couth. I was asked multiple times about finding James' body, something that was quickly shut down by the adults in the group. I had a strange feeling that the reason for the censorship had little to do with my feelings and more about not wanting to talk about James.

No one spoke of him. At almost every funeral I had attended, the family was aflutter with stories of the deceased. An outpouring of love and humor was constantly streaming from those who were close to them. Instead, the Alludy family seemed more preoccupied with their own personal lives. The only time his name was uttered was by the aforementioned children.

The Right Reverend did not speak at all, let alone towards me. It seemed that I had offended him with my earlier inquiry about James, and now he made it an important task to avoid me at all costs. I heard Mrs. Allude try to strike conversations with him, all of which were quickly shut down by a lack of response. It was a stark contrast from his earlier flirtatious behavior towards his wife.

I slept on the floor in the living room that night, not even given a blanket to cover with. I was not too terribly offended, as the house was considerably smaller than even my meager childhood home, and was warmer because of that. I could also say that, seeing as how I did not ask for a blanket, not receiving one should be expected. But I could not fully believe that excuse, as I did not think that anyone could not see that as a basic hospitality. I laid beside the living room fire and thought about the day's events as I drifted off.

I slept fitfully. I could not stop thinking of James.

The next day was more of the same. Countless hours of the same doppelganger people flitting about the house. James' father sat on the ground, playing with homemade blocks as children sprinted through the house getting prepared for the next day's burial. The information that was being gathered by my eyes could not have been accurate. I knew that it was improbable that it was James' grandfather playing blocks, and I knew that it was still not the case when his middle aged cousin was doing the same. I felt startled to see Eli flirting with Mrs. Alludy's sister, but I knew it had to be The Right Reverend and his wife continuing in their antics. I did not care for the amount of times my father and uncle made themselves known among their ranks. Almost every time they made an appearance, it became clear that it was the same man each time: The Right Reverend. It was no wonder that James had clearly not felt safe at the mention of his father.

"See as I do." The downpour said to me.

I was quickly becoming disoriented by the figures that teleported throughout the house. What at one point was a young girl with braids became a decrepit old man tottering throughout the halls. At another, a man stood on all fours and barked. The only one who maintained his personhood was Peter, who was quietly loitering by the kitchen. He seemed deep in thought, as he tended to be permanently now.

I had not even noticed that quiet downpour in my ears. It was nowhere near as harsh as before. Another layer added to it as well; a quiet mewling. The sound of a newborn calf.

James was no longer common among the ranks of his family. He only made himself known in the purest of moments. He could be seen in the child playing with its siblings. He could be seen in the man dozing on the couch after a meal. But never once could he be seen in the actions of his father. And as time passed his appearances ceased all together.

The day swam through my eyes, disorienting and viscous. People were visibly concerned at my state, as what started as an inability to remember the names of those who introduced themselves to me turned to a feverish and pale appearance mixed with very apparent confusion. They began to treat me as if I were having a mental break.

It was an understandable response, as I was.

I decided to close myself off. My body language made it apparent that I wished to not be referred to, and quickly most decided to let me be in my devolution.

I could not shake the comment that the Putrid Cloud had made.

"See as I do."

He saw nothing more than epithets and behaviors. To him, every man flirting with his spouse was the same being. Every child that built a tower made of blocks. Every vile creature looked the same as the last.

And it was for that reason I felt more and more anxious around The Right Reverend. The fact that he was no different from my uncle and my father worried me greatly, and I knew I could not be at ease around him. I could not let myself fall to the same fate as James. I could not be stopped from protecting him, and the best way I could do so was to distance myself from the Alludys. The Right Reverend felt ever present, the only person among the masses that dared wear the face of my uncle and father.

The shifting forms all huddled and shuffled about, morphing and changing from person to person instigating a severe nausea that could only be brought about by the worst case of vertigo. I had refrained from eating several meals at this point, causing the inner lining of my stomach to begin to digest itself instead of any contents that may have lied within. The hunger pangs made the nausea even more unbearable.

In addition, a new stressor had introduced itself to me in my psyche.

How did that putrid thing that had granted me sight, see me? Did it see me as just another one of the common folk, or was I among the children? Even worse, was I seen as some sort of heinous thing like The Right Reverend?

I could not bear the thought that I may be as bad as those who had hurt James. I looked about the room, hoping that I may be found somewhere among that undulating masses of Alludys and others I had met, but I could not view even a glimpse of myself.

I wracked my brain for anything that might cast me amongst my enemies.

Could it have been something as benign as the trouble James and I caused among our peers and professors? I dismissed that thought quickly. Something so trivial would not even put me in ranks with Benjamin, let alone the elder Teendyths. Not even my assault on Quill would warrant such a harsh judgment.

I felt my eyes swing from figure to figure, becoming even more desperate to glimpse myself. The pains in my stomach were becoming more and more excruciating. It was becoming harder and harder to breathe.

Could it have been James' death? Had there been a chance that I were to blame for what had occurred, I would take any punishment granted to me. But I had not been at fault, despite the guilt I felt for playing even a small part in it. The fault was purely on Eli.

Every time I saw my father or uncle reflected in The Right Reverend I felt my chest cease moving for a slight moment. Seeing something so familiar to myself made me convinced I saw my own figure multiple times, only to feel the anxiety of the situation collapse back in ten-fold. I knew that the form I saw currently was that of Eli, but could I be so sure that it was my father and not me who was there a moment before? The Teendyth men all looked so similar it could be hard to distinguish between them sometimes.

Benjamin's death was inconsequential and an act of mercy. There was no way that his death would rank me as evil, as it was a blessing for all involved. If you were to ask some, Benjamin himself was even better off dead. If he was in Hell he could have all the booze he wished, and in Heaven he would feel no craving for it.

Despite the fact that I had no reason to believe that I would be seen as my uncle or father, my anxiety was not calmed.

It was then I realized I was not afraid of being seen as evil.

I was afraid of being seen as anyone other than myself. That was something I could not reason away.

I rushed towards the washroom as I felt my nausea begin to get the better of me.

The crowd parted amongst me, clearly worried that I may vomit on them if they did not move away in time. I had not been far from it in the first place, yet it felt further away than even the clearing with the graves had been. I slammed the door behind me and almost immediately began unleashing torrents of bile and water into the latrine, nothing of substance to be removed from me. The bile burned my throat as I evacuated my stomach. As I stood up, washing my mouth in the sink, I noticed the mirror hanging behind the faucet.

At first I shied away, worried that I may see the reflection of my uncle or father in my stead. I was afraid of what I might see, but I knew I had to overcome that fear. I had to know that I could not be considered of the same ilk as those demons who masqueraded as men. I had to know who I was to my God.

I looked in the mirror.

At first I saw myself, but I could not assuage my fears so easily. I stood, staring at the flush image of myself while I waited for the shift. I leaned forward against the sink to steady myself as my feet faltered.

The figure shimmered.

It was no one else I had seen. I mean, I had seen this figure before, yet I never knew who it actually was. I had no name for it.

A shadow stood in my place. A man-shaped hole punched out of earthly space.

That featureless thing.

My stalker stood before me.

I was confused at first, but elated to think that I was not greeted by the face of my father. The image shifted again.

He had on a strange hat, an apron of poor quality, and a tag that bore my name. He was still me, though. He looked just like me. Another appeared - me but in long flowing robes, much akin to priestly garments. Another, wearing something that looked akin to an officer's uniform that emanated a strange light. It felt like my form flashed and shifted endlessly, an infinite myriad of myself flashing in the mirror before me. Each and every one of them looked vastly different from the others, yet I could still see that it was no one else other than -

Me.

With each shift I felt my body become more and more at ease. The assurance that I was not seen as the same horrendous thing as my kin brought me nothing short of pleasure. It did not even pain me to see the forms laid before me become more and more inhuman.

For the slightest moment, I saw nothing in the mirror. Just a sickly hue. It left as fast as it had come. After that moment, the figures ceased looking human all together. One figure towered past the mirror, its skin stretched across limbs that had too many joints. For another moment it was just a mass of flesh. Beasts innumerable flew past my vision. I did not mind in the least - they were not my father, and they were not my uncle, either.

It brought me peace to see the uniqueness of the forms that could be seen in the reflection. I could not help but feel as if each were familiar, at their core being me, despite their grotesque appearances and strange outfits. The flutter of figures became so quick that I was unable to process more than the shifting patterns of colors in front of me. The information had become too vast to process in such a short time. I felt my body begin to seize as it became overwhelmed by the flickering images.

I steadied myself against the sink and forced myself to find peace in the overstimulation. The peace of knowing without a shadow of a doubt that these were still all just me. I felt a cold wind exude from the mirror as it relayed its information.

A storm front.

I began to pray that the experience would soon cease.

What felt like an eternity passed as more and more images flitted across my retinas, until finally it slowed. For a moment, it rested upon that lightless form that had stalked me for so long.

And then it returned to my present form. The way that the man standing in front of the mirror truly looked. Save for one change.

A light shone behind my eyes, sickly and purple. Then stark and red. Deathly and blue. The light swam, morphing from color to color as if some living and luminous thing had taken up residency in my eyes.

And then the light left. Leaving nothing but me, in true and current form.

My head felt clear for once since I had stepped foot on this damned property. I was still me. I would always be me. I knew not why, but the Putrid Cloud cared for me.

I stood before the mirror for a moment longer, reassuring that my already rough breathing could return to some sort of normalcy. I questioned if I had even been breathing during the duration of the visions showing to me. Air stung my lungs as it flooded them, as they felt as if they had been vacant for at least a full minute, if not more. I looked deep into my reflection, the color slowly returning to my cheeks. My stomach still burned, but I found that it was not quite as bothersome as it had been before. I no longer had the anxiety about myself exacerbating the situation.

It took a minute before I fully was able to comprehend what I had been shown. Even though I could not fully process what each image was, I was able to comprehend what the images meant. I *was* a rarity to him. I knew within me that no matter how grotesque the form is, it was always me that looked back from the glass.

I was important to the cloud.

I was His Chosen.

As I walked back into the commons area of the Adully home, I still saw only the shifting faces of the family. I could no longer tell them from each other, but I no longer cared. They were now beneath me. The only things worthy of my care now, were Martha and James.

I still did not comprehend why Peter's form did not flicker, but I did not mind. The shifting forms were at the very least somewhat nauseating, and the familiarity of his form was soothing. Even without the anxiety that had found its home in my chest, the sea of shifting forms still made the pains in my stomach worsen. Peter was an excellent way to keep my balance moored, with the added bonus of him looking so similar to James.

THE NEXT DAY WE ALL awoke early to make the trek towards the gravesite. Even with the upcoming burial, the family remained cheerful and full of glee. They wore bright colors, chittering among themselves without any recognition of what they were about to do.

It disgusted me.

I had held out hoping that the mismatched air was nothing but an attempt to stave off depression, yet it was made abundantly clear that they simply did not care enough to mourn. James' own mother was more preoccupied with what she would serve for the banquet after than her son's burial.

Peter was still different. His gloom had increased tenfold, barely looking up from his feet as he trekked through the woods towards the clearing. He stood at the back of the gaggle of Alludys, barely lifting his feet save to cross over high branches. I walked beside him, perhaps to keep him company, perhaps as an excuse to avoid the disrespectful crowd.

When we all arrived, the family crowded around the casket that contained James' body. They still chittered about. The children were running through the clearing, picking flowers, playing tag, and all other behaviors that did not belong in a funeral procession. Of course, to me it looked as if grown men were wrestling in the damp ground of the clearing, but I assumed they at least had enough couth to refrain from that. Their voices betrayed them as well, as only the outward form of those around me shifted. The shrill giggles coming out of the mouths of the elder Alludy's may have been comical in concept, but was thoroughly disturbing when brought into reality. A gaggle of children and adults alike stood at the coffin, chattering away as if they did not fully grasp what sort of event it was they were attending. The few mentions of James I did hear were things that should not have come out of the mouths of loved ones.

"He would have been truly wonderful if he could have gotten past his... stumbling blocks." A matronly voice spoke to my right.

"I honestly don't understand why we're holding a funeral for him. Should've let my pigs eat him." A gruff and angry voice said to my left.

"Mama said he's in hell." A little girl's voice said behind me.

"My papa said it's where he belongs." A little boy said in response.

I could not comprehend how any person could think so lowly of my James. None of the people present were capable of shining a light as bright as he had, yet they did everything in their power to diminish it. Even after his death they would not allow him to shine brighter than any among them.

Worse yet were the forms in which they took.

The more the crowds talked about James as they waited for the service to start, the more I saw my father, my uncle, and The Right Reverend sprinkled throughout the crowd. By the time The Right Reverend had taken the stand almost every person present was bearing the faces of those devils.

All of them, save Peter. He was still just Peter.

I found myself keeping to the back of the group, trying my hardest to refrain from mingling with the crowd of evil around me, as mothers called to their children to join them and be still before The Right Reverend began to speak.

"Family members and... others." He glared in my direction. "We are gathered here to bury our James."

A series of platitudinous murmurs echoed throughout the crowd. It seemed they only cared when pomp was involved. Even the voices of those who had said the most heinous of things whispered sad amens.

"James was a beautiful man." At least we can agree on that. "A son that truly shined in all of our lives. A man quite so joyful has never existed before, and to see such a bright young man leave us so soon is nothing short of terrible tragedy."

I was shocked that the words of The Right Reverend remained so pleasant for

so long.

"I remember ever since he was a child, his sweet innocence could always bring light to a room. He was the gentlest of us all, though for an Alludy that's not a difficult feat."

An obligatory chuckle echoed throughout the crowd.

"But his sweetness and gentleness was not something that could simply wash away the horrible sin in his life." A deep sigh left through The Right Reverend's lips."Which is why it saddens me even more to say that we all know of his fate. To think that we will never see our lovely James with his beaming smile again, chills me to the heart. But it is a simple fact that we all know that he lived deeply in sin."

This was a different man than I had seen in my short interaction with him when I first arrived at the Alludy homestead. This man was colder. This was a man who prided himself on his office before his familial duty. He spoke differently, too. A cold, calculated vernacular took the place of the jovial and lighthearted man I met before. His body seemed more rigid, more stalwart than it had been. An air of sadness pervaded him, but I could not say for sure that it was genuine.

"It was no secret that James' habits had been perverted by the devil. At the very least, we can take solace in the fact that he felt remorse for the way he seduced that poor professor at his college."

My jaw dropped. My uncle had very clearly ensured in the past few months that he would be seen as the victim in this event, telling stories in an attempt to avoid any sort of incrimination.

"That being said, the actions of his guilt are in themselves another mortal sin. To take one's own life most assuredly means that he could not be with God."

Disgusting.

"Before we continue with the speech given, I would like for us all to have a moment of silence for the departed." Everyone bowed their heads in unison, as if they had all been rehearsing. The silence lasted for minutes, as if a lengthy silence could replace any sort of legitimate mourning.

Once the moment passed, The Right Reverend continued.

"I can only blame myself." The Right Reverend declared. "I thought that seminary would set him straight; that he would denounce his wicked ways and return to the fold. I should have known that he was too immature to be left alone with so many men. I should have known he would have attempted something.

The crowd all nodded in a sort of agreement, as if they all thought that James would rove about the moment he was surrounded by men.

"To think that our sweet James will never be with us in Heaven is something that I am assured we have all come to terms with."

A cluster of murmurs and nods came from the crowd. I looked to Peter to see his expression. He was standing underneath a tree on the outskirts of the crowd. Glinting tears were forming in his eyes. He nodded his head as well.

"I can only hope that God is merciful to him down below." The Right Reverend cleared his throat. "Now that I have said my peace I would like to invite any others to the front to speak."

I felt the world spin again in the sea of shifting forms and looked for Peter so he could become my rock once again. I looked towards the tree he had been resting against for the majority of the service, yet he was no longer there. When I looked back to the front of the group I saw The Right Reverend stand next to himself.

The second figure at the front began to speak.

"As is tradition, James is to be buried with a rosary." He held up a small strand of beads with a cross at the end. "May his body be with Christ forever."

The Right Reverend walked forward again and began to speak. "I felt it was only right that he be the one to place the rosary, as he and James were the closest out of all of us. They loved each other dearly, almost never separating."

A large grin spread across The Right Reverend's face, a look of pure pride in the figure next to him. "He always had

James' best interest in mind, making sure that his faith was always on track with what it needed to be."

It must have been one of the other Alludy sons standing next to The Right Reverend, but I was unsure of which one it might have been. James never spoke of his other brothers, so I found it hard to believe that the two of them were as close as The Right Reverend claimed. "In fact, when he learned of James' deviant sexual appetites, he went out of his way to inform me so that we would be able to set his path straight."

The figure next to The Right Reverend flickered, shifting to my uncle.

"That is correct, Father." The other figure said. "I thought that if we had intervened we may have been able to save his soul before it was too late."

There was no emotion in this new voice, yet it was somewhat familiar. It sounded so much like The Right Reverend's voice, yet different all the same. The form shifted to that of
my father.

"Exactly," The Right Reverend cleared his throat. "We both agreed the best course of action would be to send him to seminary. Honestly, despite the outcome I would make the same choice over again if it meant saving James' soul."

The figure was my uncle again, a false look of pain spread across his face.

"It seems he was too weak to handle temptation. We should have known that he would have attempted to seduce another attendee of the university."

The Right Reverend shot a glare at me.

I met his gaze and challenged it.

And when I unlocked my gaze from him I saw that it was no longer my uncle standing next to The Right Reverend. Not my father, nor The Right Reverend either.

Standing next to the ever shifting form of his father was none other than Peter, a false yet solemn grimace spread across his face.

I watched on in horror as Peter's form shifted in tandem with his father's. Whether it had been that the Putrid Cloud had withheld the way he saw Peter, or be it that this was the defining moment that molded how God saw Peter, I did not know.

I did not care, either.

The two of them carried on with the service. Not a single member of the Alludy family felt it important to say anything about James, so they quickly moved to the shoddy sermon that had been prepared by the Right Reverend.

Ironically, Peter remained my mooring point, but for a different reason than before. I had hoped that he could feel the hatred that was irradiating from my eyes, as I had truly felt nothing quite like it before. I could not claim that it was more unexpected than the betrayals I had faced before, but this one felt far more cutting. My father and uncle had committed their atrocious deeds out of some primal, disgusting need that they felt they were entitled

to satisfy.

Peter's evil was born from something more intelligent, more conniving. Watching his face twist from utter despair to the same false grin that his father used was nothing short of terrifying. It was not just another dark trait coming to the surface of his personhood. This was a betrayal of himself.

This was a different Peter than the jovial man I sat and shared gossip with in the late hours of the night. I had a strange feeling that this was not a new facet of Peter.

Suddenly I fully processed the information that had been given to me.

He had been the one to out his brother.

He had been the one to suggest that James be sent to seminary. Even worse was that Peter had fully known the threat that lurked in the lecture halls of that accursed place.

He knew James would not be safe.

The two chattered on about James in front of the masses that had finally decided to mourn. Every member seemed to be fully in agreement about James' mortality. Every person in attendance was assured that they would not see James in the afterlife.

For all I knew, they were right.

I was becoming disturbingly aware of how unsure I was about the afterlife. The God I had thought I had known my entire life had finally made himself clear to me, and he was far from the being I expected. For all I knew James had been sent to eternal damnation.

He may be in paradise.

He may be in some in-between place.

Wherever that place may have been, I could not allow those who would harm James to be there. I had to ensure that they would not be allowed either the blessing of heaven or the curses of hell.

And the Putrid Cloud had already informed me on how to do that.

THE SERVICE DID NOT go on for much longer, punctuated by James' coffin being lowered into its hole. They refrained from burying it until later, as the masses were beginning to get hungry from the hike, and it was reaching supper time. They would most likely bury it the next day

We trekked back through the woods again, heading back to the Alludy family's homestead. They sat and snacked on fairly mediocre sandwiches that looked like they had tough meat on them and nothing else. We would be having a banquet style meal later in the evening, but most agreed they would not be able to last until then.

During that time I decided to fully embrace the Alludy family. As awful as they had treated James both before and after his death, I could not fault them. Honestly, to mourn properly may have been past their mental and emotional capacity. Instead of secluding myself, I made sure that I would interact with the family as much as possible. I made conversation with the men of the house, all save Peter and The Right Reverend. They seemed fairly content in each other's company. I assisted the women with any food preparation as they prepared for the larger meal of the night. I made a fool of myself, crawling around the floor and tussling with the young children in the family. I made myself loved out of nothing but spite. I had learned how to be likable in the few months I had been leading Afton Assembly, and I exerted that experience here.

The Alludy family's strict adherence to the roles they were given made it easy to discern that the women were in the kitchen cooking while the men sat around under the guise of "watching the children." Even more so, none of the men in the family seemed to be the type that would go out of their way to fully interact with their children.

As time continued, the Alludy family's opinion of me shifted. They no longer saw me as the mentally ill man who had led their little boy astray. Instead, I was now something just less than a son to them. It was somewhat easy for them to accept me when I alluded to not returning James feelings. That was a partially true fact, but they did not need to know the complexities.

For the most part, everyone still refrained from mentioning James in any capacity. I did not attempt to breach the topic either.

When the meal was ready everyone gathered at the table, jostling and joking with each other. I was no longer banished to the children's table, but instead invited to the table with the men. The Right Reverend folded hands and led the group out in prayer. It was as pompous and meaningless as every other word he uttered about God.

Mrs. Alludy had again proved that some people simply could not produce a good meal, as the table spread was nothing more than sludges of various shades of grey. Despite going on two days worth of time with no sustenance, I refrained from putting the horrid mix near my mouth. I forced myself to accept that they were no lesser a person due to their inability to cook. That did not mean that there were not a myriad of other things that made them lesser.

Everyone present choked down the mess, pretending that it was the most delicious meal they had ever been served. For all I knew, it was. After everyone had cleared their plates, the men retired to the back room to smoke as the women lounged
amongst themselves.

"Why don't you join us for a smoke?" One of the men asked, offering an invitation to be one of them despite refusing to look me in the eye the day prior.

"Oh I would love to, but I neither have my lighter nor my smokes."

"Well I ain't got no smokes to spare but I have a lighter you can borrow." Said another man. The shifting was happening so quickly now that I could barely discern what form they were taking. I had grown accustomed to it.

"Why thank you. If you give me a moment, I actually think I left my smokes in the wagon. It would be a shame if I lost them as they are made with premium, high quality tobacco. I'll let you all try one when I get back, if I am able to find them, that is."

The men all seemed excited to try whatever quality smokes I had, giving me leave to go find them. I walked out of the house, lighter in hand, and locked eyes with the shed full of firewood located right next to the house

"Can I ensure that these men and women will never see James again?"

"You know how."

Splinters dug into my hands as I placed pile upon pile of of wood against every door and window of the small house.

There was plenty of fuel meandering about the inside so there was no need to ensure that the interior was stocked with fire wood. I had emptied out the entirety of the wood shed by time I was finished building the fire. I lit the light and threw it onto the wood pile..

They did not notice for a minute or two, going about their business and chatting with each other all the same. I watched as the figures passed by the uncovered fragments of the windows. I stared in from the outside, the warmth of the small fire bringing me comfort in the cold of the early spring.

I think they smelled the smoke at first, large clouds of it flooding into the house from underneath the doorways. They scrambled about the house searching for the smell. It was then that one of the figures walked by a window and saw me looking in.

He stood and stared at me.

I stared back.

Panic formed in the eyes of the figure as I stared into them. More and more members of the Alludy family gathered in that window.

They could at least be granted the fact that they somewhat knew how to handle disaster, as the window was located at the very back of the house, farthest from the source of the fire. That being said, to flee from the deadly sources of heat was an instinct that even rats had claim to. The figures pleaded with me, begging that I might unblock the window and release them from the oven their house had become.

I stared at them, unwavering.

I watched as the bright tongues took hold of the forms and began to devour them. The bright light of the flame began to drown out any sort of image that may have been seen from the inside. The screams of those inside became more and more faint as one by one every member of the family became silenced by the heat. It was not long before the only sound left was the roaring and cracking of the fire.

Let it be known that one should never put their trust in strangers, as a stranger ended the Alludy family in one night.

Ordinatio

One would think I would have run from the blaze, fleeing the scene as quickly as I could. The more distance I could create between myself and the screaming casket that I had set alight, the better.

But I did the opposite, staying on the property for longer than most arsonists would have been comfortable with. I was no run of the mill fire starter though, and I knew that no matter who happened upon the scene I would be protected. My God had chosen me for this. I had been given permission to enact whatever I felt was just. The moment I felt any sort of assurance that these people would never set eyes on James again, I felt comfort in

ending them.

Of course, the children could not be considered innocent either. They were so young, yet already held such contempt for their cousin. They were not worthy of him either.

The Putrid Cloud, the God who had claimed me as his own, had made me a promise. He had promised to hand me both the keys of heaven and hell alike, and I would use them as I saw fit. I just had to ensure I took the required steps to claim them.

Before I started back for Afton, I made my way towards the burial site. I could not allow James to be left at this place that rejected him so emphatically.

The grave they dug was shallow. They couldn't even be bothered to ensure his comfort in the earth. Any sort of rain would have quickly washed any soil away, letting the elements and those that would devour him in. He surely would have become food for the scavengers and starved predators.

I hefted the casket out of the hole and pried open the lid. I saw his beautiful face and took a moment to caress his cheek before I picked him up and carried him through the forest. He looked as if he were simply sleeping the most peaceful sleep of his life. I thought of all the snoring he uttered those nights in our dorm.

His pleasant mutterings of the goings on of his mind.

His heavy breathing.

Nothing could bring those back to me. I would never revel in the presence of my James again. He was forever lost to me, scorned by everyone who should have loved him.

My stomach began to growl as I trekked through those woods. I had not eaten any of the banquet, its tastes too mediocre for my liking.

I tottered over roots, ensuring that no harm came to James. I would much rather any scrapes and bruises came to me than him. I could heal. He could not. At times it felt as if the ground itself was working against my efforts; rocks crumbled from underneath my feet and damp leaves robbed me of my traction as I hiked down the steep incline that separated the Alludy home from their burial grounds.

Through the trek I could hear a rustling coming from behind me, matched with the soft mewling of a calf in my ear. I knew it was not there. It was James.

The pangs in my stomach grew stronger as I walked through the woods. I had not eaten in days and the exertion of today's events would make the most grizzled of men want for sustenance.

I felt my body become weaker with each step I took.

The blaze continued on through the night, illuminating the sky in a hazy hue of demonic orange, red, and purple. The oppressive heat that spread throughout the forest exacerbated my already growing discomfort from my lack of food. James looked as if he was overall unaffected by the heat, unsurprising as he was much sturdier a man than I.

The screams of those trapped inside that house turned crematorium had long since dwindled, leaving nothing but the crackling of the house wood and flesh resting inside.

As we came up to the Alludy homestead we were met with little more than an overgrown funeral pyre. The house was nothing but a pile of ash and rubble at this point. It seemed that none had escaped the fire. I fell to my knees the moment I reached the stable ground of the house's yard.

My stomach continued to growl, a persistent and growing pang that pervaded my body. My body was weakening fast. Any sort of fuel that kept my body in order was diminishing fast. There was no food in sight.

"Eat." The cacophonous voice said in my ear.

"There is nothing for me to eat, lord." I replied. A dizzying rumble ripped through my body.

"EAT."

The voice said again more forcefully. I looked upon the rubble of the Alludy house and saw a small bank of fog resting upon the corpse of a small child. It seemed that he had crawled away a small distance from the rubble before succumbing to the fire.

I looked at the child, encased in a glistening crust of char. "I cannot," I insisted.

"It is a gift." The voice assured me.

I gently sat James on the ground and began hesitantly walking towards the cooked child. "But lord, is it upright for a man to eat another man?"

"You are higher." I replied.

I looked down at my feet and saw a small puddle had formed from the still moist ground that had not fully dried from the heat. My form flickered and in my stead I saw a man, South Asian of descent. His eyes looked panicked.

It was not me.

"Yes, Lord."

I refused it. I would not be another failed apostle and I would most definitely not be one to refuse my lord's kindness.

He was right.

I had committed actions that would be atrocious for any man to commit, multiple times over, and I would commit more.

It was my right.

I was no longer any sort of man.

I was higher.

Mightier.

I looked down, able to see myself in the puddle again. I strode forward with newfound conviction, then bent down next to the charred remains of the child. I grasped it by the wrist. It had been roasted in such a way that made it quite a simple task to break off the arm at the shoulder, tender meat being hidden underneath the crisp exterior. I sunk my teeth into the forearm, the skin crackling under my teeth before sinking into the flesh underneath. The muscle fibers needed no seasoning, having a flavor not unlike veal.

The more I ate the more vigorous I became. It had begun to finally dawn on me the fullness of being ascended passed mankind. It did not simply mean that I could take lives if I felt it just, but meant I could take even without the excuse of justice. I did not need to act within the responsibilities and moralities of man. Concepts such as ethos were beneath me.

I could eat as I wished, judge as I wished, and love as I wished.

As the meat ground between my molars I could not help but laugh at how truly pitiful those men had been - My father, Uncle, The Right Reverend - Even the man that my uncle had received the knife from. All of them had attempted to grasp godhood, something that was never meant for them. That is what made them so evil; they were members of mankind enacting vicious and vile things upon those of their own kin.

I was not the kin of the child I devoured. I was no longer even of the same species.

He was little more than a burnt offering.

Grissle popped between my teeth. I finished the arm, picking the meat off of the fingers.

IT WAS FOR THAT VERY reason that my uncle and father deserved punishment. The very same reason that the Alludy family deserved punishment. They were humans that thought they had earned the right to the pleasures of gods and they needed to be punished for their pride. No matter how many times the Tower of Babel is built, it must always be torn down.

I sucked the meat off the ribs, the most tender section yet. I was in luck that the Alludy family was so stocky in nature, as a gaunt child would not have sated my hunger. It would not have been enough for me to consume.

By the time I finished I had devoured all of it. I had sucked the marrow from the center of its bones. I devoured the offal from inside its shell. I crunched the bones between my teeth.

I left nothing of it.

For the first time in my existence, I felt in control. The lungs that betrayed me so often when I was younger could be fully filled. My main tormentor had been removed from existence by my own hand. I was on the path to ensuring those who were pure, those who I cherished, were never threatened again. I was born into this world less than human, raised to be the second to every other thing.

But for once I was not only first, I was above.

I did not feel like the most important man in existence, because I no longer felt as a man.

I was angelic.

I knew how Moses felt when he parted the Red Seas. I knew how Moses felt when he taunted Pharoah. I knew how he felt when he struck the rock.

Once I had finished my meal, I stood and excused myself.

"Alright James, it is time for us to make our way back to Afton." He did not respond.

I hoisted James back into my arms, then made way to the carriage that we arrived in. I let him rest as I retrieved the horses and hitched them to the cart. In those quiet moments I talked to him again, but this time not in mourning. We talked the way we did during those restless nights in the dormitory.

He was quiet, but I was thankful for his listening skills.

I told him of the months past. I told him of Martha, and how we were to be wed. I told him of what happened to Benjamin and I told him of how old Deacon Willith had gotten his justice. I wept with him over my father and his evil. Most importantly though, I told him of my dreams for the very first time. I told him every single detail that had been shown to me in the visions I had seen, and I told him that I knew how to save him.

I told him to be patient. I told him he would be safe soon.

I gently placed his body in the cart and climbed onto the front seat, making headway back to Afton. Easter service was in a few days, and it was important that I arrive there in plenty of time for it.

I ENCOUNTERED VERY few people on the road back to Afton, as night had fallen hours beforehand. The few I did pass did not have their own face, instead being a clear mimicry of another. The faces that shimmered stopped being reserved to people I had met, instead being a myriad of men, women, and children that I had never met. Sometimes I saw my loved ones. Sometimes I saw my father. Sometimes, my mother. At times I saw my uncle as well. I kept note of those people. I would deal with them at a later date.

I spent most of the journey back taking the back roads. It would be no good if someone caught us. Yes, I had full trust that the Putrid Cloud would ensure that I was safe from any authorities that would wish to remove James from my care. They were too small minded. They would not care that what I was doing was a righteousness beyond

their understanding.

At times I found paths so secluded that they were still fully wooded; paths that only children paved. The horses must have been of strong breed, as they did not waver on the

unsturdy trails in the dark.

The Cloud stayed silent for the majority of the trip, only occasionally answering any inquiries I had. James, on the other hand, refrained from speaking entirely.

"Was this destiny, my Lord?" I asked the cloud.

"No such thing." It replied.

It gave me solace to think that I was not born for this. The God that had found me had not simply been stuck with me due to fate. He had outright sought me and hunted for me. His love for me was so great that he had chosen me amongst the infinite to be

his champion.

I thought back to what it had said to me all those nights ago. The insinuation that the Cloud and the God I served as I child were one in the same had become asinine to me. The God of my childhood had made me far too powerless for me to think they were one in the same. The God of my childhood, or at least what I was told of him, was a being that expected me to accept the abuse and let him handle the judgment made on others. Under the glory of the Cloud I was allowed the right of defense and protection. Under my new God I was given the right to my true nature. And the differences did not end there.

As a child, I only had myself.

Now, I had my god and myself.

I could not reconcile that I was so very neglected under something that told me to trust in it, yet now that I was allowed to do as I wished, I was never left to myself.

"Lord, do you care for me?" I asked.

"Yes." It replied. That was all I needed.

I felt him in all things. I felt him in the eyes of the birds that watched me as they perched in their nests. I felt him in every crawling thing that scurried away from the trampling hooves of the horses. I heard him in the wind and the cracks that echoed through the sky as the clouds moved through. I felt him in the memory of those peering gazes from the seminary. Now that I had fully accepted his embrace, I had never felt more in the presence of love. And to think that my care for him was returned to me was overwhelming.

The rest of the trip was quiet as I relished in the knowledge of love. Those moments with James and the Cloud was the most love I had ever felt.

WE ARRIVED BACK IN Afton in the dark evening of the next day. I guided the horses around the town to the church to avoid any unwanted attention.

I had no luggage, save the knife still strapped to my hip and the clothes on my back. I hoisted James from the back of the wagon and made my way towards the inner sanctum of the church. I cradled him in my arms and carried him towards the back of the sanctuary, directly towards the small ladder that led to the steeple.

It would be important that I seclude James away as quickly as I could. Most would not understand what his presence in my life meant. It was less that I was worried that my goals would be halted and more that I would rather avoid the drama of being seen carrying

a corpse.

I gently laid him over my shoulder and carried him up the ladder, careful to not bump or snag any part of his person on anything that may harm him. I would not forgive myself if I brought any harm to James, even if it were unintentional. I laid him gently down on the wooden floor of the small alcove, then curled myself around his body. He still smelled like himself. His muscles were rigid. His body remained miraculously intact for the time he had spent deceased. Yes, he had been embalmed with arsenic, but even then his body was in pristine condition. I kissed his cheek and heard a gentle mewling sound escape his lips.

I said goodnight to James, then made my way back down the ladder.

Someone was standing amongst the pews of the church in the darkness. They were watching closely, confused as to who was rummaging through the church at such a late hour.

I heard a familiar voice call out.

"Abbi, is that you?"

I walked towards the source of the voice, trying to discern who was watching me. I squinted in the direction of the voice and responded in kind. "Yes, it is me. I am back from my trip."

"Where is Peter? I see the wagon outside the church."

"Oh pay no mind to that. He fell ill and they allowed me to use their wagon to return by myself." I reasoned with the figure. "The real question is what are you doing here so late..."

I crept forward at an even quicker pace, then was finally able to make out the figure standing in front of me. My heart stuttered as I looked at the person standing in the moonlight streaming from the small window beside them.

"James?"

He stood in the light, his cheeks flushed with color. A dove sat on his shoulder, gently pecking at his ear. The gentle light highlighted his arms, free of any wounds or scars.

It was James.

It was James as I remembered him, beautiful and perfect. Free of any sort of blemish or mark.

"The funeral must have taxed you quite a lot, Abbi. You're acting unwell." James said to me. I did not question why James could be both standing before me while slumbering in the inner room of the steeple. I merely basked in his presence even more so. I said nothing, merely falling into his arms again. I was exhausted from the energy I had exerted.

"I am so sorry that I have refused to let you love me the way you wish to." I said in his ear.

"Whatever do you mean?" He replied.

"You always wanted me physically, yet I never let you have me fully." A fragrant scent flooded my nostrils. A safe and familiar scent.

"It would have made you uncomfortable, you were not ready." James reasoned.

"I am ready now." I lied. I did not know if I would ever be ready. But here he stood before me, alive and well again. I could not deny him his wants. Not again.

In that moment, we knew each other carnally. I hated every moment of it. I could not erase those flashes of my uncle with James. I paid no mind to what was happening to me as I struggled to confront the horrible images that flashed through my head.

After, I held James as we laid on the floor of the sanctuary. For some reason, I thought of Benjamin for a moment, then I cleared the thought from my head and hugged my precious James closer.

WE AWOKE TO THE SUN shining through the windows of the church. Thankfully, no one had felt the need to check on me as James had the night before. Our tryst had been completely and totally hidden from view of all.

He seemed happy as we awoke.

"That was fantastic, Abbi." He said. "Arguably the best I have ever had."

I shied away. I really had no wish to discuss the previous night's events. He seemed to understand and did not speak of the subject again. I dressed, prepping for the day ahead. The next day would be Easter Sunday, an important day for the church. Not only that, but it would be an important day for showcasing my pastoral leadership. It was my first year preaching an Easter service, and I needed to ensure that all who could be there would bear witness to it. I felt as if my sermon to them would be truly inspired.

"Will you be at service in the morning?" I asked James.

"Yes, I'd never miss it." He replied. He seemed to put on an air of excitement for me, yet I could still tell he was disheartened by my callousness regarding the night's events.

I headed out of the front door and made my way towards downtown, towards Mr. Sterling's bar. I did not expect many to be present, as almost the entirety of the town had neglected their alcoholic ways. Mr. Sterling waved to me as I walked through the front doors of the dimly lit establishment. He was the only one who was allowed behind the bar, which was the only way I could discern it was him.

"Absolom!" He called to me as I walked in. "Strange seeing you here, kid! What can I do for you?"

I sat down on a stool and leaned towards him.

"I just wanted to ensure all of you would be in attendance in the morning." I said.

"Ahhh, I see you're excited to preach your first Easter service, huh?" He said with a large smile.

"You could say that. I feel that my sermon will truly inspire everyone, as I have something important for all in the town to hear." I insisted.

He grinned again and nodded, agreeing that he would ensure that all who used to be his regulars would be in attendance for the service. I was not overly worried. Not a Sunday had passed since I had become the pastor that all the town did not ensure attendance.

Except my father.

"Damn it all." I whispered to myself.

I had not thought about that. Even if I were able to convince my father to make a showing, my uncle was not readily available at any given moment. I stashed those worries away. The Putrid Cloud would ensure that I had everything I needed. He had done so so far.

I thanked Mr. Sterling on my way out and trekked out across Afton, heading towards my parent's home. The moment I entered I could tell my father was home.

My mother was in the kitchen, the melancholy air from my childhood pervading the room. I could hear my father's voice in the other room, talking in a hushed voice with someone else. For a moment she looked not dissimilar to Willith. Strange comparison, but I deduced that the Putrid

Cloud saw the both as battered and beaten people. Seeing Willith in a kitchen apron was a sight to behold, so I did not mind.

"Absolom! I am happy to see you, but right now might not be the best time." She tried to usher me out the door.

"No worries, Mother, I will only be here for a moment. I just had a request to make of you and father."

"Your father is busy at the moment."

"I can hear he has company. Who is it?" I inquired. The voice was

becoming familiar.

"Your uncle. I really do think it would be best if you come back at another time."

My God truly did provide.

"Absolutely perfect! I would like to ask him my question as well."

A stunned look spread across her face. Last they knew of the situation, I would sooner end myself than speak to my uncle again. To see me so incredibly ecstatic at the prospect of seeing him seemed foreign to her.

She tried to block me from entering the living area a second time, but I pushed through and entered the room. My father and uncle stood in the living area, speaking seriously about some tedious subject. I could tell merely from the voice who was who, yet their forms shifted with every new sentence. No one new was added to the myriad of forms, still simply remaining as my father, my uncle, and the two Alludy men.

"What are you doing here?" My father asked with an icy twinge to his voice.

"Oh you know exactly why I am here." I replied, a clear sort of aggression in my voice. My uncle refrained from saying anything, instead remaining behind his brother. I wondered if word of what happened to Benjamin had gotten out, as he seemed somewhat nervous of my presence.

"I would rather hear it from your lips." My father growled.

I forced a grin across my lips, letting out a hearty laugh as I rushed forward and embraced my father. His body made me feel nauseous.

"Well actually, Father." I said as I broke my embrace. "I was going to extend an invitation to you. You and Uncle both actually."

Uncle Eli stepped forward, a move he would only make if he felt as if he were in control of a situation.

Idiot.

"What would that be, Abbs?" Eli laughed out, at ease with the situation.

"Tomorrow is Easter!" I exclaimed.

"And...?" My father asked expectantly.

"I felt that I should do something important for the occasion. I mean, it is my first Easter pastoring over the church. This is something that has been four generations in the making!" I said with forced excitement in my eyes.

"And you would like your old man and dear uncle to be there, huh?" Eli questioned.

My father furrowed his brow, somewhat suspicious of my newfound love of the family. He spoke in a tense voice.

"Last I had experienced you acted as if you wanted nothing more of the Teendyth family."

"I have had a change of heart." I puffed out my chest slightly.

"Oh, and how might that have come about?"

"You see, when I was with James' family, I was utterly disgusted by my experience there. Apparently the Alludy's had not heard of refraining from speaking ill of the dead."

"Oh really? Was James that disliked by his family?" Eli asked.

I almost vomited the moment the name "James" left his lips.

"Oh, extremely. James was an outlier from the rest of his family. You know how it was, Eli." My uncle seemed to get nervous again, tripping over however he may respond.

"He was a Protestant!" I blurted out. "And the rest of the Alludy's are die hard Anglicans! They really could not get past their difference in denomination and treated James poorly for it."

Eli seemed satisfied with my little anecdote. Father, on the other hand, was not.

"And how did that experience make you have a change of heart?" He asked.

"You see Father, I had to think of my own mortality. I had to think of yours as well, and Uncle's and even dear old Deacon Willith's. And I realized I really did not want to have to bury either of you with bitterness in my heart, nor did I want you to bury me and think of me as nothing more than a wayward child. After all, what son does not want a relationship with his father?" I replied, a layer of fake admiration over my words.

"And your invitation to service tomorrow is your olive branch?" My father alluded

"It is not just an invitation to be there! This is an invitation to help me with the service. Seeing as it is my first Easter preaching I felt that I should do something special. There is an object lesson I would like your help with."

Both my uncle and father seemed interested.

"What's the object lesson?" Eli asked.

"Well, all present know that Christ was the final sacrifice of our salvation. But I feel as if the congregation, young in their faith as they are, will not understand the full impact of that. So, to show them how burdensome the process used to be, I will be performing a

mock sacrifice."

"And what will our roles be in this?" My father asked.

"Well, I will be acting as high priest."

They looked at me as if I were a child who was playing pretend as a king. I noticed the look they gave me and quickly continued. "Honestly, I would have had either of you both take the role as high priest in my stead, but I felt that as I would be the one preaching it would make the most sense." I explained. "You two will be acting as priests as well. You will be playing the *most important role* of making sure I have all the tools necessary."

They both looked rather pleased at being considered "most important".

Prideful oafs, the both of them.

They exchanged looks before Eli spoke up. "I think I would be willing."

"I would as well." My father claimed. "But we need to address the matter at
hand first."

I forced a grim expression on my face. "Yes, I think that is of importance as well."

"You have been out of control recently, David Absolom. I honestly do not think that you have earned either the role of pastor nor the title of being a man. To me, you are still nothing but a boy." My father chastised me.

I hung my head low, the stance a child takes after being scolded for making a mess.

"I understand Father. I agree."

"Your uncle and I have every reason for our actions, and it really was not your place to question them. You are far too young to understand why we may do what we do."

He continued.

"I understand."

"Can I expect a change in behavior from you from here on out?" My father asked.

"Yes, Father." I said, feigning defeat.

My father clapped his hands together and smiled. "Good! We would both love to partake in the service tomorrow. We will be there bright and early."

"I'm incredibly proud of you, Abb." Uncle Eli interjected.

"Thank you Uncle. It means alot. Now that all of that is settled, I need to leave for the church. I have many things to get in order for the morning. Thank you both again for your assistance." I turned and walked out of the house, a large grin spreading across my lips.

I was given permission to take action against them, and I would do as such.

The rest of the day was more of the same, flitting around the town ensuring that everyone I could possibly invite to the service would be present. In all honesty, it was not an imperative to have any others at the service, but I felt that any who possibly could should take part in the celebration.

Next was James. I had to ensure that he would be present. He was another one of the most important guests, and while the version taking residency in the steeple would be easy to convince, the one who traveled with a dove would be a tad more difficult to ensure their presence. I did feel it would be an easy task as I knew I would simply have to ask.

The rest of the day was more of the very same, skittering about the town ensuring the presence of all who could attend. Even Willith himself agreed to appear, saying that it would be wrong for a man of faith to miss out on a sermon for a holy day.

I could not help but think of how my father and I used to solicit the town in the very same manner as I was now. It felt so long ago now, even though a year had barely passed. At that time, the demolition of the deacon's wills felt like such a large victory, yet in hindsight it was such a mediocre and lifeless event. To think that my father had been treating my mother in the same manner that the Williths had treated me was abhorrent. I almost wondered if she never truly was sickly, and instead so intensely battered by her husband that her body would not function properly. The fact that I had inherited her disposition meant otherwise though. It was even more sickening to think that my father would be willing to lay hands on the enfeebled.

All in all, the horrors I witnessed from the effects of that event were something that had brought me such tremendous growth. While that one meeting felt so mundane in the present, it was the catalyst for such wonders I now was experiencing.

I was almost thankful for Willith. Had he not been a moron, I would have never heard the voice of my God.

The responses of the rest of the town were the same as the others.

"We wouldn't miss it for anything!"

"Of course! The whole family will be in attendance."

"Never missed a service yet, don't plan to this week."

Every single resident of Afton agreed. I found pride in myself having done what my father could never hope to accomplish. I had convinced every member of the spiritually dead town that was Afton, New York to accompany me in worship. They would all be present in the worship of my God, and they all would have the pleasure of reveling in
  his glory.

The day came to a close, and I found myself drawing near to the church once again. It had become my home, a place where I could take solace in far away from the abuse and corruption of those around me. I walked in to the sanctuary to see James standing amongst the pews, the dove resting upon his shoulder. His orange hair glinted in the evening sunlight of the chapel windows.

"I must ask you, do you plan on attending service tomorrow?" I asked him, pausing near the end of the rows. He walked forward and placed his hands on my cheeks, holding them tightly.

"Of course, Absolom. If you're the one preaching then I have no reason to miss."

"I actually have a favor to ask of you. I have an important role for you in the sermon." I said, moving his hands off my face to hold them in my hands

"What is that?" He asked.

"I plan on having a sort of play to help some of the newer members of the church grasp what salvation means for them." I went on to explain. "I would like you to play a part."

"Oh yes!" James exclaimed. "Just tell me what I must do. What are my lines? I guess I should ask first, what is my character?" An excited glint shone in his eyes, a clear want to assist me in any way he could.

I patted his hand."Oh it's simple, you will not have lines. What I would like for you to do is actually a surprise. Think of it as a gift between brothers."

"A gift?" He said. He seemed excited for the most part, but also furrowed his brow in confusion. "Could I at least have a hint?"

"No." I chuckled.

James began to pout, but I was insistent on keeping the surprise as secret as possible. I could not have him guessing the circumstances beforehand, on the slight instance he may be able to discover what I may have in store. I was not too intensely worried, but I did not want to take any sort of chance. "You will just have to wait until the morning."

"Fine." He continued to pout.

I held him close and wished him well, but then excused myself to sleep. He asked if he could stay the night, but I requested to spend it by myself. I used the excuse of needing to prepare for the morning to uninvite him from the night's affairs. Had he been present, I most likely would have spent the night speaking with him ceaselessly. The less I spoke to him the better, as it increased my chances of mistakenly calling him James to his face. I had managed to avoid it so far, but any flub up could cause an uproar leading to a questioning of my sanity. The next day was necessary, it could not be derailed.

I said my goodnight and farewells to James, then excused myself to the upper steeple of the church.

James' body remained in pristine condition, a miracle that could have only been caused by the God I was now worshiping. The smell of rot had not yet even set in. It was as if he had perished yesterday. To me, it felt like he had fallen asleep only yesterday.

I laid awake next to his body, questioning how everything had drifted in such a manner since that day I first met him in our musty dorm room. I felt the knife that was shoddily attached to my hip. The weight had become so familiar to me in these past months. It felt as if that damned blade had become a part of myself. I wondered if I had always had this attached to my hip. I thought back upon the times that I felt harassment from Benjamin. Had I felt the weight of this even back then? I could no longer remember. I thought back to that train ride. The day my uncle gave it to me.

It felt as if my life had happened all at once, every single abuse and trauma had happened on the same day. Time stopped working effectively in my mind. I felt as if I were both a newborn and an immortal. Both too young and too old.

I held James close and cried into his shoulder. I had not felt anything but confusion in such a long time. He was the only thing that had helped me feel stable, yet he abandoned me. I could not... I could not hate him for it. I had failed to protect him. Maybe if I could protect him a second time he would not abandon me again.

It felt as if his corpse in its refusal to decompose was holding onto me. I thought back on the things I had done.

Maybe he was right to be afraid of me.

I asked myself in that moment if James truly would wish for the justice I was about to enact. Would he be okay with the drastic measures I was about to partake in so that I may ensure his safety?

"Yes."

The voice responded in my ear. The full cacophony of my God's voice resounded in

my ears. Men, women, children, beast, plant, stone, energy.

All things resounded in my ear the simple response of my question.

"YES."

The drumming of dead birds. The mewling of calves. All swam in my ears with infinite voices of my God, all stirring in response to my doubt. I continued to reason with the voices that swam through my mind, and quickly came to a conclusion.

The conclusion that it did not truly matter.

James, in his perfection, would never comprehend the things I would have to do to save him. The "yes" that responded to my thoughts felt less a response to his approval, and more as a goading to do what I must either way.

My attachment to James and my need for his approval made me forget what I had already learned, a lesson I came to terms with in that alley with Benjamin. It did not matter if James approved of my actions, let alone outsiders who were beneath me. What mattered was that I asserted my authority as the God dwelling within me, and took those actions regardless of the opinions of others. He may not have understood what needed to occur to ensure his safety, but he was not burdened with the enlightened wisdom that had been gifted to me by the Cloud.

I stood up and dried my tears. I could not wallow tonight, as service was in the morning and I had no want to dally. I descended the stairs and began to prepare for the coming morning.

I spent the night bustling around the church, preparing things so that they may be spotless for the upcoming ceremony. Any sort of major damage from Benjamin's stint making the chapel a whore house was erased and washed clean.

I thought back on the hours I spent in these walls with Martha. I had loved her just as I had loved James. She was nothing more than a victim of her circumstances, angelic in her nature just as James had been. I thought about how I may save her from the same fate that James had befallen. She would be safe from those demons in men's clothes that had taken my brother from me.

I went through, stitching together any rips that may have formed in the cushions of the pews. Any sort of dirt that may have been tracked in on the carpet I made careful attention to ensure that they would be scrubbed clean. I even managed to remove the stain that Benjamin left.

I chuckled at the thought of Benjamin. To think that anyone would even dare claim that I caused that monstrosity was comical. Anything the elder Willith tried to claim about me was a clear indication that he was lying.

I placed the broken pulpit at the front and center of the altar, making sure that it was perfectly in its place. I disturbed James from his rest and placed him in front of the pulpit, in view of those who would be sitting in the pews. I covered him, returning him to his rest. I scrubbed the walls, polishing the wood so that they may shimmer with a gleam that was worthy of the first coming. I waxed the pews as well, leaving a mirror-like reflection in

the wood.

I saw the sun rise from the windows that lined the church. Morning had struck as I was flitting about the building, and with it I took comfort in the state of the church. I had somehow miraculously stayed clean throughout the night, not a hint of the grime that I scrubbed away had landed on my clothes.

It was not long before members of the church began to flood through the doors, almost every member of the town taking up residency in the pews. I went to the entryway, greeting every member of the congregation that I had amassed. My father and uncle were one of the firsts to arrive, both with stern faces and my mother in tow.

"Well, we're here." One of the men groaned. I could only tell that they were my father and uncle as they were the only ones who held their forms. That being said, I could not discern which was which. The task was made even more difficult taking into account how very similar the both of them looked, the major differences between them only coming down to hair color and slight variations in their build.

"Amazing, I just need you both to stand by the pulpit." I said as I gestured to the front. Both carried on without another word, finding their places exactly as they were intended. A form I could only assume was my mother took her place near the front of the church, sitting within view of my father. She still somehow loved that man so much. It worried me.

More passed through, former prostitutes hanging on the men who had decided to take care of them so that they may quit their profession. Mr. Sterling passed through, ducking under the doors so that he may not hit it. He grinned at me as he passed; a

proud grin.

James came through, wearing baggy clothes and a dove perched atop his shoulder. He embraced me as he walked through.

"Where do you need me for my role?" He asked.

"Up next to that sheet," I gestured.

He gave me a look of concern as he saw my father and uncle near the pulpit, but I reassured them by wrapping my arms around him and kissing his cheek.

"Do not worry, I will keep you safe." I whispered in his ear. He looked even more confused, but thought nothing of it. He took his place there as well.

It was not long before all of those who would be in attendance had arrived, the pews filled and overflowing with the townspeople. I shut the doors to the church, placing a bar through the handles, then made my way back to the front.

All present turned and watched as I made my way up the center aisle. I could see many familiar faces; the older Willith, the former deacons, the town drunks. Everyone was in attendance. All seemed to watch me in anticipation. Those at the front made equally sure to gaze into me, wondering what it was that they would be doing for this special Easter service. All heads turned to follow me as I walked.

The skies outside were grey.

I could hear rain in the distance.

I took my place next to the broken pulpit, my knife heavy on my belt.

"Good morning to you all, people of Afton." I said to the crowd.

"Good morning to you, Reverend." They replied in kind.

"I know it may sound strange to do such a thing, but this morning I am going to forgo our usual order of service and get immediately into the sermon. I have a very important message to give you all this morning." The crowd remained silent, hanging on my words. "Over the last week I had gone away to remember a dearest friend of mine. James was his name. He was a close friend that I met in university; a close friend that took his

own life."

My uncle looked uncomfortable as the crowd let out sorrowful gasps.

"It was a strange experience. You see, they were an Anglican family. A bit of a culture shock for myself, as you know I was born and raised Protestant. One large difference between the denominations is that they do not even refer to their pastors as pastors, instead they are known as 'Right Reverends'. I certainly found this very strange."

I paused for a breath."Another strange custom was that they buried my dearest James with this." I pulled the rosary from my pocket, displaying it to the crowd. The James with the dove seemed concerned, seemingly being the only one to notice my insinuation of it being the same rosary.

"And as I spent more time with this family, I began to think even more on a thought that has been ravaging my mind lately. Do any of us truly know what God it is we

are serving?"

An angry look flashed upon my father's face.

"I was raised believing in certain ethics. For example, I was raised to believe that my father was the pinnacle of God's soldiers." I warmed up, feeling the blood rise to my face.

"But I was lied to. You see, my dearest father is the worst of sinners. A wife beater, a cheat, and all around a hateful man." I raised an accusing finger to point out the man standing beside me.

A clamor began to rise amongst the people.

"SETTLE DOWN!" Mr. Sterling boomed from the back pew. Everyone followed his orders.

"And my uncle, well he was the reason my dear friend took his life. My dearest uncle assaulted him at his most vulnerable time. My poor, dear James felt as if he had no other option but to end his life to avoid living with the burden of assault."

Both my uncle and father began to move forward, rage displayed across their faces.

"RETURN TO YOUR PLACE!" I screamed at them, louder than Mr. Sterling, the forceful tone of a general informing them of their place in the world.

I pulled the knife out of my waist coat at the same moment, a pure implication of what I would do if they attempted to step out of line again.

The congregation seemed unfazed by my threats. They trusted me as their God.

My mother seemed almost relieved by the threat against the life of the husband that laid hands upon her in secret for so many years.

I cleared my throat and continued. "My entire existence was one that I had been lied to, and to find out that my two biggest spiritual idols were frauds, was mind numbing. I began to doubt the God I had been told about all these years."

I looked down and noticed that a small red spot had begun to form on the white sheet I had placed over James' corpse. Quiet mewling noises began to rise up from under the cloth.

"But then, my God spoke to me. He reassured me. But something was off. He told me of things that I had never once been told about by my God. In all my years as the son of a pastor, I had never heard of the things and concepts He promised to me."

I looked over my doting congregation.

"Would you all like to hear what my lord told me?"

Faces rippling with a myriad of emotions were given from every member of the congregation. Every moment that passed, more rage shone on the faces of the elder Teendyths. I held the perfect attention of everyone in the room. I smiled and continued.

"He told me that I had the same authority that He held. He told me that as his child, I could enact the same anger that I had always been told was reserved for Him. In all fairness, we are made in the image of God, are we not? That only means that I have been given, at the very least, some of the authority that he has."

"What is the extent of that authority, Father?" A voice asked.

More blood began to stain the white sheet over James. The James with the dove companion began to take notice and shot me a concerned look.

"Limitless!" I replied. "My God has christened me with his limitless authority. It is as He said in Exodus 7:1: 'And the LORD said unto Moses, See, I have made thee a god to Pharaoh: and Aaron thy brother shall be thy prophet.' I have been picked by our Lord to be the new Moses, a new Prophet to lead his children!'"

A cacophony of gasps rang through the sanctuary. A few cries of celebration rang out as those that hung on my words became prepared for a new revival of the Christian faith. Pride could be seen on the shifting faces in the crowd. One raised up among the congregation and shouted out.

"I can't let this madness go on any longer! I was right to insist that you not take this position!" Willith cried from the back pews. "You've become worse than your father, and cannot for a moment let this continue! The boy on the pulpit is a killer! And I cannot let you all continue to believe that he is some sort of emissary of our Father! This demon in our midst was the one who killed my dearest Benjamin. He cannot be of God!"

There was not even a sniffle of grief from the crowd. None responded except to shoot glances of disapproval his way.

I smiled reassuringly towards the congregation and nodded as I spoke.

"Yes, I will admit that I was the one that caused Benjamin's demise. What else would I have done? Look at the glory his death has brought upon this town! Had I not taken his life the men would still be in a drunken stupor and the women would still be whoring themselves out!"

Various exclamations of 'Amen' and 'Hallelujah' rang out from the crowd.

"And even Moses had to end the lives of many to make sure his people were safe. It is a right of the gods to do as such!"

James strode forward and struck me across the face, a look of betrayal and anger across his face. Blood was pooling underneath his sheet while the living version stood before me with nothing but rage in his eyes. "You despicable man! Benjamin may have been nothin' but rot but that gives you no right to up and kill people!"

"CAN YOU NOT COMPREHEND THIS IS FOR YOU, JAMES?!" I screamed as I struck James across the cheek. He crumpled to the ground as a large black welt already began forming under his eye. The crowd still did not respond. More and more hatred formed in the eyes of my uncle and father, as if *they* had any right to feel as if my actions were heinous. James looked dazed, confused under the actions I had just taken against him.

"You are not a god, Absolom." James whimpered underneath his tears.

"I know." I replied. "Not yet."

I looked back up at the congregation and let a grin spread across my face again, ready to begin the events. I could hold no ill will against James. He was too pure. It was reasonable that he would still be incorruptible.

"And that leads me to the bulk of our sermon today. Today, you all have the pleasure of witnessing my ordination!"

The voices in the crowd cheered.

"And of course, I could not have an ordination without my priests. While I have no brother Aaron, I do have a father and uncle that can very much play the role."

I walked around the pulpit and stripped the sheet off of James, revealing his bleeding body. Sick mewling noises came from his mouth. Blood had pooled underneath his body, though it was unnoticeable against the crimson color of the carpet. I had worried about his deceased nature interfering with the event, but my God provided as He always did.

I need not worry about the details under the cover of His love.

I heard a thud against the roof as I stared at James' body.

The living James screamed.

The congregation did not.

"Let us begin!"

I removed the retaining knives from the Kukri's sheathe and passed them to my father and uncle. The moment their fingertips passed over the blades the light behind their eyes dimmed. They were forced into their role.

I settled into my role as well, unsheathing my beautiful blade and grasped it tightly in my hand.

"Eli. Bring me the calf."

Eli hoisted the now breathing corpse of James over his shoulder and brought him before me. While the shell was alive, I still felt a great sadness at the diminished state of my James. He was in a state that could technically be considered living, but clearly not having any mental capacity or thought. I embraced his body for a moment, my arms wrapped around my brother one last time before I would have to be forever separated from him.

It was a price that had to be paid for his safety.

It was a price I had to pay for my godhood. There was no way for *us* to continue.

I held James' corpse in my arms, cradling it as if he were a child. It was then that the first dove broke through the roof, coming down with such force upon the head of one of the church goers that they were killed immediately. I called my uncle forward.

"Thank you for the offering."

Eli dragged his knife across James' throat, flesh and blood pouring from the wound. More doves came crashing through the roof, the downpour beginning to drown out all noise. More and more congregants were snuffed out by the falling birds. Shadows of beasts and men alike flitted past the windows, making grotesque shadows that danced through the sanctuary in celebration. I laid its body down onto the altar.

"David, present the dove."

My father ushered the living James over to me. James' small frame tried to struggle against my father as he pushed him forward, but he was too small and my father too large.

James continued to scream.

"It is okay James, you will be safe soon."

He had the confused look still upon his face, tears forming in the corners of his eyes.

"Why do you keep calling me that, Abbi?! That's not my name! I'm begging you! Please I just..."

"You are to be the second sacrifice. Though my father never caused any harm to you, you are still of the caste of innocents that he spent his life trampling on while claiming to

be holy."

I held the living James in the same way I held the deceased, cradling him like

a child. "Please, I'm begging you Abbi, I'm not James. Can't you tell who I am?" He said frantically as he weakly fought against my hold. "I know you always said..." I held him tighter, giving the living James one last sign of affection before I was cut off from this one as well.

"...I know you always said I reminded you of him..."

My father leaned forward, retaining knife in hand.

"Abbi, it's me. It's Martha." He whispered in terror.

I held him tight and pressed my mouth against his ear.

"I know."

The retaining knife slid across her throat. The blood bubbled out as she gurgled in confusion and pain. The birds thudded against the roof, a discordant war drum. Chants began to form from outside of the church. They were nonsense, but they were clear. They were the cheers of the healed. The cheers of they who were at one time dead, but were now alive again.

They were the chants of my God.

I laid Martha on the altar next to James and stood behind them, kukri in hand. I looked out into the congregation. Crushed pews littered the sanctuary, viscera and grey matter strewn about the chapel. The birds were thick, a torrential downpour that nearly drowned out the chanting.

I boomed out in a solid voice to the carnage spread out before me.

"These two souls that have been given over to me are the flesh of my ascension. I have earned these through tribulation." I looked lovingly upon my sacrifices.

"These two, the objects of my love, will carry me to my Lord!"

I knelt and began to devour the flesh of James and Martha. It tasted so much sweeter than that of the young Alludy. More empowering. Though I had been given that meal out of nothing but a need for sustenance, these two were much more than simple nutrition. As I chewed through the tendons of their joints I felt as if this were right. They were a gift, as if they were woven in their mother's womb specially designed to be sacrificed unto me.

I engorged myself on them as I watched out into the crowd. More and more doves began to crash through the ceiling, each one emulsifying another one of the church patrons with its strike. It was as if my God was eradicating anything that was unworthy to be in

his presence.

Anything that was unworthy to be in mine.

The room was silent despite the terror that was taking place. The birds did not land with a crash, but instead with a drip. It was pleasant weather to enjoy a meal in. The sweetness of the meat paired with the roar of the storm and the scenes played before me was an experience that no man could pay or beg for. It was a stage show reserved only for the gods. I ceased engorging myself, instead deciding to take a moment to savor the meal and the view before me.

Poor old Mr. Sterling had tried to rush at me from the pews when a bird careened into his leg, snapping it in half and forcing him to the ground. He tried to crawl towards me, screaming curses and profanities. His flailing was put to end by another carcass impaling itself into his skull. I smiled as I swallowed a small chunk of meat.

Willith seemed to have become catatonic in his seat, staring glassily as those around him tried to flee. It seems that the things I had put the man through had been far too much for his mind to handle. I felt as if he deserved some sort of mercy, as he really had changed at least a little. Rare for a beast to do. I pointed a grease covered finger in his direction. A dove crashed through the roof, much faster than the others. He would not have felt any pain.

Others tried to escape through the doors of the church, but they were blocked by the beam I had placed in the handles. No one dared leave through the windows, as they were swarmed by creatures that were all too familiar to me. They all chanted in such similar voices, crying out about the joy of being seen.

The people of the town all screamed prayers to their savior. Their God did not answer, and neither did the one they prayed to.

My mother, may she be blessed, was not given the same mercy as Willith. I truly wish she had, yet it was too late for me to deal with her mercifully. She had been grazed by a multiple of the deceased birds, leaving her unable to move and crumpled to the ground. I shed a metaphorical tear for her and dealt with her in the same manner as Willith.

Seeing my mother in such a state soured my mood, so I returned to my offering. I ripped into the sinew of both of them. James was lean, his sinew tough and hard to chew through. Martha, on the other hand, was softer. Fattier. It was as if they were different creatures entirely. The doves hit both my father and uncle as well, each time somehow avoiding a killing blow. Their legs and joints cracked under the impact. The light behind their eyes had returned, and I knew they were feeling every moment of the pummeling.

The creatures from outside began to pound on the walls in rhythm with the rain. It was not an attempt to break in.

It was music.

It was worship.

I devoured the bodies with speed. Just as I had in my dream, I picked their veins from their wrists and chewed, savory the blood. I bit into their organs, the fat that coated them more delicious than any other part. I cracked their bones in my teeth. It would be wrong of me to spare a morsel. This was their love. This was me accepting their love for the very first time.

Nothing was left of them.

I looked out into the crowd of those who had attended. All of them had been crushed by the pouring doves. The chanting continued, but had unified into the one voice of my God. Thick mist began pouring into the sanctuary, all glowing that same sickly red and violet hue. It was my God. He had shown himself to me in the physical. They began to twirl around me, intertwining over my skin. It was a pleasant feeling, gentle and loving. It was caring. It held me there in the silence of the chapel. No light shone through the gaps in the roof. Only the hue of my God.

I felt his love more than I had ever felt any feeling before, an intense pulsing pervading my entire being.

In that moment, We became One.

I asked again.

"What is your true name?"

"We are Cha' Ush."

Praise Be the Putrid Cloud

Printed in the USA
CPSIA information can be obtained
at www.ICGtesting.com
LVHW090836061223
765391LV00024B/125